FRANKLIN HORTON

COMPOUND FRACTURE

BOOK THREE IN THE LOCKER NINE SERIES

Copyright © 2019 by Franklin Horton

Cover by Deranged Doctor Design

Editing by Felicia Sullivan

ISBN: 9781099498893

ALSO BY FRANKLIN HORTON

The Borrowed World Series

The Borrowed World

Ashes of the Unspeakable

Legion of Despair

No Time For Mourning

Valley of Vengeance

Switched On

The Locker Nine Series

Locker Nine

Grace Under Fire

The Mad Mick Series

The Mad Mick

Masters of Mayhem

Stand-Alone Novels

Random Acts

ABOUT THE AUTHOR

Franklin Horton lives and writes in the mountains of Southwestern Virginia. He is the author of several bestselling post-apocalyptic series. You can follow him on his website at franklinhorton.com. While you're there please sign up for his mailing list for updates, event schedule, book recommendations, and discounts.

1

Robert Hardwick's eyes snapped open and he immediately checked his watch. It was 5:25 AM. He decided he might as well get up since his alarm would be going off in five minutes anyway. He was never one for lingering in bed. He wrestled free of the blankets, sat up in bed, and glanced out the window. The curtain-less window looked out onto the southern Appalachians and he found only the palest glow at the eastern edge of his view. The sun wasn't up yet and there was no reason Robert had to be either but he couldn't break routine. This was when he got up — winter, summer, weekday, weekend, normal life, or not-so-normal life. Like now.

He went to the window, leaned his head against the cool glass, and thought of his family. His wife and son would probably not be awake for hours. His daughter Grace was different, though. She was probably up now, just as he was. He hoped they were all safe and that he would be back with them soon.

Robert was not a person who stepped into his day like it was hot bath water, testing it first with a toe before easing in. Robert dove into his day like a drunk belly-flopping off a diving board, springing from the bed into a state of full wakefulness that drove his wife nuts. She required more time to ease into the day.

Normally, a few weeks ago, his routine would have been to get up, suck down some black coffee, and get in four hours of writing before doing anything else. The world was quieter then and he was better able to resist the temptations of the day — business matters, farm projects, or mountain biking. He'd gone without writing for several days now and it made the world seem wrong. The process of putting down his thoughts, of writing stories that engaged people, helped him process the world around him. It purged demons and emotions alike.

What point was there in writing now? If there was a story here in this broken world, he didn't know how it would end yet. Would he live to be the narrator or would that responsibility fall to someone else because he died here, far away from his home and family? He didn't want to think about it. It was a pointless spiral of negativity and pain.

He dressed and went to the kitchen, boiling some water on the gas range for a single cup of coffee. When it was ready, he poured it through a French press, then moved to the back porch, placing the cup on the rail to cool in the chilly morning air. The camp was quiet but he knew he wasn't the only one awake at this hour. There were men on perimeter security, ready to sound the alarm and shoot back should anyone try to breach the unfenced boundary between this compound and the area controlled by the interlopers.

While his coffee cooled, he dropped to a pushup position, feeling the grit and dust of the floorboards beneath his hands as he knocked out twenty-five pushups. He transitioned to a plank and stayed that way until he felt the muscles of his stomach and lower back start to spasm. From there, he did squats until he felt fire in his legs.

"This the morning routine?" Arthur asked as he came out onto the porch with his own cup of coffee.

"No," Robert said. "Usually it's coffee, writing, and exercise after that. Then back to writing in the early afternoon. Everything's off schedule now."

Arthur shrugged. "You might as well relax into it. Not a lot can be done about it right now, other than what we're already doing."

"*Relaxing* and *accepting* aren't qualities I'm known for. I feel like a caged animal," Robert said, taking that first, magical sip of strong coffee. "I'm going nuts here. All I can think about is my family. Wondering if they're safe, if they're comfortable, if they're eating well."

"You're doing this to yourself," Arthur said. "Take back control. Rein yourself in. Push the emotional bullshit to the side. Process what's in front of you and nothing else. Besides, you know they're okay. You've talked to them. Grace and Tom are there now. Everything is going to be fine. You guys will be back together soon and this will just be a footnote in your story."

Robert laughed. "Push it to the side? Easier said than done."

"What else is there? What else can you do? We're in a holding pattern."

Robert had no answer for that. He took a seat in a creaky wooden chair and sipped his coffee. "Any new developments?"

Arthur leaned casually against a porch post, one hand in his pocket, the other holding a Shark Coast Tactical coffee mug that was always close at hand. He took another sip. "Kevin and I were up late. I think we've come up with something. Not sure if it's a good plan or not but sometimes you just have to shake things up and see what falls out."

"I think I'm about ready to make another run for home," Robert said.

"Your call, but I think that's your emotions talking," Arthur said. "If you keep butting your head against the wall you're going to get yourself or Sonyea killed. You've been lucky too many times and I think you're running on borrowed luck now."

Sonyea was a friend of Robert's. His daughter Grace had stopped over at her place while finding her way home from school in Oxford, Mississippi. Robert had come to Arthur's compound to bring Grace home but had stuck around to give Sonyea a few days longer to heal from her wounds. Grace and Sonyea's son, Tom, were already home, having managed to hitch a ride aboard the chopper that delivered Kevin here to the compound. It was killing Robert to be stuck here away from his family but Arthur was right. With Tom and Grace already home, his family would do fine.

"I don't like it a bit," Robert said.

Arthur shook his head. "You think I like the feeling of being pinned down like a bug beneath a shoe? You think I like those guys breathing down my neck, waiting for us to make a mistake? Waiting for us to give them an opening?"

"You don't seem stressed."

"Because you can't let it get to you, Robert. You have to get your head right and play the long game."

"I know it."

"Then *do* it. You're in control. Burn the emotions out of your body. You're not going to do it with a couple of pushups and a handful of squats."

"What do you suggest?"

"Go down to the shooting range and tie off to one of those tractor tires. Drag it back and forth for a while. Carry some railroad ties up and down the shooting range. Do something that knocks you in the dirt."

"I might take you up on it," Robert said, taking another drink.

"You've got to do something, man. You're wigging out. People are noticing. You've got Kevin concerned about your mental health."

Robert shot to his feet, downed the last of his coffee, and gave Arthur a nod. "I'll tighten it up, Arthur. You don't have to worry about me."

He went back in the kitchen and rinsed his mug out at the sink. The gravity-fed water was not pressurized, coming from an elevated tank near the cabin, but it beat the hell out of hauling water from the creek in buckets. It wasn't just the fact that he was separated from his family that was bothering him. Robert was a loner. He was a person who spent most of his time either alone or among the trusted circle of his own family. He wasn't used to having to work in tandem with other people. He wasn't used to having to arrive at a consensus before making a decision. He was used to doing whatever the heck he wanted, whenever the heck he wanted to. Except now he couldn't.

Arthur was right. He needed to get himself together. People probably were noticing and concerned that he was a flake. The big bad writer who wrote such engaging stories, such taut action sequences, who didn't shy from blood and gore, was crumbling under the pressure of a tactical standoff.

Maybe he did need to spend some time dragging tires and toting railroad ties. Maybe he did need to cook the worry and self-doubt out of himself. He stowed the coffee cup and went back outside.

"I'll be at the range," Robert said, not slowing as he strode across the porch and skipped down the steps. "I'm going to spend some quality time with your tractor tires."

Arthur held his mug up in a toast. "Go for it. When you get back, check in at the commo shack. Kevin and I have a little recon operation planned. You might find it interesting."

2

The communication shack at Arthur Bridges' compound was a rustic plank building painted in Forest Service green. Corrugated steel panels of a similar color made up the roof. There were two double-hung windows recycled from an old house. The structure wasn't much bigger than a suburban backyard shed. The only hint that the shed held anything interesting was that the window glass was painted flat black.

Arthur, owner of both the property and the shed, had not wanted to include any windows at all but his radio operator friends had assured him that the heat from the equipment would make the shack stifling in summer with no ventilation. The heat could even damage the sensitive electronics. Arthur's compromise was to allow windows on the condition they be blacked out to contain the glow from the electronics after dark.

The shack only had one chair, intended for the single radio operator using the equipment. The room was packed to capacity now, the radio operator surrounded by eager faces waiting for an update from the man they'd just sent beyond the wire. Recon was always risky work. Arthur and his men were aware that the men surrounding them had thermal and night vision capabilities. They'd also heard a

.50 caliber sniper rifle, an utterly devastating weapon in capable hands.

The presence of such a rifle, of night vision and thermal gear, did not necessarily imply that the enemy had access to military gear. All of those items could be purchased off-the-shelf at a local gun or sporting goods store. While there had even been some full-auto fire during the brief skirmishes between the compound folks and the outside force, that didn't mean much either. Most local police departments had access to full-auto weapons now through government re-utilization programs. Whatever select-fire gear these men had probably came from a law enforcement agency with access to military surplus weapons.

The radio operator, a young guy named Carlos, threw a hand up to silence the room even though no one was speaking at the moment. It was purely a reaction. Carlos nodded as he listened. "Roger that," he said. "Jim Beam over."

"What is it?" Arthur asked. His impatience, his desperation for an update, mirrored the anxiety of everyone else in the room.

"Jim Beam Delta in position," Carlos said calmly, not taking his eyes off the meters, buttons, and LEDs in front of him.

"Remind him to keep under that thermal blanket," Arthur said, nervously flexing the sides of a thin plastic water bottle. It made an irritating crackling sound. He tried moving around, wanting to pace, but there was nowhere to go in the tight quarters.

"He knows that," Kevin said.

Kevin Cole was an old friend of Arthur's and maintained a bug out location at Arthur's compound. As a resident of the Washington, D.C. area, he needed a safe place to go if the shit ever hit the fan. He never really expected it to happen but it had just a short time ago. Kevin packed his toys, flagged down a chopper, and arranged to have himself dropped off at Arthur's compound.

"It never hurts to remind folks," Arthur pointed out. "I feel a responsibility to look out for my guys."

"Brandon is a sharp kid," Kevin pointed out. "He's obsessive about details. He'll be fine."

Arthur shrugged and conceded the point, though the whole thing left him a little uneasy. Weapons and tactics had always been a hobby for Arthur, never his trade and profession. When it came to operations like this he had to trust the people among his group with operational backgrounds. This was their sandbox.

Arthur came from a construction background, having built high-end safe rooms and secure vaults for people in the Washington, D.C. area. It was amazing how many people needed such things and what they were willing to pay for them. A lot of his work had been for upper-echelon folks employed by the government's intelligence agencies. In those cases, the government often picked up the tab for his work, allowing Arthur the pleasure of recouping a portion of his tax money by sticking it to the government.

It was an eye-opening experience for him. The more he worked with people in the military and security fields, the more he learned just how precarious the security of the United States was. Arthur began thinking seriously about building a secure bug out retreat in the Appalachian Mountains. He'd grown up there and felt it was one of the safer places on the East Coast. When he realized he wouldn't have enough money to do what he wanted on his own, he broached the topic with other like-minded folks and began to build a network of people who wanted in on the project.

Arthur was highly organized and made the decision to set up his retreat as a corporation, allowing people to buy in at different levels. Some levels of ownership bought you a cabin on the property, which Arthur would build to suit your needs. Other tiers of ownership allowed you to cache a shipping container of goods on the property and stay in communal bunkhouses. Regardless of the level you bought into, all the paperwork made it clear that Arthur was in charge. This was his baby. He made the rules. He surrounded himself with people with an array of useful skills and experience and he sought their input, but they had to understand that every final call rested with him.

Carlos touched his headphones, listening, then relayed the info to the group. "He's in position with eyes on."

The forward observer they'd dispatched from the compound was armed but his primary tool was a spotting scope that would allow him to collect intelligence on the opposing force. The scope was equipped with a killflash, a specially-designed screen that prevented light from reflecting off the optic and giving away his position.

Kevin placed his hand on the radio operator's shoulder. "Remind him I don't want analysis, just a description. He should start video immediately."

Carlos repeated the message, touched a button, and twisted the volume knob. The observer's voice began pouring out of the loud-speakers in the commo shack. He was whispering so the volume was turned up enough that everyone could hear what he was saying. No one in the room spoke, afraid they would miss a detail.

"I've got one RV. It's huge. Like the size of a tour bus. Behind it there's a line of vehicles stretching down the road. I can't see how far the line goes because of the trees. There are other campers of different sizes. Some are trailers, like you'd pull with a truck, but they've been unhooked from their trucks. There's at least a half-dozen individual vehicles—Jeeps, SUVs, and pickup trucks. Most are seriously loaded down with gear. They have shit tied to the tops and packed into every available space."

"Does he see any people?" Arthur asked. It was nearly 8 AM. Surely there were people out there moving around already.

Carlos relayed the question and the speakers crackled back to life with the hushed response.

"There's a couple of those square pop-up canopies close to the RV with camping chairs and plastic tables set up under them. There's a campfire nearby and it's still burning. A couple of older guys that look like they're on a deer hunting trip are standing around there sipping cups of coffee. I think one of them must be the congressman based on the picture I saw.

"Another of the men is wearing what looks like a military uniform with insignia but he appears to be in his seventies. If I had to call it, I would say he was retired military. I got two other high-and-tights standing with these guys. Looks like they've got on a mix of hunting camo and tactical gear. I know you don't want commentary but if I had to put money on it, I'd figure these guys for state troopers. They've got some kid working as their cook. I

would put him at eighteen to twenty years old. Looks like he's heating dish-water now. Doesn't appear to enjoy his work. I'm getting a pissed-off, resentful vibe from him."

Kevin shot a quick glance at Arthur and the man nodded at him. Comments like that were good information. It was good to know there were chinks in the armor that could potentially be exploited.

"Give me a description of that dishwasher," Kevin requested. "Is he armed?"

Carlos relayed the question and waited for the answer.

Brandon's whispered voice returned again. *"Scrawny guy. Bad skin. Cheesy mustache. Dirty T-shirt with some logo I can't read. Oversized jeans. He's got a big-ass knife hanging off his hip but it's nothing I recognize. Reminds me of those cheesy zombie killer knives that kids are obsessed with. I don't see a holster which would make this the only guy I've seen with no sidearm."*

"Brandon's getting all this on video?" Arthur asked.

Carlos relayed the question and a second later nodded. "Affirmative."

"Ask him if there's anything else we need to know," Kevin said. "Anything that sticks out to him."

Carlos did as he was asked. The whisper came back across the speakers again.

"You'll see this on the video but they have a flagpole attached to the RV, flying the American flag. It kind of rubs me the wrong way considering what they're trying to do."

Arthur gritted his teeth. It also rubbed him the wrong way that these men would hide behind the flag while trying to illegally seize his property.

Kevin leaned over the desk and picked up a microphone. "Jim Beam Delta, this is Jim Beam Actual. Your sentiments are acknowl-edged. Pack it up and retreat with the utmost caution. We'll alert perimeter security to expect you at the reentry point. Safe travels. Jim Beam Actual out."

Robert observed the operation from a position close to the door in the hot, overcrowded communication shack. He was already overheated. He'd taken Arthur's advice and done an intense workout on the shooting range. He'd dragged and flipped tractor tires, carried railroad ties, run sprints with cinderblocks. None of it helped. If anything, he felt his anxiety had risen to hair-trigger levels. He felt ready to blow but who was he going to blow up on? None of these people were deserving of it.

Maybe what he needed to do was slip through the wire and take it out on the people who were really at fault. Slip inside their campers at night and slit throats like some shadowy assassin. Such action wouldn't be his call, though. Not to mention that he had no practice at being an assassin, though he'd written about one. Once. He'd probably end up getting killed.

With the group still processing the operation, Robert shoved his way out the door. His frustration was evident and did not go unnoticed by Arthur, Kevin, and some of the others. After a few moments, Sonyea followed him and found him stretched out on a wide wooden bench.

She nudged him with her foot, causing him to remove the hand shading his eyes. When he saw it was her, he moved his feet and sat up.

"What's the deal?" she asked.

"You know the deal. The deal hasn't changed since yesterday. Nothing has changed. That's the problem."

"People were watching you in there," Sonyea said. "It was clear what they were thinking. They think you've checked out. You've moved on. You're not one of them anymore."

Robert opened his hands in a gesture that indicated he wasn't sure what he was supposed to do about that. He had a sour expression on his face. "I'm *not* one of them. This isn't where I'm supposed to be."

Sonyea's mouth tightened. "You know, I've only met you in person a couple of times. Obviously we've spent more time together in the last few days, we've gotten to know each other better, but I have to tell you you're not what I expected. You come off as being more *together* in your interviews and public appearances."

"Those are under ideal conditions."

"We don't get to choose our conditions, Robert. Your books preach about flexibility and adaptability but I don't see any of that here. What I see borders on a tantrum. You're mad at the world because you're not getting your way."

Robert gave her a bitter look. "Sorry if I'm a disappointment. Excuse me if I don't beg for forgiveness."

Sonyea shook her head at him. "You just don't get it, do you?"

"At this moment, I don't really care about disappointing people. I'm more concerned about the people that aren't here. Like my wife and kids."

Sonyea sighed deeply, coming to the conclusion that arguing with Robert was a waste of breath. She rose and walked off, returning to the commo shack. Robert laid back down on the bench and slipped into the familiar murky waters of his thoughts.

3

"Jim Beam Delta is safely behind the wire," Carlos relayed when the forward observer reached his reentry point.

No words were exchanged but there was evident relief that the operation had gone off without a hitch. There was no such thing as a routine operation under the current circumstances. Arthur, Sonyea, and Kevin filed out of the radio hut and walked back across the gravel lot to Arthur's cabin. Arthur lived at his compound full-time since retiring and, as the only permanent resident, he'd built the most elaborate home on the property.

Arthur spotted Robert sitting on the bench. "You want to join us for some breakfast?"

Robert stood and gave a sullen nod, falling in behind the others.

While other investors had cabins, tiny houses, or stayed in the various bunkhouses that were scattered around the facility, Arthur had built his dream home here. It was fully off-grid with solar power. Secondary power was provided by diesel generators but it was unlikely Arthur would be using those very often since he didn't know when fuel would become available again. There was even a micro hydroelectric generator installed on a spring-fed brook that ran off the mountain all year long.

With his construction background, Arthur did most of the work himself, building everything exactly how he wanted it. He performed the work with the attention to detail that made him successful when he built for a living. Doing the work himself also meant that he could reduce the number of outsiders he had visiting his property. No utility workers, no excavation contractors, no electricians, and no carpenters. The only thing he subbed out was concrete and metal roofing. Both were jobs that required a crew, and most of the time he was a crew of one.

There were times he preferred things that way. The end of the world, when numbers could make the difference between life and death, was not one of those times. That was a time to circle the wagons and join forces with people you trusted.

In the kitchen, Arthur cracked fresh eggs into a stainless mixing bowl and preheated the oven for biscuits. Sonyea was used to cooking for her son Tom, now safely living with Robert's family outside of Damascus, Virginia. She didn't take well to sitting on her hands and watching other people cook so she jumped in to help, mixing biscuit dough from scratch. The stove ran off a thousand gallon propane tank sitting a distance from the house. Now that they were under siege, Arthur was glad that the tank was not sitting immediately beside his home.

Robert and Kevin sat at the table, watching Arthur and Sonyea work their culinary magic. It was one of those moments where, a few months back, both men would have been scrolling through their phones, checking calendars and reading emails. Without those devices, they had nothing to resort to but conversation.

"So, what's your play now?" Robert asked.

He'd been silent in the communication shack but was curious what Arthur and Kevin were thinking now that they had more information. He was a guest here and felt he had no business asking questions during the stress of that operation. He was not one of Arthur's shareholders. He had his own relatively secure compound in the mountains of Virginia. He imagined that his family was experiencing some level of hardship but should be fairly comfortable when contrasted against the unprepared.

As long as there were no complications, anyway. And as long as they had no unexpected visitors.

Robert could not help but live a prepared lifestyle. It was a hazard of the job, so to speak. The collapse of society was his bread-and-butter. He lived and breathed fictional death and destruction every day, writing stories about apocalyptic events, constantly inventing new ways for the fabric of society to be torn asunder. As much as he understood the fragility of society, he never really expected anything to happen. He was fortunate, though, in that all of his research helped him to see the writing on the wall when the collapse began. He was able to understand where things were headed as soon as the first reports started coming in about the scope of the terror attacks. He knew it was time to batten down the hatches. Time to implement the bug-in plan he'd been perfecting for years.

The perfect bug-in plan didn't help Robert now. Just outside Arthur's compound was a United States congressman fully intent on taking Arthur's compound for himself. Apparently the *Honorable* Congressman Honaker had picked up on the same early indicators of collapse that Robert had. He'd also known that it was time to batten down the hatches but he went an entirely different route in preparing for hard times. His plan went back to a period in time when Arthur Bridges first showed up on the congressman's radar.

They'd met years ago when Arthur built a safe room in the congressman's Washington residence. Congressman Honaker had not paid for the job himself. It was a gift from a "concerned citizen." Through conversations between the two, the congressman figured out that his safe room contractor, Arthur Bridges, was a serious prepper. The common term at that time, the 1980s, was *survivalist,* and there were a lot of bad connotations associated with it.

At one time, Arthur considered Congressman Honaker to be his friend. Like many inside the beltway, the congressman had developed a different definition of friendship. Although he may once have been a country boy from the hills, he'd forgotten what real friends meant to country boys. Decades of deal-making and backstabbing changed him. He was more interested in what people could do for him than what he could do for them.

Years later, in the wake of the Y2K bug and 9/11, as prepping became more mainstream, Congressman Honaker recalled his encounter with the survivalist contractor Arthur Bridges. He began to wonder how far Arthur had progressed in his dream of having "a place to get away to if things get bad." Using, or rather *misusing*, the powers of his office, the congressman kept tabs on the growth of Arthur's compound. He developed a bug out plan of his own, based on booting Arthur off his property and taking it for his own friends and family.

It was not exactly working out like he'd planned, though. The residents of Arthur's compound, needless to say, had no plans to go off quietly and surrender the facility they'd worked so hard to build. Hence the current stand-off.

At the island in his bright, open kitchen Arthur whisked his ingredients together in a stainless steel bowl, dumping in spices and a healthy squirt of Sriracha chili sauce. It was his favorite condiment.

"After I have another cup of coffee and I've enjoyed this nice breakfast, I'm going to try to get the good congressman on the radio to see if he's had time to recognize the error of his ways. Maybe he'll realize that since we're not rolling over on our bellies like scared pups he should just pack up and go home."

"I think he underestimated what he'd come up against," Kevin said. "I'd bet he wrangled together his hunting buddies, some of his law enforcement contacts, and asked them if they wanted to be part of his plan. I doubt they knew the details of what they were getting into. They probably thought they were just going to roll in here and you would give them what they wanted."

Arthur carefully poured the eggs into a cast-iron skillet heating on the gas range. "Well, you know what I bring to the table in terms of gear. I've been seriously preparing for this for probably thirty years. I know some of the equipment you and other folks staying here brought too. All of us came into this expecting the worst. We've spent years accumulating good weapons and high-tech gear. Beyond what we've talked about and shared openly, I bet we've all got a secret stash of even scarier stuff held back for a rainy day. Honaker and his guys are outclassed here. They have no idea how big a bear they've poked."

Robert smacked his hand on the table in frustration. "Then why not make that readily evident to them? A show of power and weapons capability might send them scurrying back down the mountain."

Arthur shook his head. "The problem with taking action like that is that you give way too much information. If we show our cards and allow the congressman to leave, we could be giving him the information he needs to go off and build a force that could eventually take this place down. It's better to be vague and keep them guessing about what we have. I'd rather imply force than demonstrate it, when the situation allows."

"Then what does that leave you?" Robert continued. "I wouldn't let those bastards linger out there any longer. If you're that much better trained, that much better equipped, then don't give them any more time to probe your defenses. They'll eventually find a weakness and someone will get hurt. Put snipers on them. Plant a bomb and blow them all to Kingdom Come. Take out everybody in their head shed and then send in your foot soldiers to mop up the mess."

Arthur stirred his eggs. He looked grim. "That's not the only option. I want to try to talk to him one more time. He's had time to think about this. He could still do the right thing."

"I just don't get it," Robert mumbled, unable to let it go. It was his frustration speaking, the desire to clear out everything standing between him and getting home to his family. The comment was ill-timed, and exactly the wrong thing to say among this group of men.

"You sound like a politician," Kevin spat. "That 'sending in the foot soldiers' comment is the kind of shit you hear out of rear echelon desk jockeys who have never seen combat. You know what a *fobbit* is? Look it up some time."

This was not the first time Robert and Kevin had exchanged harsh words. There had been a little tension since their first meeting, when Robert angrily implied that Kevin's chopper ride into the compound went against the idea of maintaining a low profile. He went on to speculate that it may have even led Congressman Honaker to Arthur's place, thereby preventing Sonyea and him from getting home. They knew now that wasn't true. They had learned that Congressman Honaker had been tracking Arthur's progress for years as he built and stockpiled the compound.

Robert shrugged. "I know what a *fobbit* is, but I'm just trying to be realistic here. Times are different. You have to be prepared to make the hard calls."

That was the wrong thing to say to Kevin. He crossed his arms and shook his head with disgust. There was a look in his eyes that said, under different circumstances, he would probably be throwing a punch. "You're in no position to talk to me about hard calls, buddy. I've made more of them than you'll ever have to make. How many times have you *ever* sent anyone off knowing they might not come back? And when the worst happened, when they didn't come back, how many times have you ever had to visit a family and explain to them what happened?"

"Obviously, I've not done any of those things," Robert said. "Our experiences in life have been different."

"Damn right you haven't! When you have done those things, we can talk. Until then, everything that comes out of your mouth is just ignorance and noise."

"Look, I appreciate your service to our country, Kevin. I would never try to minimize that. But being a contractor, an operator, a fixer, or whatever the hell you really are doesn't make you any better prepared for the collapse than I am. I have access to most of the same gear you can get. I've had plenty of shooting and tactical training. Having a military background doesn't make you any more of a prepper than the next guy."

"And writing about being a badass sure as hell doesn't *make* you a badass!" Kevin exploded. "You can take all the same trainings I've taken, you can own all the same weapons I have in my safe, and you can be prepared for every survival scenario out there, but that doesn't prepare you for the consequences of taking a life. There are long-term emotional and psychological consequences. There is *responsibility*. Only experience prepares you for that, and you've got no experience. Right now you just sound like some keyboard warrior. Like some punk on an internet forum with all the answers."

Robert was silent, both surprised at Kevin's fury and embarrassed that he'd let his frustration push him to this point. He hadn't wanted this to happen. He hadn't intended to trigger Kevin in this way, but he clearly had. Sonyea slid the biscuits into the oven, wisely choosing to stay out of the argument.

Arthur scrambled his eggs with more vigor than was necessary. He was stewing too. Everyone saw it. Finally, he decided he could no longer stay silent. He pointed the oversized food service spoon at Robert.

"Those men out there, the ones we're fighting, are still Americans. Honaker, I don't give a shit about, but I don't want to kill those other men if I don't have to. They have families on the way here. What am I condemning those families to if I kill every man out there? To death, that's what," he said. "When the lights come back on, when the gas is flowing again, will I have to answer for that? Would killing the congressman be considered self-defense under these circumstances or would it be a war crime? I'm not saying it won't come to the point where we have to take him out, but you have to think about these things. You have to consider the potential consequences even when there's no law."

Robert had no answer to that. He didn't know what the right answer was and apparently no one else knew either.

"Just because you *can* kill someone doesn't mean you *should*," Kevin said. "Arthur is right. If we have to answer for this one day, for killing a congressman, I want to be able to say with absolute certainty that we tried everything. Your daughter told me that part of how she survived so successfully was that you taught her to think several steps ahead of every action she took. Think several steps ahead now. It would be easy to kill all those men out there but will it be as easy to explain our actions to their families when they show up? Do you think they'll accept our response? Are you prepared to kill them too if they threaten to go out into the world and bring more people back here?"

"Then what is the answer?" Robert demanded. "Do you just open the gate and invite them in? Do you give up this place and hand everything over to them? Do we stay trapped here forever?"

"There is no clear answer yet," Arthur growled. "But there may be one around the corner. We're not forced into action yet. Congressman Honaker and I will talk at least one more time. That idiot will hear all the same arguments you just heard. He needs to gut-check his own level of commitment. He needs to understand the very real possibility that their families might arrive to find them all dead."

Robert pushed his chair back abruptly and stood. He shoved his way through the back door and went outside to stand on the back porch. He crossed his arms and examined the mountains. Frustration percolated inside him. He thought about everything, from the things he'd heard in Arthur's kitchen to the fate of his own family at home. He thought about himself as a father and as a writer. He thought about his legacy and his future. He wasn't certain how long he dwelt on those things but at some point he felt a hand on his shoulder. He flinched, then turned to find Sonyea standing there.

"I'm sorry for startling you but breakfast is ready if you want some."

Hunger overcame his anger and frustration, leading Robert to go back inside and sit down at the table. The other men were already filling their plates. The tension was thick, the disagreement not sitting well with any of the men. They weren't best friends but, like it or not, they were a team thrown together by circumstance. They had to work together, which would be difficult with so many emotions swirling around between them. Robert accepted he was responsible for it and needed to attempt to fix it. If they thought he was losing his shit before, they probably thought worse of him now.

"I apologize. I was out of line," Robert said. "It's easy to just drop in here and make suggestions when I don't have to stick around and face the consequences of those decisions. I'm sorry."

"Acknowledged." Arthur shrugged. "We're all a little stressed out. Nerves are bound to fray under these conditions. We've got to hold it together and stay cool though."

Robert extended a hand to Kevin and the man took it. "We good?"

"We're good," Kevin replied, perhaps a little too quickly to mean it.

Robert hoped it was true. He hoped he hadn't damaged things beyond repair. For the rest of his stay, no matter how long it was, he would have to work harder to rein in his frustration.

4

Arthur barged through the door of the communications shack, startling Carlos. The radio operator spent most days monitoring frequencies in relative peace and quiet so any guest was unexpected. He jumped, and Arthur realized he may have entered a little more abruptly than was usual for him. It was that damn *discussion* with Robert at breakfast. It still had him feeling a little raw.

"See if you can raise the congressman on the radio," Arthur ordered. "Then give me some privacy. It may take a while to talk sense into the hard-headed son-of-a-bitch."

"You sure you don't me to stick around?"

"What part of the word *privacy* do you not understand?" Arthur snapped.

Carlos looked stung by the sharp response. "I just meant that I wasn't sure if you were familiar with this radio setup or not."

"Who do you think put all this crap together?" Arthur frowned at the younger man. "Besides, I was tinkering with radios when you were sitting at daycare mining nose nuggets. I think I can manage."

"Yes sir," Carlos said efficiently, punching a preset button to return to the frequency he'd used to contact the congressman before.

"Bridges' Survival School for Congressman Honaker. Bridges' Survival School for Congressman Honaker, over."

Carlos continued repeating his request at intervals. After nearly two minutes, a snide response unfurled from the headset speakers.

"Bridges' Survival School?"

Carlos recognized the voice from earlier radio transmissions. It was the congressman. "Hold for Arthur Bridges, sir." Carlos slid his chair back and offered it to Arthur, then excused himself to sit on the steps and have a smoke.

Arthur waited until Carlos was closing the door behind him to address the congressman. "This is Arthur Bridges. That you, Honaker?"

"Well, it is, but people typically address a sitting congressman with more respect than that."

Arthur gritted his teeth. "If you were acting within the responsibilities of your office, I might tender more respect. As it is, you're acting like a bully and a criminal so I'm probably addressing you with more respect than you deserve."

There was a long pause. *"Bridges' Survival School,"* Congressman Honaker finally muttered dismissively. Over the years, his voice had lost some of the twang of the region. Now it sounded like more of a cultivated southern accent, the kind that a speaker might adopt on the campaign trail to demonstrate that he was just a decent, home-spun country boy. *"I never did buy that training school bullshit. Your place is a survivalist compound. Pure and simple."*

"We never broke any laws," Arthur replied. "In fact, if you were having us surveilled for your own nefarious intentions, then maybe it was *you* who was breaking the law."

"I will neither confirm nor deny that I might have monitored your activities over the years but I guess none of that matters at this moment, does it? It's not like you can sue me. We're kind of at a stalemate, aren't we? Waiting to see who flinches first."

"Thinking you're up for a showdown with us is going to get you killed, Honaker. And you'll be taking a lot of men with you. You'll also be condemning their families to a slow and miserable death if there's no one around to help look out for them."

"Well," Congressman Honaker drawled, *"the solution is simple. It's already been presented to you. All you have to do is gather your men together and march your happy camouflaged asses out the front gate. Make no mistake about it—we will eventually be occupying your compound and there is not a damn thing you can do about it."*

Arthur sighed loudly into the microphone. It was pure frustration, not intended for dramatic effect, but it was certainly audible across the airwaves. "That's where you're wrong. You might have planned for this. You might have come here thinking you could actually do this. You probably even convinced those men dumb enough to come with you that you could do this. But you can't. We won't let you. Taking what's rightfully mine will not be as simple as just knocking on the door and asking me to leave."

"You anti-government types are all alike. Paranoid, misguided, and misinformed. Your only choice, Arthur, is to leave on two legs like a man. If you can't see reason, your decomposing corpse can fertilize the forest," the congressman bellowed. *"You'll be worm food."*

Arthur chuckled. "Now when you say shit like that, it shows me you've got an audience. You're probably sitting over there right now trying to impress a roomful of people. That always seemed to be the thing that you liked most about being a congressman. You always liked an audience. You liked being the big man. Since you've got an audience, let me take the opportunity to tell them a few things at the same time I tell them to you. You came in here with a leg up on us. You had more advance knowledge of our capabilities than we had of yours. Now, though, we've been collecting our own intel and I think we have pretty good picture of what we're dealing with."

"Is that right? Well, despite what you might think, I can assure you that you have no idea what you're dealing with," the congressman boasted.

"There you go again, showboating for your audience. Do I need to point out that half of your force is middle-aged and soft? That half includes you, by the way. The other half appears to be from a law enforcement background. While they may have been good at their jobs, law enforcement training is well below what even the most poorly-trained of my men has gone through. You are outclassed here. You and your men are going to die."

"You sound awfully sure of yourself over there, Arthur," Congressman Honaker said.

"I am."

"Your confidence is misplaced."

Arthur shook his head in disgust. There was no reasoning with this man while he had an audience. He enjoyed acting tough. He enjoyed putting on the appearance of hard-nosed negotiation. He was one of those congressmen you often saw in the televised congressional hearings, asking questions purely for the drama of the moment. Purely for getting himself on the evening news.

"And your families are heading here with the expectation that you've arranged a safe haven for them?" Arthur said, changing tactics.

"That's exactly right. And you should understand a man will fight for nothing with such dogged determination as he will fight for his family."

"I completely understand that, but I can't agree that you have the well-being of your families in mind. If every one of you gets killed you'll have family showing up here for nothing. How do you think the death of all these men will affect the odds of their families' survival? For each of your men who gets killed, does his family have someone equally as capable, ready to assume the role of leading the family? Or will those families be reduced to scavenging? Will they become slaves to someone with better resources? Will they have to become prostitutes in order to eat and put a roof over their head?"

"The same could be said of your own families," the congressman retorted.

Arthur let out a low laugh. "You obviously missed something significant in your intelligence gathering. There are *no* families here. We have women soldiers and men soldiers but no families. Everyone who lives here has *nothing* left to fight for except this compound. They'll fight to the death because this place is their last stand. They see your attempt at an invasion as an affront to everything they believe. They will risk everything to see you killed."

Arthur gave the congressman a minute to process this new information, then another, and when there was no reply, Arthur continued.

"I want to add one more thing. I have no doubt that you used your resources and the resources of your men to scour police arsenals for tactical gear and weapons. You probably feel like you're pretty well-armed compared to the average citizen. I'm sure you are. But understand that the residents here have devoted their lives to amassing the supplies we need to operate this compound. I'd venture that I *personally* have more weapons and ammunition than your entire force and that doesn't include what the rest of my folks bring to the table. If you came for a war then you brought a knife to a gunfight. Bridges out."

Arthur slipped off the headset and stood up from the chair. He hoped he'd given the congressman something to think about. He pushed his way out the door. Carlos was hunched on the steps like a gargoyle, sucking at the stub of a hand-rolled cigarette.

"All yours," Arthur mumbled, heading back to his house.

5

Arthur had given the congressman a lot to think about. In fact, he hoped Congressman Honaker was at that very moment involved in a deep discussion with his cohorts as to whether they should continue this endeavor or not. However, Arthur knew the congressman wouldn't give up. He was too hard-headed, too persistent, and his ego too large to risk the embarrassment of backing down.

After Arthur finished his radio conversation, Kevin persuaded him there was a mission they needed to undertake. The surveillance Arthur's group had conducted that morning had given them some useful pieces of information. For one, the enemy had a hot breakfast and hot dinner each day but lunch was usually canned or freeze-dried fare taken whenever they had the opportunity to eat it. That was only of interest because it meant the cook was probably unoccupied during the middle of the day. If he was alone and unobserved, that would be the best time to launch an operation against him.

Kevin surmised that the cook might be the one person who knew the scope of Honaker's plan but, at the same time, was probably the least likely to be able to defend himself. Kevin had watched the video their observer shot several times over, focusing on the sections showing the cook. There was a definite sense that he resented his assignment. Whatever circumstance put him in that particular role was not of his choosing. Those kind of people could be exploited. They often felt unappreciated and under-utilized. They were the weak link.

In Kevin's assessment there was only one man among them cut out for the job of kidnapping the cook; the same military-trained sniper who had collected the footage in the first place. There were many among Arthur's group with the skills for precision rifle shooting but there was only one who had completed the U.S. Army Sniper Course. Part of that training was mastering the intricacies of camouflage and stalking. That was exactly the type of skill that would be required to pull off this job.

The perimeter around Arthur's compound was porous, mostly wooded and ill-defined. It wasn't fenced or walled-in. The congress-man's force was monitoring this perimeter by means of snipers and gunmen placed at intervals around the compound. During the day they used rifle scopes or spotting scopes. At night they used thermal and night vision. In daylight they had no difficulty spotting overt breaches, such as when Sonyea and Robert tried riding out in a vehicle or on horseback. Perhaps a heavily-camouflaged man in a perfectly-designed Ghillie suit creeping along a single inch at a time might not be so easily spotted.

The sniper's name was Brandon Barton. He was a stout young man with a buzz cut, incredibly fit and focused. He'd done twelve years in the Army with half of that as actual combat time served in the Middle East. Kevin, Arthur, and several other men from Arthur's team met with Brandon in the command bunker. They explained the assignment to him. Brandon listened with conditioned stoicism, never a flicker of concern, indecision, or questioning in his eyes.

"Think you're up to it, son?" Arthur asked.

"I'd be honored, sir. What are the rules of engagement?"

Arthur and Kevin smiled at the same time and looked at each other. They'd chosen wisely. You had to like a fearless, no-bullshit young man like that.

"You can drop the *sir*," Arthur said. "There's no rank here. We're all in the shit together."

"Old habit," Brandon replied. "What are the rules of engagement, *gentlemen?*"

Arthur took a seat on the edge of the table and rested his hands on his thighs. The homemade table creaked under his weight. "You'll be issued a suppressed .300 blackout with an EOTech. No sniper gear on this trip. You're cleared to engage anyone who engages you or anyone who threatens to compromise your mission."

While Arthur was trying to avoid the wholesale slaughter of the congressman's group, he was okay with the selective removal of targets as part of an effort to put an end to this siege. He understood this was perhaps selective morality but these were complicated times. In the back of Arthur's mind, he understood there was a possibility that they might even have to take out all of the enemy before the dust settled. He hoped to avoid that, though.

Kevin handed Brandon a picture of the cook captured from the video shot earlier that morning. "This is your target. The cook you saw this morning. Notice that he's one of the few not wearing a hat. He's also wearing jeans and not cargo pants. We've never seen him with a sidearm or weapon but that doesn't mean he's defenseless. Approach with the same level of caution you'd use with any other target."

"What am I supposed to do with him when I find him?" Brandon asked.

"Snatch and grab. We think he's staying in a tent on the edge of the camp. This time of day, he's probably one of the few remaining in camp. Everyone else is either in the command RV, out on assignment, or sleeping because they've come off-duty. If he's like most of the other cooks I've met, he's probably taking a nap before he has to prep for dinner. You'll approach him with utmost stealth and discretion, then disable him with a stun gun. While he's incapacitated, you'll gag and cuff him, then deliver the package to us."

Brandon nodded, completely unfazed by the nature of his mission. His cool head was part of why he was here. He'd only been able to buy into the compound because Arthur had cut him a break on the lowest tier of ownership. It was moments like this that demonstrated what he'd seen in the kid—total detached coolness, total professionalism.

"When you've bagged your target, you head home. If you hit trouble, put out a call on the radio. We'll launch a diversion. Once you get within visual range of our perimeter I'll have assistance waiting for you."

"Roger that," Brandon said. "When do I go?"

Kevin and Arthur looked at each other, then back to Brandon.

"Now."

6

The mountaintop compound was made up of several hundred acres of hardwood and pine forest. The majority of the structures were clustered in small groups or pods around the property. There was a shooting complex with an elaborate range which, before the collapse, was used to train paying students in different shooting and tactical situations. There was a precision rifle range that allowed shooters to stretch out to four hundred yards. That was a pretty long shot for the steep Carolina mountains but was useful for training both the precision shooters and the hunters that signed up for the long-range classes. Both ranges had classroom facilities, a covered bench area, and a composting toilet facility.

The main complex, where Arthur's cabin was located, was also referred to as the Command Pod by some of the residents. Besides his cabin, there was a green metal shop building containing tools and equipment. There was a repair shop attached to it for maintenance on the various machines and vehicles used to work the property. There was the commo shack, and a firewood storage shed. Out of view of Arthur's cabin were two bunkhouses, a solar shower facility, and more outhouses.

Located at a remote site, away from the roads travelled by students and guests, there was a fuel facility with several five-hundred gallon tanks of gasoline and diesel. Fuel was dispensed by twelve-volt pumps operated by solar power and a battery array. This was the only convenient way to manage refueling the many ATVs, tractors, mowers, and other machines used on the property. There was also a site where logs were processed into firewood for bonfires and the many woodstoves used to heat the buildings.

Cutting firewood was not allocated to a certain time of year. It was a continual process. Arthur and the other folks that lived on the grounds spent all year dragging fallen trees to the wood yard where they could be cut to length and split into firewood. Several open sheds contained wood in different states of curing. One shed contained pine logs which were used in bonfires but not in the woodstoves. Other sheds contained oak, poplar, walnut, and cherry all cut to length for the woodstoves.

Robert walked to the wood yard, deep in thought, rifle dangling over his shoulder. He was pleased to find a pile of logs waiting to be split. A splitting maul with a yellow fiberglass handle was sunk into a stump. Robert retrieved it and checked the edge with a thumb. He leaned his rifle against the wall of a nearby shed and removed his gun belt, snapping the belt back closed so he could hang it from a hook near his rifle. He rolled a short log onto the chopping block, took a wide stance, and heaved the maul up over his head. His first stroke cleaved the log neatly in half with a satisfying *thunk*.

He made short work of several more logs, cutting them into halves, then quarters, and even some smaller pieces. He worked up a sweat, relishing the feeling of physical labor. It was satisfying and made him miss home. On his small farm he could find work like this every day, something to get the heart pumping and ease the mind. He wanted to get back there. To get back to his life. His routine. His family.

"Is this splitting for exercise or clearing your head?"

The voice startled Robert and he spun, nearly stumbling over the growing mound of split wood encircling his feet. It was Sonyea.

He leaned the maul against the chopping block and wiped his forehead with the tail of his flannel shirt, squinting against the sun and the sting of sweat in his eyes. "Maybe a little of both."

She turned a fat log on its end and took a seat. "I've been there myself. It's therapeutic. When my son Tom first came back from the Middle East and the VA doctors had nothing but bad news, that's where I always ended up. Splitting wood. Sometimes I'd be cussing. Sometimes I'd be crying."

"I miss home," Robert said.

As soon as the words were out of his mouth, he immediately regretted saying them. After all, Sonyea's entire home had burned to the ground and she wasn't certain she'd ever see her farm again. She didn't respond to the comment but he could tell he'd pushed her to a dark place. He seemed to have a talent for that, also known as *insensitivity*. From the look on her face, she was reliving the whole thing— getting shot, the fire, having to bury Grace's friend Zoe. He forgot sometimes that he'd lived a pretty comfortable existence for most of this crisis. Sonyea and Grace had both gone through a lot more than he had.

"Look, I'm sorry. That was thoughtless."

Sonyea gave a strained smile. "Well, now that you mention it..."

He smiled back, thinking she was joking at first but she wasn't. Sonyea looked distracted. Something was on her mind. Something besides the memories he'd just dredged up for her. "Everything okay with you? How are you feeling today?"

She shifted on her log seat, leaning forward to rest her elbows on her knees, her head in her hands. She looked at the ground. "I've thought a lot about the breakfast conversation today."

"You mean the breakfast *altercation*?"

"Yep. That one."

Robert sighed. "Me too," he said, halfway hoping he could preempt whatever direction she was heading down. He knew that his mouth had gotten ahead of his brain, as it sometimes did. He knew that made him come off as a jerk or an asshole. The problem with *coming off* as an asshole was that it pretty much meant you *were* an asshole and just didn't want to admit it.

"Your friends have been really good to us," Sonyea said. "They helped us without question and without regard for how it affected their supplies or their personal safety. At no point in our stay have I ever felt like they were pushing us out or were concerned about the supplies we were using. Heck, their doctor saved my life with medical supplies they can't replace. They never made it seem like we were imposing. They did the same for our kids when they arrived here too. They kept them safe until we could get to them."

Robert was nodding in agreement the entire time she spoke. "They're good people."

"That's my point," she said, raising her face to him. "Are we being good people?"

Robert waved his arms in the air as if the answer was obvious. "Of course we're good people. I'm not even sure what you mean by that."

"That could be part of the problem."

He looked at her, confused and frustrated.

"That you don't know what I mean by that," she clarified. "That you don't understand."

"What's the problem?" he asked a little too loud. "I'm still not seeing any problem."

"If I thought Tom was in danger, I would move Heaven and Earth to get to him. I know you would do the same for Grace because I've seen it. The thing is, our kids are not in danger now—at least no more danger than anybody else. They're at your compound. They have access to gear and supplies. They're looking after your family. For now, the people we love are as safe as they can be."

Robert shook his head. "That doesn't affect me wanting to be with my family. Just because they're safe doesn't mean I'm not obligated to get to them. It doesn't mean they won't need my help again."

"Of course it doesn't. The tides could turn at any time and they could be back in danger again. *Could.* But these folks here need our help now."

Robert still wasn't getting it. This happened to him sometimes. It was the way his brain worked. As a writer, he spent so much time in the nuances of language that he often missed the obvious. He was never actually in the present but instead miles ahead or off to the side of what was really going on. "So what's your point, Sonyea? Just tell me."

"I'm not sure I can just walk away from this fight. To be totally honest, if *you* can walk away from this fight and return to your family with a clear conscience, it makes me wonder how I could ever really trust you. How could anyone ever trust you? I don't want to align myself with someone who can turn their back on me as easily as you're turning your back on these people. Your *friends*."

"I'm not turning my back on anybody," Robert said defensively, annunciating each word loud and clear. "I'm just trying to get to the place where I'm supposed to be. I had a plan for this possibility. That plan didn't include me being somewhere else while my family was at home alone facing whatever dangers show up on their doorstep."

"Well, I had a plan too and it didn't include any of the shitty things that have happened to me in my life. It didn't include a dead husband and an injured son. It didn't include some nut killing a beautiful young girl in my house. And it sure as heck didn't include my house burning to the ground."

Robert flipped up a log and sat down by Sonyea. "I think we need to try breaking out of here one more time. We go on foot. We sneak out just like the observer did this morning. We travel light. We can walk it. I know we can."

Sonyea shook her head. "No. Have you even been listening to a word I said?"

"Yes, but we have to try," Robert pleaded. "I can't just sit here and not try."

Sonyea looked him in the eye, her expression one of sadness, of disappointment. "If you go, you go without me. I'm staying until this is settled, for better or worse. I may not be a sniper, a soldier, or even a doctor, but I can shoot. I can help. That's the kind of person I am. You really need to think about what kind of person you are, Robert."

A lot of nuance went over Robert's head but there was no

mistaking the accusation in Sonyea's expression and her words. He hated feeling like he was being interrogated or questioned. He hated this loss of control. He hated it when people made him doubt himself. It was part of why he wanted to be back in the little world he'd made for himself, behind his fences and private road.

He got to his feet and angrily snatched up the splitting maul. He lined up another log, heaved the maul over his head, and split the chunk. He used significantly more force than was necessary and the maul buried itself in the chopping block, sending the split sections flying in opposite directions like they'd been tossed. He tugged on the handle, worked the maul loose, his mind processing what had just happened between him and his friend. When he finally came up with the words he wanted to say, he turned to Sonyea, ready to rebut her arguments, but found her stump empty.

7

B randon tried to make his steps blend in with the natural sounds of the forest. Nothing rocked his single-minded focus —not the men anxiously waiting on him back at the compound, not the objective that lay ahead of him, and not the risk that lay in between. It was just like being back in the Army Sniper Course. His only goal was to not make noise and not be spotted as he went about his mission.

With each step he paused, listening for any reaction to his movement. During that pause, he searched for his next foot placement. It was to his benefit that the leaves had not fallen yet. When that happened in a few months, there would be no stealthy movement in this forest. For now, the forest floor was mostly ferns, moss, sparse grass, weeds he couldn't identify, and the thick mulch that came from the endless cycle of plants living and dying in the deep forest.

He gave the enemy camp a wide berth, circling and approaching from the back. He assumed most of their security effort would be directed toward the side of the camp that faced Arthur's compound. That would be the logical place for their eyes and assets. They would not be looking for visitors to wander in from the rear.

Within visual range of the encampment, Brandon slipped a pair of binoculars beneath his camo net hood and observed the scene before him. He'd re-watched the videos from that morning's incursion. They'd gone over the layout of this camp a dozen times and he was fairly certain he knew the basics. They'd even mapped it out on a whiteboard, wanting to imprint a visual map into Brandon's brain. Besides, he knew if he had any trouble it wouldn't be from his failure to recall the exact layout of the camp. It would be from something unexpected. That was how these things always happened.

He studied the pop-up awnings and the campers. He saw the huge RV that served as the command center, or "head shed," and the long tent that served as the mess hall and meeting space. The sides were rolled up and the tables empty. That was good. It was what he expected to find.

Adjacent to the mess tent was another square pop-up tent where the cooking was done. There was a prep table, plastic storage totes, and another table with a line of propane camping stoves. Just as they'd hoped, no one was cooking a meal. The cook was elsewhere.

Beyond the dining area Brandon found a two-man backpacking tent set up in the shade of a hemlock. The proximity to the cooking tent, combined with the intel from the morning, led Brandon to think this was the cook's tent. He changed positions to get a better look. From a different angle he saw the person sleeping in the tent had removed the rain fly to improve ventilation on the muggy day. It occurred to Brandon that the thin mosquito netting would allow him to see inside the tent if he got close enough.

Using the same stealthy approach that got him to the camp, he maneuvered tree-to-tree, edging his way down the shallow slope. At one point he froze in his tracks when he heard raucous laughter coming from the RV. This erased any wonder about whether there were men inside there. His assumption had been confirmed.

The owner of the backpacking tent, apparently wanting a little separation from the main group, had positioned his tent so that it was blocked from the main encampment by trees and underbrush. Brandon figured as long as no one came down to the mess tent he should be okay. If they did, that might be a little too close for comfort but he felt confident he could disappear into the forest and lose them before chaos erupted. If that failed, he had the suppressed .300 over his back and clearance to use it if he had to. Still, if it went to either of those options, it was likely that his mission had failed and that wasn't how he wanted this to end. As trite as the saying may be, failure was not an option.

He warily closed the distance between himself and the tent. With each step he paused and listened, then repeated the process. While it was painfully slow, that was the nature of stalking a target. You only had the one chance. There were no do-overs.

Brandon broke from the last of his cover around thirty feet from the tent. With no rapid movements, he performed a careful 360-degree check of his surroundings. No threats. No movement.

He proceeded. One step. Another step.

Another.

At fifteen feet from the tent he did hear a sound and froze. While the forest was far from silent, this was not a naturally-occurring sound. It was something alien, abrasive. While the normal gut reaction of most folks might be to turn tail and retreat to the last cover, that was not how Brandon worked. He examined the sound. He wouldn't react without thinking it completely through and determining the best course of action. He listened and at first it sounded like a person choking. Brandon didn't move as he struggled to decipher it. He was frozen like a deer hoping to disappear into its surroundings. Then it hit him. It was snoring.

Brandon almost smiled. It was an optimal condition, a sleeping target.

He checked his surroundings again. There was the murmur of loud conversation, the occasional raised voice, coming from the distant command RV but they were completely obscured from him by woods and underbrush. Brandon moved forward again, walking slowly enough that the knee-high weeds barely whispered as they brushed against his legs.

He kept a consistent cadence. Step. Listen.

Step. Listen.

Inside the tent, the snoring continued, the rhythm of the breathing unchanged even as Brandon closed on him. Then he was at the side of the tent, his toes within inches of the nylon sidewall, and he leaned forward to peer through the netting. Sometimes people woke from the sensation of being watched. What would Brandon do if he looked inside to find an awake man staring back at him?

Fortunately, he was spared that circumstance. He found the sweaty cook out cold on top of his sleeping bag. His hand was draped across his eyes and his mouth gaped open like that of a dead fish. Even in this disheveled and unflattering condition, Brandon was certain it was him. He remembered the clothing, so distinctly different from that of the other men in the party.

He needed to strike before something went wrong. Any delays could give the cook time to wake up or allow someone else to show up on the scene. Brandon couldn't let any sense of urgency force him to rush and become careless, though. He'd made it too far to screw this up now. He moved forward with cool, determined efficiency.

He crept toward the end of the tent where the cook's head lay. He considered the zipper but decided even that small sound could be too much and might wake the sleeping man. He only needed a small opening in order to carry out his assignment, perhaps six inches. Just enough to get his hand and the Taser through.

Brandon dropped a hand to his belt and slipped the custom James Huse bowie from its sheath. The knife was a beast, designed for both combat and survival. It was honed to razor sharpness, the cutting edge polished to a mirror finish. Brandon eased the blade toward the netting. It slashed the fabric with such ease that he couldn't even detect the moment it penetrated the fabric. He moved the blade upward and then withdrew it, leaving behind a slit of more than sufficient size.

Brandon returned the knife to its sheath, coming back with the Taser Bolt he'd been issued for the operation. When it was in his hand, he paused to focus. This was the moment of truth. He slid the protective cover back from the trigger and verified the green LED was glowing. The device was ready. He carefully pushed the Taser through the netting, aimed at the cook's neck, and pressed the trigger.

The cook's eyes shot open, his jaw clenched, and he grunted as slobber ran from the side of his mouth. Brandon let the device do its job, watching impassively as the man's body clenched and seized from the burst of electricity. When he felt it was safe, Brandon yanked the probes free and rolled the wires around the device. He shoved it into a dump pouch on the back of his belt. He knew he had a brief window before the effects of the neuromuscular incapacitation began to wear off and the man might begin to react. Brandon wanted to have his prisoner securely packaged by that time.

He unzipped the door, grabbed the cook by his shirt, and yanked him swiftly out the opening. A special carabiner on his belt held a partial roll of duct tape. Brandon yanked off a two foot strip. He slapped it over the cook's mouth and wrapped it around his head until he ran out of tape. Brandon could feel the cook regaining control of his body, encountering some feeble resistance as he manipulated the man's limbs. Before the cook totally regained his faculties, Brandon dug a hand into a cargo pocket and came out with one set of flex cuffs and one long zip tie. He secured the cook's hands with the cuffs and his ankles with the zip tie, then straightened the body out on the ground.

Dead weight was difficult to deal with and a man could easily exhaust himself trying to pull an unconscious man up into a fireman's carry. Everyone thought they could do it until they tried. Most gave up when they realized it wasn't as easy as they made it look in the movies, but Brandon had a trick for that.

He propped his weapon against a tree and laid himself perpendicular across the cook's body, resting his back on the cook's chest. He hooked his left arm under the cook's knee and grabbed a handful of his pants. Brandon rolled hard to his right side, pulling the leg with him, and using his momentum to roll efficiently onto his knees with the limp body across his shoulders. The technique was called a *ranger roll* and designed exactly for this scenario.

It still took significant effort and Brandon used all his power to force himself to his feet. The cook was comparatively light as grown men went—it was nothing like lifting another soldier across his back —but heaving a human body across your shoulders and moving with it was never an easy task. Brandon trained obsessively, often with sandbags. He'd sling them around, drag them, or carry them for long distances. Although he couldn't explain to people why he did it, this was precisely why. It was for moments just like this, when an injured buddy or a high value target had to be carried to a location they weren't able, or willing, to go.

Brandon grabbed his weapon, then did a quick check to make sure he had all his gear with him. He was certain these folks would eventually figure out what happened but he didn't want to make it easy for them. Maybe they'd assume the cook wandered off to answer the call of nature, or perhaps took a walk and got lost.

He aimed for the woods and began marching in that direction. He climbed steadily away from the encampment, taking long steps and feeling the burn in his quads almost immediately. When he hit the woods he reached into his radio pouch and keyed the mic. It was the signal. He had his cargo and was coming home.

He tried to maintain as much stealth as possible but with the man on his shoulders there was no blending in this time. He focused on moving as quickly as possible, with sure and certain steps, while still trying to minimize the noise. He was constantly processing input from his environment. He monitored comms, did a visual scan of his surroundings, listened for unusual sounds, and kept track of what messages his own body was sending him. With each step he reminded himself that climbing a peak wasn't over just because you reached the summit—you still had to get home.

8

"*Jim Beam Actual, this is Jim Beam Romeo. I have a visual on Jim Beam Delta. He's returning under load. Over.*"

Brandon heard the message in his earpiece and knew Arthur's perimeter security had spotted him.

"*Jim Beam Delta, this is Jim Beam Actual. Be advised we'll meet you at the border unless you request an alternative pickup point. Over.*"

Brandon freed up a hand to click his mic in response. It was a pre-arranged signal. He lowered his head and chugged away, focusing on his steps. Focusing on not falling and injuring himself. Focusing on not getting killed.

A hundred yards shy of Arthur's boundary, a side-by-side ATV with two rows of seats intercepted him. The armed crew relieved him of his burden, sandwiching the sluggish prisoner between them in the back seat while the front passenger provided overwatch. Brandon, legs spent but feeling considerably lighter without the body on his shoulders, rolled into the cargo bed and held on for dear life. The ATV spun around, spraying dirt in all directions, then shot toward the safety of the compound.

Back inside Arthur's borders, the ATV hit a trail and accelerated madly, the engine racing. Branches whipped off the roll cage, sending leaves spiraling in their wake. The trail soon joined one of the compound's interior roads, wider and smoother than the trail. The driver punched the throttle. The machine slewed sideways before the wheels caught traction and it accelerated forward. In less than a minute, they were at the command pod, skidding to a stop in front of the communications shack. Arthur was waiting for them, along with Sonyea, Kevin, and a glum-looking Robert.

"The hay barn," Arthur ordered, pointing a finger in that general direction. It was all he had to say. He didn't want this prisoner out in the open for too long, not banking against the devious Congressman Honaker having access to drones or satellite surveillance.

The driver did as he was told, accelerating toward a different gravel road and travelling deeper into the interior of the property. He was gone from sight in seconds.

Arthur called back inside the radio shack, "Carlos, transmit the code for radio silence. I don't want anyone using a radio unless it's an emergency. Got it?"

"Roger that," Carlos called back.

"Bailey!" Arthur yelled, calling to a stocky man in the distance wearing camo and carrying an AR-10 with a long-range scope.

"Yes sir?" Bailey asked, jogging toward Arthur.

"Put some guys on the electronic security measures. Plug any gaps. I want this place wrapped tight."

The compound was nearly surrounded by a boundary of trip-wires and electronic notification devices. It was low-tech for the most part, with many of the electronic measures being of the simple home improvement store variety. There were intentional gaps in the perimeter security so men could come and go without being concerned about tripping over them. This didn't seem like the time to err on the side of convenience, though. Any gap that would allow a friendly to access the camp might also allow an enemy to stroll into the camp undetected.

His assignment clear, Bailey jogged off. Arthur walked briskly to his own ATV. He waved at Kevin. "Come on. Let's interview a cook."

"Arthur!" Robert called.

"What is it? I'm kind of in a hurry here."

Robert looked sheepish. "Any chance of me coming along?"

Arthur cut his eyes to Kevin but the other man gave no reaction that Robert could see. Settling his eyes back on Robert, Arthur pulled his hat off and scratched his head. "I just don't see the point. This isn't your fight and you've made it clear that your priority is getting out of here."

His message delivered, Arthur didn't wait for a response. He hopped into his own side-by-side and cranked the engine, not even waiting for a reaction.

"Wait!" Robert shouted, stepping in front of the vehicle.

Arthur sighed and turned the engine off. He looked pissed. "Make it fast."

Robert cast a quick glance at Sonyea, who appeared uncertain as to where this was going. They'd barely spoken since she'd expressed her opinion to him while he was splitting firewood.

"I had some time to think about your problem while I was splitting wood. Sonyea and I talked about it. Until this is resolved one way or another, this is our fight as well. Our families are safe for now and we're not walking out on you. This is where we're needed. I'm sorry it took me a while to realize that and I'm sorry about...being a dick."

Kevin cast a quick glance at Sonyea, raising a questioning eyebrow.

"He's right," she confirmed. "We're here until this is done. It's not up for debate."

Arthur merely nodded and waved Robert toward the back seat of the side-by-side. Sonyea started to follow but Arthur held up a hand. "No, ma'am. This is one place where I draw the line, Sonyea. If the cook doesn't speak freely, this may get ugly. The threats I'm going to make will not be pretty. It may even get physical. I don't want you to have to see that. Some things won't leave your head once you let them inside."

Sonyea nodded with understanding, a little embarrassed that she'd not grasped the full implication of what was about to take place. This was not to be a friendly conversation. This was an interrogation. If the answers weren't forthcoming, there would be the threat of torture and perhaps even the application of torture. She was tough as nails but the sight of a man being tortured was not something she wanted to see. Bad memories were never as easily forgotten as the good.

Arthur started his machine again and punched the gas. The light vehicle spun the tires and barreled toward its destination. Robert caught Sonyea's eyes as they parted ways. There was a lot in that brief glance. There was appreciation for her setting him straight while he was splitting wood. There was apology that he'd put her in a position of having to say those things to him in the first place. There was also a flicker of concern at the things he might soon have to watch. It was one thing to write gore, violence, and human ugliness. It was another thing entirely to experience it firsthand.

9

Arthur's compound made the majority of its income from survival training and the firearms school. They had contracts with state police and local law enforcement agencies for firearms training, and contracts with the military and some alphabet agencies who required a low-key place to train or needed something specialized that the military schools didn't normally offer. It was not operated as a farm commercially but they did maintain some livestock as part of their long-term, sustainable preparedness strategy.

There were some sheep, goats, a few head of cattle, a contrary bull, and a dozen free-range hogs that rooted around in the woods. There were chickens and ducks in coops and running loose. There were several hayfields carved from the forest and Arthur allowed a trusted local farmer to cut the hay several times a summer, with Arthur and the farmer each getting half of the yield. For hay storage, Arthur built a cavernous pole barn with mammoth rolling doors that allowed a tractor to stack bales inside. A couple of solar panels on the roof powered a simple twelve-volt lighting system.

Arthur skidded his ATV to a stop in front of the hay barn, practically launching himself from the seat and barreling into the barn. He was laser-focused on the task at hand. Kevin and Robert were on his heels, trying to keep up with him. Inside, the cook from the opposing force was sitting upright on the dirt floor. His hands and ankles were bound and a burlap feed sack had been pulled over his head.

Brandon and the other men who'd played a role in recovering the prisoner stood around him in a circle, their weapons at low ready, watching him impassively. They were all men who'd been in this very situation before in numerous regions of the world. At different times, in different lives, the man on the ground before them had been Taliban, Al Qaeda, a suspicious local villager, an insurgent, a cartel member, an Iraqi Republican Guard, a Somali pirate, or a host of others. Regardless of who the high value target was, they all knew how this went. They all knew their role.

Arthur went to Brandon first, patting him on the back and offering a smile at a job well-done. No words were exchanged. Brandon gave a silent nod of acknowledgement, meeting Arthur's eyes before returning them to the prisoner. Arthur then strode to the prisoner, dropped to a knee, and yanked the sack off the cook's head.

"Welcome to my side of the fence, shitbird."

The cook was wide-eyed, panicked. He struggled, but with his hands and feet bound, only succeeded in falling over to his side, unable to sit back up.

Arthur smiled. "The Taser just scrambled your wiring a little bit. Your coordination will come back. You'll be fine."

The cook rolled to his back and awkwardly struggled to a sitting position again, glaring at Arthur. He tried to speak but the tape over his mouth limited him to muffled swearing.

Arthur reached forward and pinched a flap of the tape that had worked its way loose. The cook stared at him, fear in his eyes.

Arthur smiled. "This is probably going to sting a little."

The man gave a muffled scream when Arthur yanked like he was starting a particularly cantankerous chainsaw. The tape came loose but didn't break, whipping the man forward. As the tape unwound itself from the cook's head, it brought a generous amount of hair along with it. When his mouth was no longer covered, his voice no longer muffled, the cook had a lot to say.

"You old bastard!" he screamed, his face burning crimson. He writhed on the floor, wanting to rub his aching scalp, his stinging flesh, but he couldn't get a hand loose to do so. He worked himself to a sitting position, yelling and complaining until he was done. When he got no response from Arthur, he settled down and glared murderously at the older man.

"You done?" Arthur asked with a grin.

"You are so screwed right now!" the cook bellowed. "You're a dead man. You are so *dead*!"

Arthur's smiled faded. "What's your name, son?"

"Screw! You!" the cook spat.

Arthur lashed out and slapped the cook across the face. The blow knocked him over on his side again. The gesture wasn't intended to injure the cook but to establish that violence wasn't off the table. Better to get that out of the way now so there would be no doubts and no misunderstandings later. The rules in any negotiation should always be established at the beginning. Less time was wasted when everyone knew the rules.

Arthur stood, grabbed the cook by his t-shirt, and hauled him back to a sitting position, making sure he was able to hold himself up before he released him. "What makes you so certain that we're screwed?"

The cook hesitated, giving Arthur a wary glare. His eyes watered and his face stung from the tooth-rattling blow to his cheek. "Because my dad is *Congressman* Honaker. You understand that? A United States Congressman. He's part of the government. He was trying to be nice to you guys and give you a chance to leave quietly, but you were too stupid. Now you've left him no choice. He'll probably have to kill all of you and it will be your own fault."

The way the cook offered up his dad's name and title indicated that he thought this information might carry some weight with the men surrounding him. He seemed to think it would instill fear or maybe regret at the path they'd taken. If he expected them to back out of the room like a primitive tribe mistaking technology for magic, he was mistaken.

Arthur grinned and looked around the room. "Did you hear that, boys? That's the government outside. We're supposed to be scared." He chuckled and his congregants followed his lead.

The cook looked from man to man, infuriated that they weren't taking him seriously. Then it occurred to him that, if this was their reaction, maybe *he* was the one who needed to worry. He thought they would be alarmed at the revelation he was the son of a sitting United States congressman, the very man leading the attack on the compound. His father had led him and many of the other men to believe taking the compound would be a cakewalk. Any resistance they met would be purely a token gesture and would be dealt with quickly. These men gathered around him appeared serious and dangerous. Worst of all, they apparently didn't give a crap who his dad was.

"You won't be laughing when my dad's done with you," the cook spat defiantly, trying to regain some of his bravado.

Arthur squatted down. He spoke more intimately to the young man but loud enough for the rest of the room to hear. "What's your name, son?"

The cook stubbed up and twisted his head away like a defiant child refusing to eat broccoli.

Arthur sighed for dramatic effect. "You can tell me the easy way or you can tell me the hard way, but I guaran-damn-tee you'll tell me. In fact, you'll tell me everything I want to know before the day is over. The only question here is whether you'll survive the telling."

The cook flicked his eyes in Arthur's direction, his escalating fear apparent. He was obviously weighing those words, trying to gauge just how much trouble he was in.

"Let me tell you a little story. I grew up on a farm in the country not too far away from here," Arthur said. "We had a lot of livestock. When hogs were born, my daddy and I would track down all the males. He taught me to push them over and hold them down with my knee. I'd grab the scrotum, just above the balls, and squeeze like I was trying to wring out a wet rag. That forced their balls down tight into the sack, you see. Then, just like my dad showed me, I'd take my pocket knife and make a quick little cut in their scrotum. From there it was just a matter of squeezing their balls out that little slit and snipping the cord that attached them to the hog. That was it. No medicine, no stitches. The cut healed on its own. We did dozens of them in a day sometimes. There would be little balls everywhere—dogs eating and carrying them around, cats batting them like toys, kids throwing them at each other."

Arthur paused and forced a look of compassion onto his face. "You're okay, aren't you? You're looking a little green. This story isn't making you uncomfortable, is it?"

The cook shook his head hesitantly. "No," he croaked.

"Good. The point is that I'm a little rusty after all these years but I still remember the basics—grab, squeeze, cut. Some things never leave a man. Now I'm going to ask your name again. I'll ask nicely but this will be the last time I ask nicely. Do you understand where we're headed here? Do you understand there's a point from which we can't back this thing up?"

The cook nodded.

"Now what is your name?"

The cook swallowed hard, deciding that a name was a simple thing, in the end. He could give that up much easier than he could a testicle. It was not information worth getting cut over. "Jeff. My name is Jeff."

Arthur reached forward to pat the young man on the shoulder with a folksy gesture of appreciation of their progress. "See, that wasn't too bad was it?"

"What do you want with me?" The young man looked Arthur in the eyes. The icy look he got back from Arthur demonstrated that his concern for his safety was completely valid. The man interrogating him was deadly serious. He was not lying when he said he would stop at nothing to get what he wanted.

"I need information."

Jeff tried to give a laugh of exasperation but managed only a pathetic seal-like bark, fear constricting his throat and choking it off. "Why would I just hand you any information?"

Without breaking eye contact with Jeff, Arthur gestured dismissively to the barn door and the world beyond. "All those men out there, the men that brought you here, they're already dead. I don't care if they're your friends, your family, whatever. They're dead. They just don't know it yet. Nothing you say will either save or further endanger those men. Those cards have been dealt. All you can control is what happens in this little circle right here." Arthur gestured around the room to emphasize just what circle he was referring to.

Jeff considered this for a moment. He sighed and slowly released a breath. Arthur detected the slightest hitch in his exhalation. It was a choked-back sob. Jeff was about to cry. He was losing his shit. He was breaking down. It was exactly what needed to happen.

"If you're going to kill those men, then you're probably going to kill me anyway. What would be the point of me telling you anything?"

"Oh, there's different ways to die, Jeff. There's good ways and there's bad ways. There's easy ways and there's hard ways. There's taking a quick bullet to the head and then there's dying inch by inch, piece by piece. But before you get too worried about how you're going to die, you need to know that our little talk, this exchange between you and me, isn't about saving those men. It's not even about saving you. It's about saving those other people out there on the road that haven't got here yet. The people related to you. The people you love."

Jeff looked even more concerned now. Wherever his mind had been, it snapped back to center with razor focus. Perhaps he hadn't realized that Arthur knew they had families coming. For Arthur's part, it hadn't even been a serious feat of intelligence-gathering to arrive at that tidbit of information. It had been the Congressman's own arrogance, his bragging that he had people on the road. He had been *so* confident in his ability to take the compound that he didn't even have the families wait for confirmation it was safe to come.

"Do you have family coming, Jeff?"

Jeff dropped his head and looked at the ground but he nodded.

"I used to know your family but it's been a long time. You were a kid and probably don't remember me but I visited your home," Arthur said. "Who's coming? Your mother? Brothers and sisters?"

"My mother, my little sister, probably my grandmother. She's been living with us."

The fight was gone from Jeff now. He was relaying information with no coercion at all. He was beaten.

"This is where the burden falls on you, Jeff. Do you love those people?" Arthur was speaking lower now, just above a whisper. It was not the voice of an interrogator. It was the voice of a counselor offering solace, offering assistance with a problem of some gravity. It was the voice of a grandfather passing on wisdom.

"Yes," Jeff replied, as if the very question was absurd. "Of course I love them."

"Did you ever watch those movies, Jeff, where the hero saves the day? This is *your* opportunity to save the day. You could be that hero, but you have to be man enough to make the tough calls."

Jeff didn't respond. He was spiraling into a dark place. Arthur looked back over his shoulder. He nodded at Kevin, who tossed a canvas tool bag to the ground beside Arthur. It landed with a metallic clank. Arthur reached for it and tipped it over, shaking out the contents. An array of tools spilled out. There was a rusty scalpel, pruning shears, a sharp, pointy awl, needle nose pliers, and several zip ties.

Arthur looked up at Jeff, who was staring intently at the pile of tools. "You know what these are for?"

Jeff shook his head.

"I don't believe you," Arthur whispered. "Are you sure you don't know what they're for?"

When Jeff refused to bite, Arthur picked up the awl and drove it into the ground with his palm. He reached into the same pile and withdrew the pruning shears, snapping the jaws shut. The metallic clack echoed in the quiet barn. "Little pig, little pig," Arthur whispered.

Arthur had Jeff's undivided attention now.

"These are tools for the extraction of information, Jeff. These are tools for punching tiny, painful holes into large muscle groups. These are tools for pinching bits of flesh into bloody paste. That rusty scalpel? That's for what we discussed earlier—the thing about dropping your severed nuts onto the ground. And you know what? If I want to do any of those things, you can't do a damn thing about it. The only tool you have for saving yourself from the pain is freely giving me the information I want."

Jeff knew it was true. He sat rigid with fear. He knew the cutting could begin any moment. He hoped, if it did, he would pass out and be spared the agony of a slow death from torture.

"The way this goes down, Jeff, is that you tell me what I want to know because you want to be a hero. You're not doing it because you're afraid of me. You're doing it because you want to be the guy in the movie who saves his family. You want to be the guy who saves *all* those families. You tell me what I want to know and maybe I can find a way to stop them from coming here without having to kill them. If you don't tell me what I want to know then you die, the men outside die, and every family member that shows up outside my gate probably dies. That includes your mother, your little sister, and your grandmother. Is that what you want, Jeff?"

Jeff shook his head. "Am I going to die?" He asked it with such sincerity that he sounded like a small child asking a question for which he dreaded the answer.

Arthur gave an exaggerated shrug. "Honestly, the jury is still out on that one. Whether you live or die doesn't change the facts of the situation. You can still be the hero, even though you might not be around for the little pat on the back at the end."

Arthur stood. "I've given you a lot to think about. Unfortunately, you don't have a lot of time to make your decision. I'll give you a little time but it won't be much. That's just the nature of the situation.

When you see me again in a few minutes, things will get real serious. You got me?"

Arthur didn't wait for an answer. He was done for now. He felt dirty and slightly nauseous for manipulating the cook but he'd done what he had to do. Hopefully the kid wouldn't force him to take things any further than he already had.

10

Outside the hay barn, the interrogation complete, Arthur stood ramrod straight, his palms shoved into his back pockets, staring off at the mountains. It was how rural men processed the world, immersing themselves in their surroundings, ruminating over their thoughts. He was pulled from that process by the scuffing of gravel behind him. He found Robert approaching, his brow furrowed as he too processed what had just taken place in the dim barn.

"Kevin still in there?" Arthur asked.

Robert gestured back toward the barn. "He's going over some details with the guards. He doesn't want this guy snatched back from us."

Arthur nodded absently. "That's probably a good idea." He was still distracted, gazing and thinking, trying to figure a way out of the hole they found themselves in.

"I've been thinking," Robert began.

Arthur shot him a sour look. "I've been trying to think too but I'm not getting too far with it. Some thinkers are apparently louder than others."

"I'm sorry. What have you been thinking?"

"If we heavily engage the main camp then the congressman will be forced to pull in all his troops to defend it. That should leave gaps in their coverage. You and Sonyea can try to make another break for it with the horses."

"Arthur—"

Arthur ignored him and continued. "Once you're gone we'll see if we can use Jeff in there for leverage to make the congressman pull out and go home. We need more info out of him first but I think we're off to a good start."

"Arthur!" Robert said loudly.

Arthur snapped his head in Robert's direction, both surprised and angered at the man's tone. He glared at him. "What?"

"Would you listen to me for a second?" Robert said. "I might have an idea."

"I thought your only idea was to get back to your family as soon as you could. I thought that's what you wanted."

"That *was* my idea. Earlier," Robert said. "But it was the wrong idea. I told you, I'm here until this is done."

"What was wrong about that idea? About leaving? What changed your mind?"

Robert anguished over his response. Honestly, he was unsure of how to put it into words without making himself sound like an asshole but maybe that wasn't possible. Maybe that was the truth of it. Maybe he *had* been a selfish asshole and he just needed to embrace that fact and move on with things.

"I think I've had a case of tunnel vision, Arthur. Ever since Grace left for college my biggest fear was how I would get her home if the shit hit the fan. That's dealt with now. She's the one who's home and I'm the one stuck on the road away from my family. It's a consuming, gnawing fear that just doesn't let up. But Sonyea reminded me that we've talked to our families and they're safe. They've dealt with any immediate threats. I still want to get home to them with all my being but maybe I don't want to have regrets when I get there."

"Regrets?" Arthur asked, raising a single, questioning eyebrow.

"Regrets that I turned my back on friends. Regrets that I walked away and said this wasn't my fight. Years ago, when I asked if you would help my daughter if she ever came to you, you said yes with no conditions whatsoever. You never said she wasn't your daughter and wasn't your problem. You never said it depended on any conditions. You just said you'd help her in any way possible. You were true to your word. You've been a better friend than I was and I apologize for that. I hope you can forgive me."

Arthur smiled at his friend. "Of course I forgive you. If anyone understands obsessive focus on the mission it's me. This is still *our* fight, though. I don't want you to stay out of a sense of obligation. Your presence here is welcome and appreciated but you're free to go if you want. I won't think any less of you and we'll still be friends when this is over."

"I've thought it through and I'm staying," Robert said resolutely. "You may not think any less of me but I'd think less of myself."

"Sonyea's good with this?"

"You heard her yourself. She's already told me that she's staying whether I do or not. Even though you two barely know each other, she's apparently a better friend than I am. Maybe a better person in general."

Arthur patted Robert on the shoulder. "We're good, buddy. That's all that has to be said about it. So tell me, what's this plan that you've been trying to make me listen to?"

Robert smiled. "Do you remember the story of the Pied Piper?"

Arthur screwed up his face as he considered the question, then recollection washed over him. The glimmer of intrigue flared in his eyes like a gas burner coming to life. "I'm listening. Tell me more..."

THAT EVENING KEVIN, Sonyea, Arthur, Robert, and the doctor sat on the back deck of Arthur's house. They had just wrapped up a respectable feast of venison steaks, roasted potatoes and carrots, with hot buttered cornbread. The Appalachian sunset queued up over the distant ridges, pausing to make certain it had everyone's attention before it began a spectacular plummet behind the farthest ridges.

"An evening like this calls for a sip of bourbon," Arthur said, heading back inside the house.

"I won't argue with that," Kevin said.

Arthur returned to the porch with glasses and a drawstring bag about the size of a grapefruit. He spread his goodies on a plastic table and slipped a bottle of bourbon from the bag.

"Blanton's," Robert said with a degree of respect. "That's good stuff."

Arthur shrugged. "No use saving it for a day that might never come. Maybe the congressman will have his way with us and toss us out on our ears. If that's the case, I don't want him drinking my bourbon. Even if it's not him, maybe it will be the next band of savage marauders to show up at our gates. So I'll just live for today. If I want a sip of bourbon, I'll drink the best I have."

Robert took the glass that was offered it to him and raised it in a toast. "To living well today."

The other men raised their glasses to the toast, Sonyea adding to hers, "To living well today *and* tomorrow."

"And tomorrow," the men agreed in a staggered chorus.

Arthur took his seat in one of the plastic deck chairs and the others followed suit, sipping their bourbon and watching the sun finally crawl off to die, generating an agonizingly unhurried light show.

"I wonder why people have always been so mesmerized by sunsets," Robert said. "Is it our brains reacting to the colors or is that the sunset itself serves as a reminder we've survived another day?"

"If you're that philosophical off one sip of a bourbon then I don't want to see you drunk," Kevin scoffed.

"It must be a writer thing," Sonyea said, nodding along with Kevin. She knew Robert hated it when people accused him of philosophizing, which made her want to encourage it. Maybe she had a little bit of a mean streak, or maybe he deserved it for the way he'd been acting the last few days.

"I'll just keep my thoughts to myself then," Robert said in mock offense.

"So what was this Pied Piper thing you mentioned earlier?" Arthur asked. They hadn't had a chance to discuss it at the barn and he wasn't in the mood for levity right now. As much as he wanted to sip his bourbon and enjoy the sunset, he couldn't push away the burden that he was facing right now. The stakes were too high. The lives of his men depended on his decisions.

Robert hesitated. He'd just taken a sip of his bourbon and speaking would interfere with the ritual. It was a rare treat and not to be wasted. When the moment passed, the bourbon having run its course, he set the glass on the arm of his chair. He was an animated speaker and needed both hands free to express himself.

"You guys know the basics of the story, right? Some small town in Europe promises to pay this flute player to lead away the rats that have inundated the town. He does his job but they refuse to pay him so he does the same thing with their children, leading them away never to be seen again."

"Heartwarming," Sonyea said, a disturbed look on her face.

"Fables are intended to teach morality, not provide happy endings. That's a more modern expectation," Robert said. "People weren't always so squeamish."

"What does this have to do with our current situation?" Kevin asked.

"We know from the congressman's own mouth and from Jeff's interrogation that their families are on their way here. We also know that they have an armed escort but we don't know of what size. I would assume small because the congressman would want most of his troops at the front of his operation and not bringing up the rear. We also know where they're leaving from, thanks again to Jeff. If we can squeeze a little more info out of him we might be able to intercept those families on the road."

"Whoa! A clash with families is what we're trying to avoid," Arthur said. "I'm trying to save innocent lives."

"They're not innocent if they're party to trying to take your place illegally," Sonyea said.

"If they even know what's going on," Kevin said. "The congressman might not have explained the details. They might just think that he has a retreat lined up for them without knowing any of the specifics. They may not know his plan rests on displacing the lawful residents of this compound. It would be a shame to kill them all if they had no understanding of what was taking place."

"Excuse me. Not done here," Robert said. "Hear me out."

Arthur spun his fingers in the air, encouraging Robert to get the story back on track. Time was wasting, bourbon evaporating.

"Assume we intercept the families on the road and lead them astray, like the Pied Piper leading away the children," Robert continued. "I haven't worked out all the details yet, but the point is that we lead them somewhere else. Once we do this, we explain to them that we led them there to save their lives. We tell them that everyone they were going to meet is dead and they need to go back home. Maybe we disable their vehicles and leave them there. Take their fuel to prevent them from leaving on their own. Either way, we put them in a state of peril that we can then exaggerate to the congressman and his party. We create a situation where these men across the gate feel that they have to leave and go rescue their families. I don't think that's a move the congressman would expect."

Robert looked from face to face and the expressions of the group revealed nothing. Everyone was processing what he said, playing out scenarios and examining options. They were looking for flaws or filling in gaps where he'd left them.

"It's possible something along those lines could work," Kevin agreed. "There's a lot that would have to be hammered out. There's the matter of whether those families are in communication with the congressman's party. There's the matter of who we would send out to intercept them and whether we could spare the manpower. Then there's the matter of how they would even get out of the compound and travel that far without getting killed in the process."

"I'm willing to go," Robert said.

Arthur pursed his mouth and shook his head.

"What?" Robert said, offended. "I can play a role here."

"I'm not saying you're not capable of it, Robert," Arthur said. "I'm just saying you don't need to do it. There's no reason for you to put yourself in that kind of danger. There are people here who are better trained for that kind of operation than you. I'll also remind you that none of us have families to worry about. You and Sonyea do."

"Your men are the very people you need to keep here," Robert said. "You need them to defend this place and create the kind of diversion that would allow us to get out. We also need some way to take their comms out so we can make certain they're not communicating to the folks on the road."

"In these steep hills, they're not communicating any distance with handheld radios," Kevin said. "If they're communicating with folks on the road, they're using big antennas, perhaps mounted at a high point in the hills around the camp. That's the vulnerability. We destroy antennas and disable comms."

"I could take one of the side-by-side ATVs?" Robert suggested. "That Polaris of yours is pretty fast."

Arthur cleared his throat. "You're getting ahead of yourself here. I don't think we pinned down that you're the one going on this mission, even if we do undertake it."

"But you'd consider it?"

"Hell, I'd consider anything at this point," Arthur replied.

The sound of boots on the stairs to the deck got everyone's attention. The group went on alert, hands dropping to sidearms. A serious face appeared at the top of the steps. It was Carlos, the radio operator.

"What is it?" Arthur asked.

"I need you in the commo shack now."

MINUTES LATER, Arthur stood in the radio shack, jammed shoulder-to-shoulder with his friends and team leaders. He had the microphone in his hand, listening to the congressman's angry voice pour through the wall-mounted speakers.

"Do you have my son?" the congressman bellowed, venom in his tone.

"We have a prisoner," Arthur acknowledged. "We believe him to be part of a hostile enemy force currently engaged in an unlawful attack against our home."

He released the mic button. "They probably just noticed the kid was missing when they showed up for dinner and he didn't have their soufflé waiting for them."

"This really doesn't bode well for you people," the congressman growled. His tone was exaggerated, theatrical, as if he were again playing to an audience. *"We have tried to conduct ourselves in a civil fashion. We've tried diplomacy and negotiation. Now you've killed several of my men and kidnapped my son."*

"We killed men who were actively engaged in firing at our folks. That's called self-defense. I would also consider it rather naïve on your part to assume you could steal someone's property under the cloak of diplomacy. Did you really think I was just going to turn this place over to you? If you've done any research at all, you know how much of my own blood and sweat went into this."

"I don't give a tinker's damn what you put into that place. Consider this to be official notice that the window of civil discourse has closed. From this point forward we are no longer fellow Americans. You may consider us to be your enemies."

Arthur keyed the mic, laughing into it. "You dumbass, I've never considered us to be anything but enemies. You gave up being Americans when you decided to steal my property like some third-world dictator. Now your son will pay the price for it. His blood will be on your hands."

"I could lie to you and tell you things will go easier if you release him but I know you wouldn't believe me. In fact, I don't think there's anything you can do at this point to make this go easy for you."

"I'm prepared to make you a slightly more generous offer," Arthur replied. "Pack your little campers, get the hell out of here, and the rest of you might escape the fate that your son is going to meet."

"You better not harm my son," the congressman said through clenched teeth. *"If you've spoken to him at all, you know the boy is not a threat. In fact, he's damn near useless, which is why he's packing a spatula and not a gun."*

"The fact that you see him as an ineffective soldier does not change the fact that he is a member of an invading force. He is the enemy and will be dealt with appropriately."

"This is war now!" the Congressman bellowed.

Arthur held the microphone back up to his own mouth. "It was always war."

11

After the radio conversation between Congressman Honaker and Arthur the compound went on full alert. With diplomacy tossed out the window there was concern there might be an attempt to rescue Jeff. Arthur didn't have an accurate picture of the size of the Congressman's force. He hoped Honaker understood that throwing men at the heavily armed compound would be suicidal but the congressman could be blinded by any number of things, including his pride, his narcissism, and his determination to get his son back. Arthur wasn't even sure that last item on this list was motivated by love as much as by the congressman's desire to save face in front of his men.

Arthur gathered his team leaders in front of the commo shack. "I need every man on duty tonight. Hand out caffeine pills, energy gels, and keep the coffee flowing. Alert the men who have remote duty stations and pull them back a little tighter to the command pod. I don't want anyone so far out they can be easily separated and picked off. We protect the core of the compound and we protect each other. That's our priority. If we lose any ground we can take it back over the next couple of days because I don't think they have enough men to keep it."

The team leaders rushed off to carry out Arthur's assignments. Arthur directed his attention to Robert and Sonyea. "I want you two to get some rest. If you're still up for this Pied Piper mission we talked about, we'll launch it at daybreak. Be ready. Have your personal gear packed."

"Are you sure the timing is right?" Robert asked, surprised to be on-deck. "Won't they be all over us since they're trying to get the congressman's son back?"

Arthur threw a devious smile. "I have an idea for that."

"This should be good," Kevin said.

Arthur nodded. "Oh, it's twisted."

"What do you need me to do?" Kevin asked.

"I need somebody to weld up a jerry can rack for the Polaris Razer. Something that will hold four cans. It's fine if it crowds the back seat a little but they'll still need room for three people."

"Three people?" Robert asked. "Who are you sending with us?"

"Jeff."

Robert threw up both hands. "Now wait a damn minute! No one said anything about taking Jeff with us. I volunteered to go on this mission to help, *not* to babysit."

"I can send someone else if you're not agreeable to the plan."

"It was my idea!" Robert erupted. "I want to go but I don't want to jeopardize it by having someone along who might sabotage the whole thing."

"Then maintain control of your prisoner. Don't give him an opportunity to screw things up," Arthur said.

"Look, Robert, it makes sense from a mission standpoint," Kevin said. "If I was sending you to meet up with some group, whether it was a cartel, the Taliban, whoever, I would send you in with a familiar face. It would make them more likely to buy your story. It makes you more credible."

"I don't like it," Robert said. "I see the logic but I still don't like it."

"What if he refuses to cooperate?" Sonyea asked.

"Then we kill him," Robert said, looking Arthur in the eye.

Arthur shrugged. "I'm good with that, if that's where the road leads, but that's on you to figure out."

"So, anything else need done to the Razer?" Kevin asked.

"Yes, take one of the mechanics and have him go over it. The three of them will need food and gear for the trip. Give them two sets of handcuffs so they can lock Jeff up to a tree each night. Throw in a short length of lightweight chain so they can secure him to whatever is handy at night."

"Throw in some of that good night vision," Robert asked. "Can you do that?"

"Planned on it," Kevin said. "Two sets."

"Every time we've tried to leave this place we've taken fire," Sonyea said.

"Trust me, before the sun even comes up tomorrow, the congressman will have every man in his force watching the front gate. While he's doing that, you guys can launch out the back of the compound at seventy miles per hour. Even if they notice, they're not going to have time to react. You'll be miles away by the time they decide to come after you."

"Why will they be watching the gate?" Robert asked. "If I was him, if I was trying to breach your perimeter, I would come in through the least defended sector."

"It's all part of my twisted little plan," Arthur said. "Kevin, you know that scaffold at the shooting range that we put the instructor on sometimes?"

"I do."

"Have some guys bring every section of it up here. Also have them bring Bob from the classroom."

"The torso dummy?" Kevin asked.

"That's him," Arthur said.

"Torso dummy?" Sonyea asked. "What exactly is that?"

"It's the big rubber torso we practice self-defense strikes on," Kevin said. "It's like a punching bag except it has human features. Its name is Bob."

"This sounds utterly devious," Robert said.

Arthur broke a small smile. "You'll find out in the morning. I want you and Sonyea to try and grab some sleep. You've got a long day ahead of you tomorrow and I want you alert. The rest of us are going to pull an all-nighter."

12

It was a little after 4 AM when Arthur's core group gathered in the meeting space he referred to as his command bunker. A rubbery pink torso lay on a folding plastic table beneath the harsh glare of a halogen work light. It looked like the botched result of an alien autopsy. The blocky head, complete with grimacing face and molded hair, was attached to a long torso. There were no arms and legs but there had been a weighted stand, now removed, that kept the dummy vertical when it was being used.

This was Bob, the striking dummy used in self-defense classes. Unlike a standard punching bag, Bob taught you to aim for specific features or regions of the body. It was a better way to train. Bob wasn't here as a training prop today. He had an integral role in the new mission.

"You're on, Doc," Arthur said with a grin.

The doc frowned as if he were the butt of a distasteful joke, which apparently he was. "I guess you guys think it's hilarious to make a real doctor do this surgery?"

"Isn't it?" Kevin asked.

"It kind of is," Sonyea added with an apologetic smile. "Sorry."

The doctor withdrew a Benchmade folding knife clipped to his pocket. He flicked the blade open and looked around the room. "I'm assuming disinfection and sterilization protocols aren't necessary?"

Arthur smiled. "Now you're getting into the spirit of things. Get to it."

The doc grumbled as if he were still not on board with the humor of having to perform surgery on the dummy. He positioned himself over the torso and applied the tip of his knife to the rubberized torso with such seriousness that he might indeed be engaging in thoracic surgery. Unlike a standard surgical procedure, though, he made multiple crisscrossing incisions through the outer layer of plastic "skin." When he was done he stepped back, folded his knife and gestured at his patient.

"He's all yours. I hope you're satisfied," he said.

Arthur tore open a cardboard box of Hot Hands chemical hand warmers, normally used by hunters to keep their hands and feet warm in the winter. The packets produced a chemical reaction that generated heat for several hours. Arthur handed out packets and everyone began tearing them open.

Arthur caught the doc trying to slip away at the back of the room. "You're not done yet. Get back up here. This is a delicate surgical procedure."

The doctor rolled his eyes and stepped back up to the table. As the folks around the room opened and activated the chemical hand warmers, the doctor peeled back the flaps he'd opened in Bob and began dispersing the chemical hand warmers around the torso, placing them between the rubberized skin layer and the foam core. When he had inserted all the packets, he sealed the incisions with duct tape.

Arthur stepped forward and slapped a hand on the rubber torso. "I think he'll make a full recovery. A notch above your usual work there, Sawbones."

"Just remember, there'll be a time when you need me," the doctor said. "It's always good to keep the doctor on your good side unless you want me to repair *you* with duct tape."

Arthur was looking at the dummy with satisfaction. "Now, who has the legs?"

One of the team leaders stepped forward with a length of canvas firehose. The hose was draped in equal lengths around Bob's neck with the loose ends pulled down the front of his torso so that they would hang like legs. More duct tape was applied around Bob's stomach to hold the canvas "legs" in place. The hose was filled alternately with sand and several hot hands packets. Where the ankles would be, the canvas hose was sealed with zip ties. When this part was done, they dressed Bob in some old work clothes.

Arthur admired their handiwork. "Not bad." He gestured at the team leaders. "As quietly as possible, get that scaffolding down to the front gate. Position it beneath that big oak. I want a noose running over a branch of the oak and around Bob's neck. Strap Bob to that scaffolding so he won't fall off. I want him looking like some scared schmuck standing there waiting to die. When you're done, fall back to cover and give me a heads up on the radio."

The men were ready to get to work but Arthur held up a hand to silence them a moment longer. "Do not discuss your jobs with anyone. Do not speak to each other about what you are doing. I don't know that the enemy doesn't have parabolic microphones on us or some other type of listening device. This plan only works if they believe it. Don't say anything outside this room that might give it away."

The men jumped into action. The dummy was heavy and awkward to handle but they hoisted it like a drunken buddy and disappeared out the door. Arthur looked at his watch.

"It's about 4:30 A.M. I'm aiming for a 5:30 showtime. Robert and Sonyea, you guys get your personal gear ready and get it to the hay barn. The Razer will be there waiting on you. Make damn sure you're combat-ready—primary and secondary weapons systems hot. Don't pack to travel, pack to fight."

"What about Jeff?" Robert asked.

"We'll load Jeff at the hay barn. Don't you worry about him. He'll be cuffed to the roll cage and will have basic gear—sleeping bag, tarp, food, and water. You can make him as comfortable or uncomfortable as you want. I don't give a crap."

"Does he know he's going with us?" Sonyea asked.

Arthur nodded. "We had a long talk last night. He told me everything we needed to know about their intended route and what he knew of their security protocols. I think he was telling the truth given his level of fear. All that information will be provided for you when you reach the barn. I'm giving you guys the Taser to take with you. He had a taste of that and didn't like it at all. I told him several times last night that you guys didn't mind watching him twitch if he insisted on being an asshole. I also told him that you were clear to kill him if he became a burden."

"You really think he'll cooperate?" Robert asked.

Arthur shrugged. "I already told him he will *never* be rejoining any of his family. He knows our strength and believes we are capable of carrying out the threats we made. He's buying into this concept that this is his chance to be a hero and save everyone. I also explained to him that if you guys aren't back here in a week we will kill everyone outside of the perimeter, including the families that arrive here."

Robert and Sonyea looked at each other. Neither of them was completely certain what they were getting into but that was the nature of the beast. Missions could be like that. Sometimes you were simply launching yourself into the unknown and hoping you had the skills to keep yourself alive.

13

The congressman was roused from a restless sleep by several bursts of full auto gunfire. He sat bolt upright in the master suite of his RV, eyes wide with fear. Had Arthur launched an attack? He was trying to shake the fog from his head when there was a knock at the door.

"What is it?" He threw back his blankets and swung around to get dressed. "What the hell is going on out there? Are we under attack?"

"I'm not sure. There's something going on at the gate." It was Bradshaw, an officer with the Capitol Police. The congressman had met Bradshaw soon after being elected and they'd become friends over the years.

The congressman burst from his room and jammed himself into the cramped dinette, pulling on his socks, then hastily trying to button a flannel shirt. It started crooked but he didn't have time to fix it. "Who's firing? Is that them or us?"

"I haven't figured it out yet. I was getting ready to put a call out on the radio."

Bradshaw was staying in the command RV with the congressman. It wasn't so much an act of largesse on the congressman's part as it was in keeping Bradshaw tied into providing personal protection for him. Having Bradshaw under the same roof meant any attacker would have to go through one more person before they got to the congressman.

He pulled on his boots and tied the laces while Bradshaw worked the radio. He stood up, tucked his shirt in, then hauled his suspenders up over his shoulders. The RV door flew open and the rest of his command team piled in.

The congressman's mind was racing. He wasn't used to being in a position where he had no idea what was going on. Even in Washington he was a master of backchannel gossip and intrigue. People rarely took him by surprise. He'd been naïve to think all of his manipulative abilities and hollow threats would get him through this.

"What's the source of the gunfire?" Bradshaw asked the men who'd just come inside.

"I don't think it's our people." It was Colonel Jacobs. Actually, *retired* Colonel Jacobs, who now worked as a consultant and lobbyist. He treated Congressman Honaker very well and that was all it took for the congressman to consider anyone a close personal friend. Those were positions always open to the highest bidders.

Bradshaw returned to the radio. "Can anyone with eyes on the gate tell me what the hell is going on?"

There was a crackle of static and an excited voice burst from the small speaker on the radio. *"This is Cummings. I've got eyes on the gate. There's been some activity there but the gunfire was definitely not ours. I repeat, the gunfire is not our people."*

"Give me that!" The congressman snatched up the mic and barked into it. "What kind of activity is going on out there?"

"I have thermal capability but no night vision," Cummings replied. *"I can see a figure standing on top of a tall platform but that's all I can make out. If you want more than that, I'll need someone with night vision."*

"Can you fire on the target on the platform?" the congressman asked. "It could be a sniper nest. Maybe we should make a preemptive strike and kill their sniper."

Colonel Jacobs threw up a warning hand. "I don't recommend

taking any action until we know who that figure is," he said. "What if it's your son?"

The congressman looked at Jacobs like he'd sprouted horns. "Why in the hell would it be my son?"

"I don't know that it's your son," the colonel retorted. "We don't have that information yet. But we sure as hell know your son is in there and I'd not advise pulling the trigger on anyone we can't identity with one hundred percent certainty."

"Dammit!" the congressman muttered, conceding the point. He keyed his radio. "All teams, do not fire on that target unless you get an order from me. Over."

He waited for a response. "Can everyone acknowledge that order? There's to be no shooting unless I give the order. My son is still out there. Do you understand me?"

His voice thoroughly conveyed his irritation at both the current situation and the larger state of things. A string of *rogers* and *affirmatives* rolled in. The congressman dropped the mic and returned to his seat, sitting down hard. He raked a nervous hand through his hair. "Bradshaw, get somebody with night vision on that gate with Cummings. I need to know exactly what the hell's going on out there."

Bradshaw took the mic back up and spoke into it. "Somebody with NODS take a position on the gate and coordinate with Cummings."

"This is Rico. I'm closing in on the gate with NODS right now. I don't have magnification but it looks to me like there's a figure slumped at the top of some kind of platform or staging."

"Slumped?" the congressman echoed.

"Ask him to hit it with an IR illuminator," Jacobs suggested. "He may be able to see it better."

"Bradshaw for Rico. Do you have an IR illuminator?"

"I just activated it. That helped a little," Rico replied. *"Can somebody cover me? I need to move forward."*

"Cummings for Rico," Cummings barked. *"I have you on thermal. Got your back."*

"Roger that, Cummings!" Rico shouted.

The congressman wiped his face on his sleeve and sighed deeply. He wondered if he'd gotten in over his head. He never expected Arthur to surrender but he thought maybe the other men would flee when his army showed up. They weren't, and he had no idea at this point what he was going to do about it.

"I'm within fifty yards," Rico said. *"I see some type of platform with a figure on top. The figure is not moving and is slumped kind of awkward against a railing at the top of the platform. There's some kind of line running from the figure to a nearby tree but I can't tell what it is. It could be safety rope, I'm not sure."*

Bradshaw looked nervously around the room. "Sit tight, Rico."

"You know they're awake over there," Colonel Jacobs said. "The gunfire originated with them. Maybe we should just ask *them* what the hell is going on."

The congressman shook his head bitterly, disgusted that it had come to this. The last thing he wanted to do was go begging to them for information. He couldn't see as he had any choice, though. He returned to the radio and took the microphone. "This is Congressman Honaker calling for Arthur Bridges. What the hell you up to over there, Bridges?"

When Arthur's voice finally came through the speaker, he sounded relaxed and almost cheerful, as if he were pleased that the congressman was taking the time to give him a call. *"I'll tell you exactly what's going on, Honaker. Playtime is over. You've pushed me over the edge. That platform you're looking at is a gallows."*

"You're the one pushing things too far, Bridges. I don't know what you think you're up to but this isn't funny."

"What I'm up to is serving justice. We've held a trial and a sentence has been handed down. Your son has been sentenced to hang from his neck until dead. The sentence will be carried out in about, oh, thirty minutes or so."

"My son?" Congressman Honaker said slowly, carefully pronouncing each word. Even beyond the loss of his only son, how would he ever explain this to his wife? How could he admit that his plan had led to the death of her firstborn? She would never forgive him.

"I guess you should have thought this over more carefully. You should have understood that your actions would have consequences."

"How do I even know that's my son on this platform of yours?"

"It's a gallows, not a platform. What does your thermal tell you?" Arthur asked. *"I'm sure your snipers have already confirmed it's the real deal, a warm human body. You think I would be dumb enough to put one of my own men up there and expose them to fire? No way."*

Bridges had a point. It couldn't be anyone but his son. Concern pushed back the anger and he was pleading. "Bridges, don't do anything stupid. I'm begging you. Cross that line and there's no going back."

"The line is already crossed, Congressman. Go outside and you might be able to yell a last good-bye to your son. Of course, if you expose yourself to fire we'll take you out."

"Bridges!" the congressman screamed in rage but there was no response.

He gritted his teeth. His entire body flexed like it was building toward an explosion. He drew back to smash the radio against the wall but caught himself, knowing that would be a mistake. Instead, he keyed the microphone again. Bridges had left him no choice here.

"This is Congressman Honaker. All teams converge on that gate now. Take no action until you hear from me but get there ASAP."

14

Across the gate and up the winding gravel road into the compound, Arthur smiled at Kevin as they listened to the congressman's transmission. They'd fooled him so far. He apparently believed the warm body on the scaffold was his son.

"Let's give his people ten minutes to get in position by the gate, then we'll put Robert and Sonyea on the road," Arthur said.

"What about Bob?" Kevin asked.

Arthur looked at his watch. "What did I tell them? Thirty minutes?"

Kevin nodded.

Arthur's mouth curled into a devious smile. "In five minutes, tip the scaffold, and let Bob drop to his death. They won't be expecting that. I guarantee they'll be crapping in their pants."

"That might turn into a firefight," Kevin warned. "They may lay down cover fire in order to launch a body recovery."

Arthur shrugged. "Let them. If there is a firefight, it will be a short one. We're dug in and have protected positions. Tell the men to let them retrieve Bob without a fight. They should keep their heads down and dispense enough cover fire to make it seem legitimate."

"The chaos should cover Robert and Sonyea's exodus," Kevin pointed out. "Which I'm guessing is exactly what you hoped for."

The men stepped outside of the commo shack, enjoying the cooler air of very early morning. The radio room was a heat trap but Arthur was insistent on light discipline. He paused outside and looked around. "Where's Carlos? Every time I throw him out of there he waits for me right on the steps. He's not there."

"I don't know. Maybe he's in the head?" Kevin suggested, scanning the area for the radio operator.

"Maybe," Arthur said. "I hope he's back soon. I want someone monitoring the congressman's radio traffic and we can't do that from our handhelds. Some poor sap needs to be babysitting those radios and Carlos is that designated sap."

"Well, I'm going to deliver the news to tip the scaffold in person," Kevin said. "If I see Carlos I'll send him back this way."

Arthur nodded, sliding into his own side-by-side ATV. "I'm headed to the barn to see Sonyea and Robert off. Hopefully I'll be back in time for the party." He started the engine and floored the gas. There was something about those machines that made it impossible to resist.

15

Sonyea sat cool, calm, and comfortable in the front seat of the Polaris Razer parked in front of the hay barn. In contrast, Robert paced nearby like a caged cat. Their gear was loaded, their weapons ready, extra jerry cans of fuel stowed in the newly-fabricated rack on the back. All they could do now was wait on Arthur. When he said it was go time, they would go.

"Relax, you're wearing me out," Sonyea said. "Sit down or something."

"I can't," Robert said. "This is how I think and there's a lot to think about."

"You must drive your wife bananas."

Robert nodded. "I do. For a variety of reasons."

"I got no doubt."

Robert frowned at Sonyea, as if her agreement wasn't expected or required. He turned away from her and faced the blocky man in tactical gear who was guarding the entrance to the barn. "Can I talk to the prisoner? To Jeff?"

The guard gave Robert a blank look. "It's nothing to me, man. You're going to be riding with him soon anyway. Knock yourself out."

"Be right back," he called to Sonyea, slipping around the guard and into the dark cavern of the hay barn.

There were round bales stacked in the middle section of the structure, white plastic cinching their girth. Hidden behind them were the stalls, including the one that had been converted into a holding cell by making a welded cage of one-inch rebar with a locking gate. Translucent acrylic skylights allowed a murky light to seep in though a layer of pine needles, dust, and pollen when the sun was overhead. Now, being up before the sun, everyone was depending on headlamps.

When Robert skirted the towering stack of bales, he was surprised to find Carlos standing at the cell, his body nearly against the bars. Startled at Robert's appearance, Carlos smiled awkwardly.

"Hey, I just wanted to see the big scary cook," Carlos said. He held up a pack of gum in his hand. "He asked me for a piece of gum. I hope that's not a problem."

"It's not a problem for me," Robert said, "but I don't make the rules. How'd you get in here, anyway? I didn't see you pass us."

"The back door," Carlos replied, nodding toward a windowless steel door against the back wall.

Robert nodded. Something about the whole scene was a little weird to him. Although it didn't make sense, he had so many other things on his mind that this incident seemed trivial and unworthy of any of the limited space available.

"Well, I have to get back to the radio," Carlos said, pushing through the back door and disappearing into the dark.

Robert approached the bars and eyed the prisoner. The cook looked like hundreds of other raggedy cooks Robert had seen over the years, his clothes stained, his t-shirt stretched out and riddled with holes. He was shoving a stick of gum in his mouth. While Robert watched, the cook shoved the wrapper in his pocket, his eyes not leaving Robert.

"So you're Jeff?

The cook nodded.

"I'm Robert. Sonyea and I will be your escorts."

Jeff snorted. "My guards, you mean?"

Robert gave a gesture that indicated he conceded the point. "Yeah, I guess that's an appropriate term for it."

"I mean, it's not like we're going sightseeing, right? We're not friends. I'm your prisoner and you're taking me on a one-way mission to keep my family and the other families from reaching this place."

"That's fair, Jeff, but it doesn't have to be a one-way mission. You may survive this if you follow the rules and don't act like an idiot."

"Meaning what?" Jeff said with a frown.

"Not acting like an idiot? That means don't try to escape," Robert replied. "Don't try to interfere with us conducting our mission. Don't try to harm us."

"So just play along like a good boy and everything will be okay, right?"

"That's about the size of it."

"And if I don't?" Jeff asked, taking on a defiant attitude.

Robert stepped closer to the bars, all traces of friendliness gone. "I think the terms were already explained to you so don't test me. You know the consequences from meeting with Arthur and Kevin, don't you? A slow, miserable death, torture, or the death of your families if they get caught in the crossfire between our people and yours. You're doing the right thing so just make sure you continue doing the right thing. No crazy ideas. No change of heart."

"I'll take that under consideration," Jeff replied.

"I'd strongly advise very careful consideration," Robert said. "If I have to kill you and dump your body in the dirt, I'll do it. I'm more than capable. More than willing. It might also be relevant to mention that I'm a little on edge right now. I'm missing my family and ready to get home to them. The presence of your people outside of this compound is the only thing that's preventing that. Just keep in mind that I might have a hair trigger where you and your people are concerned. Once I start hitting, I don't know when I'll stop. And if I have to pull a gun, I might not be able to keep my finger from curling a little too tightly around that trigger."

The drone of an approaching engine was followed by the crunch of gravel and an ATV skidded to a stop outside. Robert abandoned his conversation and jogged back through the barn. He found Arthur hopping from the seat of his ATV, nimble as a man half his age.

"Showtime!" Arthur yelled. "You guys buckle in and arm up."

Robert wanted to ask if there had been any new developments but the time for discussion was past.

"Get moving," Arthur said. He pointed at the guard. "Thompson, get the prisoner out here. Cuff him with his hands in front, then use another set to cuff him to the roll cage. Put him in the front seat."

Thompson snapped into action. In seconds they could hear the echo of him barking orders at the prisoner deep inside the hay barn.

"Something wrong?" Arthur asked.

Robert still hadn't moved. He was trying to process everything and something was still bothering him but he couldn't put a finger on it.

"Then get cracking! Get in and buckle up. We've got less than two minutes until all hell breaks loose."

Robert came back to life and headed for the driver's seat of the Razer. He double-checked his weapons, then took a seat, buckling himself in. Sonyea was in the back seat, sitting behind Robert so she had a clear view of the prisoner.

"If he tries to fight me, you're my backup," Robert said. "Stab, shoot, beat—whatever it takes."

"Got it."

The massive Thompson arrived at the vehicle and stuffed Jeff into the passenger seat like it was something he did every day. As Arthur asked, he handcuffed his hands to the passenger side grab handle. He could hold on for dear life but he wasn't going to jump out and run.

"Might as well buckle his seatbelt," Arthur suggested. "Just in case Robert wraps it around a tree or something."

When Jeff was buckled in, Arthur leaned into the cockpit and patted Robert on the shoulder. "Be careful, buddy. Don't take any ridiculous chances. I don't want to have to explain to your family why you didn't make it home."

Robert nodded and started the engine.

"Be careful," Arthur warned Sonyea, taking her hand and squeezing it. "Don't let Robert do anything crazy."

"I'll do my best," Sonyea said. "But you know how he is."

Arthur nodded that he did. He patted the roll cage and stepped back. "Let's do this. Stay on the route I showed you and try not to shoot if you don't have to. It will just draw Honaker's men to you."

"Got it," Robert said.

He punched the gas pedal and the Razer spun the wheels. He didn't have a lot of experience with the machine and his nerves got the best of him. The 1000 cc engine got the light machine up to seventy miles per hour before he knew it and he had to drop off the throttle. He shot a quick glance to his side and saw Jeff was terrified. Robert was afraid to glance behind him for fear of wrecking but he imagined Sonyea had the same expression frozen onto her face. It was too late to do anything about it now but helmets might have been a good idea.

They barreled down an old logging road that Arthur maintained as a back door into the compound. They'd been turned back while trying to ride out of here before on horses but the hope was that this time would be different. Arthur was now certain that his diversion would draw all the troops to the front gate and leave them a clear path of egress.

In better times, they maintained the trail up until it crossed over to National Forest property, mowing it with a tractor on a regular basis. It hadn't been mowed in several weeks now and the summer underbrush was quickly overtaking the route. Pokeberries, stinging nettle, and blackberry vines all fought for dominance.

A blaze of two white lines circling a tree indicated the point where they left Arthur's property. Robert had a compact AR pistol in his lap, a round chambered and ready to go. Sonyea was wielding the Kel-Tec KSG with wicked custom loads Robert had gotten from a friend at Maker Bullets. Already nervous, Robert's anxiety ramped up even further after crossing that line. He expected at any moment they'd receive the same response from Honaker's men they'd gotten before—rifle rounds flying in their direction, intent on killing them.

Robert tried to maintain a high rate of speed while watching for obstacles or attackers. He quickly realized that there was no way he was going to spot camouflaged shooters at this speed so he returned his eyes to what was in front of him. Just as he did, he saw that he was about to barrel into a downed tree. It wasn't massive and he probably could have moved it with his winch and a snatch block fastened to a nearby tree but there wasn't time for that. They weren't far enough out of range yet. The last thing he wanted was to be standing still outside of this vehicle with armed bad guys running around.

He whipped the wheel and the vehicle slewed sideways. He punched the gas and the machine shot over the low shoulder, shooting the gap between trees until it was past the obstacle. Robert turned left, made sure the four wheel drive was engaged, and swung around the end of the fallen tree. On the steep slope the Razer felt tippy but he was committed now. There was no going back.

"Do you know how to drive this thing?" Jeff asked.

Robert didn't answer. With a steady throttle, he climbed back onto the road and straightened out. Flooring the gas, he sprayed sod, dirt, and leaves in all directions. They were up to a more cautious thirty-five miles per hour in seconds.

"Did you see anyone?" Robert asked.

"No!" Sonyea shouted, trying to be heard over the engine. "Arthur's idea must have worked."

"Let's hope so."

16

ongressman Honaker frantically paced his RV. His command team tried to comfort him and offer suggestions but the ideas rolled off him without taking root. The leaders all assumed the congressman was brainstorming, hence his distraction, but they were wrong. He could never have admitted the truth to them, that he was in fact wondering why he and his son had never bonded. He'd tried when they were both younger, but maybe he had been gone too much. Between growing a business and his political ambitions, he'd probably been a lousy father.

He also couldn't help but wonder how he was going to explain this to his wife. She would see it as his failure, his fault, and in the end, who else was there to pin it on? This whole campaign, this whole effort, was his idea and his alone.

Even more concerning than his son's fate was the thought of how he appeared at that moment to the men around him. Was his indecision, his paralysis, reflecting poorly on him as a leader? Was his whole effort to portray himself as a commander, a leader of men, unraveling? This was not the way this was supposed to be going. This was not the way he'd planned or imagined it over all these years. How could it be salvaged?

He stopped pacing and faced his command team. "Have all the outlying teams reached us?" he asked.

"Almost," Bradshaw replied. "The most distant, those covering the back of the compound, are double-timing it and should be here within two minutes."

The congressman nodded, processing. "Is my son moving at all?"

"I've observed him myself on thermal," Colonel Jacobs said. "We can't see features with any type of optic because the head is covered by a sack or something, but it's definitely a warm human body. He's alive. Judging by the awkward stance, he may have been roughed up a little. They may have also drugged him to keep him from panicking and falling off the tower. I'm assuming at some point they'll send somebody up there to shove him off if their intention truly is to hang him."

"That may be our best opportunity," Bradshaw said. "If someone shows themselves to climb the scaffolding we have a sniper drop them. In the confusion, we rush the scaffolding. Maybe we create some diversionary fire against their positions so we can get men to the scaffold. We send someone up, they cut him loose, and lower him to the ground. There's nothing elegant about it but it might work."

"As long as it's understood that we can't do this without casualties," Jacobs said. "We'll be operating in the open. We know Bridges has thermal, night vision, and the same sniper rifles we do. We're going to lose men. If we lose too many, our force may be sufficiently compromised that we'll need to retreat until we get reinforcements."

"I hope you're not suggesting I leave my son up there to die," Honaker said, shooting Jacobs a warning look. "That's an unacceptable option."

The colonel stood and sighed, resting a hand on the congressman's shoulder. "Look, I'm not speaking as a father but as a strategist. Is it worth losing ten operators for a cook? Those are the questions officers have had to ask themselves for years. If you're going to undertake activities like the one we're engaged in now, this won't be the last time you're faced with a dilemma like this. It comes with the territory. You may not like it but you still have to deal with it."

"Let's just be clear here that you're speaking as an officer and not as a soldier," Bradshaw said. "For a soldier there would be no question but to save one of their own. Cook, mechanic, engineer, whatever, doesn't matter. It's still an American soldier. You've probably forgotten that."

Colonel Jacobs bristled. "I wasn't brought along to win friends, Bradshaw. I was brought here to win battles, and that's what I'm trying to do. That's not a goal we'll accomplish if the game stops every time somebody's in danger. There are no time-outs in war."

"It's never a game when lives are at risk," Bradshaw said.

"And this isn't just *anybody* out there in danger," Honaker added. "It's the son I vowed to keep safe and out of the fight. At the moment, I'm not as concerned about facing Bridges as I am about facing my wife."

The colonel threw up his hands in defeat. "The decision isn't mine. I was just offering my opinion. Do what you feel you have to do."

"Command!" squawked the radio.

Bradshaw keyed the mic. "Go for command."

"This is Cummings. They must have some kind of rope system on the scaffold that we didn't see. They're tipping it over."

Bradshaw looked at Congressman Honaker with an expression of shock and fear.

The congressman grabbed the mic. "What's happening to my son?"

"It tipped! He's hanging from the noose!"

Bradshaw and the colonel stormed out the door, grabbing rifles on their way.

"Cut him down!" the congressman screamed into the radio. "Cut him down now! Charge the gate! Whatever it takes."

He threw down the mic, grabbed his own rifle, and stumbled out the RV door. He rounded the hulking vehicle and looked to the distant gate, spotting the limp body of his son dangling against the pink striations of the morning sky. Congressman Honaker was paralyzed by shock, his rifle falling from his numb fingers. Gunfire erupted at the gate, then yelling. He heard someone call his name but didn't know who it was or what they were saying.

He lumbered forward, staring at the hanging body, his child dying before his eyes. His focus was zoomed to that single point in the vastness of the universe, the point where his son hung, hopefully clinging to a spark of life.

Inside the now empty RV, a second radio crackled and the whisper that emerged from the speaker went unheard. *"It's a diversion. I repeat, the body is a diversion. It's not real. A team is escaping through the rear of the compound at this very moment. If you get men back there now you may be able to intercept them."*

When there was no response, the voice transmitted again.

There was no answer.

"Hello? Anyone?"

17

From his command bunker, the basement of his cabin home, Arthur watched the action at the gate unfold on security cameras. The congressman's men were scrambling over the gate, trying to find the rope that would lower the hanging body to the ground. Of course those men didn't know it was a dummy, and Arthur couldn't wait to see the looks on their faces when they discovered that fact.

"They're firing on us," Kevin said, repeating a message he heard through his earpiece.

"Remind the guys to keep down," Arthur said. "They can pop off a few shots to keep the men from advancing on them but I don't want this turning into a serious firefight. My guess is this is a recovery mission only."

The men on the screen found the end of the rope tied around a nearby tree. They couldn't just cut it because the body would drop about twenty feet to the ground. Men latched onto the rope and held it tightly. Someone cut the knot with a knife and two men lowered the body as quickly as possible. The body dropped into the waiting arms of two combatants who immediately noticed something off about the body but still frantically wrestled the noose off the neck. In seconds, their suspicions had been confirmed and they knew they'd been tricked.

"This is it," Arthur said, sitting up in his chair and scooting closer to the security monitor. "Wait for it…"

Cummings yanked the hood from the body and found himself staring at the rubberized grimace of Bob. He hit the microphone on his vest. "Abort! Abort! This is some kind of trick."

There was immediate radio chatter and requests for confirmation, the sporadic gunfire making it difficult to understand what Cummings had just transmitted. Cummings let out a loud whistle and directed his men to retreat.

"It's a trick! Cover us!" he shouted, fleeing toward the locked gate and flinging himself over.

While the men who came with him provided cover fire, he helped stragglers over the gate and they scrambled to safety on their side of the wire. Once everyone was over, Cummings ran straight for the command RV. He found the congressman waiting for him, flanked by Bradshaw and Jacobs.

"What the hell is going on? Where is my son?"

Cummings wiped his forehead with the back of a sleeve, sweating from both the humidity and the adrenaline. "He ain't there. That wasn't even a person. It was one of those striking dummies. I've seen the same damn dummy at my gym."

"But it was warm," Bradshaw countered. "You saw it on thermal. I saw it on thermal."

Cummings shrugged. "It was warm in my hands when I caught it. They must have put something inside it to make it heat up. It was definitely not a person though."

The congressman spun and slammed his fist against the side of the RV. When once didn't help, he repeated the gesture several more times. "What the hell! What was the point of that? Why would they go to all that effort?"

"There was certainly an ulterior motive," Colonel Jacobs agreed. "They wouldn't do this simply for entertainment."

"An attack?" Bradshaw suggested. "We consolidated our forces and left everything else open. Maybe they're circling us? Preparing to launch an attack?"

The utter sensibility of that move bore down on all of them instantly.

"Build a perimeter!" the congressman barked. "I want this camp circled-up right now. They could be moving in from any side."

Cummings was on his radio in a second, relaying the barrage of orders coming from both Bradshaw and Jacobs. The congressman stalked off, Bradshaw on his heels. He threw open the door to the RV, clambered up the steps, and tossed his rifle onto a bunk. He cursed and banged on the wall, still stinging over what had transpired.

"Get Bridges on the radio," Congressman Honaker snapped.

Bradshaw slid into a booth and began working his magic. "Congressman Honaker for Bridges. Congressman Honaker for Bridges."

The congressman frowned and yanked the microphone from Bradshaw. To heck with radio procedures. He wanted answers. "What the hell was that about, Bridges?"

The congressman's angry voice spilled from a speaker in Arthur's basement. It was his personal radio, not quite so fancy or far-reaching as the setup in the commo shack. Arthur picked up the mic, looking at Kevin. "Did we find their antenna yet?"

"I put Brandon on it since he was familiar with the terrain," Kevin replied. "He followed the wires and found two up on a ridge. He cut the wires and broke the antennas into little pieces, scattering them on his way back."

Arthur couldn't restrain a smile. "Can they reach anyone farther out than us?"

"Probably not," Kevin said. "The wire that went to the antenna will function in that capacity somewhat but won't be sufficient for long distances in these mountains. They're just going to be talking to us from this point forward unless they brought a replacement antenna with them."

"I doubt that," Arthur said. "And I'm not sure they'll find talking to us as comforting as hearing from their families."

The speaker barked again. *"Answer me, Arthur!"*

Arthur sighed and raised the mic to his mouth. "What are you growling about, Honaker?"

"What the hell are you up to? What was that stunt all about?"

"I'm pretty certain you're not supposed to use that kind of language on the airwaves," Arthur said. "They're pretty strict about that."

"I'll show you strict when I come up that hill and shove that striking dummy up your ass!"

"Bring it," Arthur said. "That may end this whole mess sooner than later."

The congressman was silent for a moment. Arthur glanced at Kevin, who shrugged to indicate he had no idea what was going on.

"What was that all about?" the congressman repeated, his voice more measured this time. He was trying to regain control of his anger.

"I'm afraid you don't have the clearance level to access that information," Arthur said, speaking in a sarcastic tone that he knew would infuriate the congressman. "It's classified."

There was no response, and Arthur pushed himself from the table, rolling casually back to the table where Kevin sat. "He's probably wrecking things about now. Or at least making life very unpleasant for the folks around him."

"He seems like that kind of guy."

"He is," Arthur said. "A jerk. Spoiled, entitled, and drunk on his own power."

"So what now?"

"I'd imagine he's a little amped up," Arthur said. "He's probably waiting for us to attack."

"I'd agree with that assessment."

"When we don't attack, he'll gradually work people back into position around us."

"You don't think he'll come after his son?" Kevin asked.

"I think he'll try to negotiate or intimidate us into giving him up," Arthur replied. "I do think we have to maintain a heightened state of alert. He may try to kidnap one of our guys or start taking potshots at us. The closer his families get, the more his anxiety will go up. He'll want to have this mess cleaned up before they get here."

"You still think those families are going to get here?"

Arthur understood that the implied question was whether he thought Robert had a chance of blocking the families from reaching the compound. "I'm not going to voice any opinion other than that I hope he's successful. Life will be a lot simpler for all of us if Robert succeeds."

18

While GPS satellites were still orbiting and functional, GPS mapping of the national forests, like many remote areas, was not always dependable. Sometimes the GPS included historical roads or trails that were not navigable in a vehicle like the Razer. Robert was relying on a USGS paper topographic map Arthur had given them. Sonyea was the navigator, calling out directions and landmarks. In his state of urgency, desperate to escape the fear of coming under fire, Robert felt like he'd been driving for hours, but that couldn't have been the case. Probably fifteen minutes was more likely.

They were doing okay. They were putting miles between them and the congressman's forces. They'd also not taken any fire, which had been one of Robert's biggest concerns in the open cockpit. If fireworks had started they'd have been sitting ducks.

Thankfully, the condition of the forest roads was not nearly as bad as expected. Since they were used frequently by hunters, adventurers, and four-wheel drive clubs much of the year, the forest service kept them passable. It wouldn't have been until fuel became more difficult to get that people would have stopped using the roads. Still, they came across several downed trees they had to go around and one they even had to winch off the road. They also ran into a sweeper—a downed tree with limited clearance beneath it. Robert was able to get beneath it and push up while Sonyea drove the vehicle through.

Each time he slowed or stopped the vehicle, Robert reminded his passenger that he was clear to kill him if he caused any trouble. Jeff still had an attitude, although was less intimidated by Robert than he had been of Kevin or Arthur. Part of Robert wanted to do something to Jeff to earn that same measure of fear and respect but he didn't have it in him to assault the man for no reason. He considered it, though.

They'd gone nearly thirty miles when Sonyea mentioned she'd like to stop to stretch her legs. The map indicated they were about to make a river crossing near a waterfall. "I'd love to stick my feet in a cold creek."

"Not there," Robert said. "Waterfalls are noisy. You can't hear people coming."

Sonyea went back to the map. "The road crosses a feeder creek a mile beyond the river. The map shows a campsite there. That might be a decent spot. We could stop there and grab a bite to eat."

There were several campsites at the river crossing. The water wasn't deep there, more of a creek than a river, but trash left at the campsites was fresh enough that Robert couldn't tell if it pre-dated the terror attacks or was a recent deposit. It reminded him of all the people who said their plan was to bug out to the hills if the power went out and things collapsed. The most likely place for them to go would be these national and state forests since those were vast public lands rich in big game.

The truth was that these mountains would be hunted out pretty quickly if everyone who claimed they were bugging out there actually did so. With most people not understanding food preservation, and with the warm temperatures this time of year, a lot of that game would be wasted. Even smoked meat wouldn't last indefinitely in the humid southern mountains.

When Robert killed the Razer's engine at the creek-side campsite, some of his stress dissipated. He didn't get out immediately but sat holding the steering wheel and forcing himself to relax. He focused on his breathing, on calming himself down.

"You okay?" Sonyea asked, wasting no time unbuckling herself.

He nodded. "Just decompressing."

Sonyea climbed out and walked around the vehicle, stretching as she went. "My husband and I used to do a lot of four wheeling. He had an old Jeep and we took it everywhere. I don't remember those trips being as hard on the body, but I guess I was a lot younger then."

Robert unbuckled and climbed out, noticing immediately what Sonyea was talking about. He'd been so distracted by his own stress while he was driving that he didn't notice he was sore all over. His back was stiff and his shoulders ached. The Razer had better suspension than any vehicle he'd ever owned. It floated over bumps and downed branches. Perhaps it was from being so tense. Robert stretched and his back sounded like popcorn popping.

"In my case, it's definitely age," Robert said. "I'm feeling my years today."

"In my case too," Sonyea admitted.

"You guys going to let me out or make me sit here all day?"

Robert gave Sonyea a questioning look, then focused on Jeff. "Is there a reason you need out?"

Jeff looked at Robert like he was an idiot. "Duh, I'd like to stretch too. I've been locked into this damn thing all morning just like you guys."

"He might need to go to the bathroom," Sonyea said.

"With that attitude, he can go in his pants," Robert said. "The seats are waterproof and we can rinse the floor with a bucket of water."

Jeff frowned. "So that's how it is?"

"Like I said, *attitude*. Show us a good attitude and we'll be a lot nicer," Robert said.

"How am I supposed to act? I'm your prisoner. I'm supposed to be all friendly and shit? I'm supposed to be nice to you?"

"I don't care how you act," Robert said. "But it will be reflected back in how you're treated. Remember, you *agreed* to this."

Jeff shook his head in frustration and groaned.

Robert noticed a sympathetic look on Sonyea's face. He gestured at her to step farther from the vehicle. "I know you're a mother," he whispered. "We can't take any chances, though. We may need him to gain the trust of those families. If he escapes in these woods, we'll never find him."

Sonyea pursed her lips. "What are you implying with that *mother* comment?"

Robert looked at her blankly. She seemed offended and he had no clue why.

"You think that means I'm weak, Robert? Easily manipulated?"

Robert was getting an idea that he may have put his foot in his mouth. Again.

Sonyea pointed a finger in Robert's face. "I may be a compassionate person but I'm not soft. There's nobody on this planet tougher than a mother."

"I have a lot of respect for mothers," Robert said.

Sonyea wagged her finger again. "Careful what you say, buster. If it comes out sexist like the rest of what you've said, I may just have to show you how tough a mother can be."

Robert's mouth was open. She'd interrupted him as he'd been queuing up a comment. What she said made him think twice. Maybe the best thing was to say nothing at all. "I'm sorry."

"That's better," Sonyea said. "But take this as a reminder to not assume you know what I'm thinking because you probably don't. Unless, of course, you're sensing at this very moment that I'm thinking you're an asshole. If that's the case, you'd be right." She spun on her heels and walked away.

"I'm sorry!" Robert called after her. It was all he could think to do.

Sonyea marched to the passenger side of the Razer.

"That guy say something mean to you?" Jeff asked. "He's an asshole."

Sonyea drew her pistol and pointed it at Jeff. "I'm going to let you out to do your business, mostly because I don't want a floor full of pee sloshing around my nice boots. Your hands will stay cuffed and I'll have a rope around your neck. Any funny business and I'll use the Tazer. If it comes to that, then it will be the last assistance you'll see from me on this trip. Got it?"

"How am I supposed to go with my hands cuffed?"

"Not my problem and I'm not going to argue with you. This is your one opportunity. Take it or leave it."

"I'll take it," Jeff mumbled, rattling his cuffs.

Sonyea made a paracord leash for Jeff and slipped it over his head. She pulled it tight and then unfastened the pair of cuffs that secured him to the grab handles in front of him. A second pair still bound his hands together. She stepped back while he awkwardly negotiated his way out of the vehicle. When he was free, she pointed him to a nearby cluster of mountain laurel.

Jeff stared at the bushes. "That's not very private. You planning on watching?"

Sonyea lashed out with her foot, kicking Jeff in the butt with a good amount of force. He cried out and tried to skitter away from her but she yanked the leash tight. His eyes were watering from the force of the blow. It had not been a playful kick. "One more disrespectful comment and it's back in the vehicle for you. You can stew in your juices for the rest of the day."

Although Jeff sulked at Sonyea's abrupt reprimand, he didn't say another word, heading directly to the bushes and stepping behind them to do his business. When he was done, he returned to the vehicle without so much as a glance in her direction.

After he'd taken his seat, Sonyea fastened his seatbelt then cuffed him to the grab handles.

"Do I get something to eat and drink?" he asked.

"When the rest of us do," Sonyea replied.

"Catch," Robert said, tossing Sonyea a bottle of water and a protein bar.

She opened the bottle and put it in Jeff's cup holder, then opened the protein bar and offered it to him.

"Those suck," he said.

"Then enjoy your water," Sonyea said, sticking the protein bar in her own mouth and walking off.

"I was just joking," Jeff said. "I'm sorry!"

"Too late," Sonyea said.

"Can you eat and ride?" Robert asked.

Sonyea nodded. "If you go easy on the bumps."

"Then let's hit it. I feel like we're a little too close for comfort."

19

In the commo shack at Arthur's compound, Carlos listened through his headset to the congressman and Arthur going back and forth. When they ended the conversation, Carlos listened for several more minutes to make sure they were done. He switched one of the radios to a memorized frequency.

"Green for White, Green for White, come in."

Just as he was preparing to repeat himself, a voice broke the silence.

"What the hell is going on over there?" "White" was the congressman and he was pissed.

"It was a diversionary tactic," Carlos said in a low voice. He couldn't take a chance on anyone outside the shack overhearing this conversation.

"Diversion for what?"

"They launched three folks, including your son, out the back while you guys were distracted."

"What?" the congressman erupted. *"How could you not warn me about that? We could have taken measures. I nearly had a heart attack thinking that was my son hanging from that tree. You have no idea what that was like."*

"I tried to warn you but the information was compartmentalized. I didn't know anything about it until a short while ago. I tried to relay the information as fast as I found out about it but no one answered on your end."

"Do we have time to intercept them?"

"That's unlikely," Carlos said. "They've got a fifteen minute head start in an all-terrain vehicle. I don't know their route but your son told me that the plan was for them to intercept your families on the road."

"You spoke to Jeff?"

"That's affirmative," Carlos said. "But just for a moment. We got interrupted."

"Have you been compromised?"

"I don't think so. It was a civilian and he didn't look suspicious."

"Why do they want to intercept our families?"

"Jeff said something about delaying or diverting them. The plan is to prevent them from getting here. Arthur doesn't want them caught in the middle of the fight."

"I don't want that either. I was hoping it wouldn't come to that. We should have been in there by now, making a place for our families."

"I guess Arthur thinks you guys might pull off this endeavor to rescue your families if you think they're in danger."

"What am I supposed to do here? This whole thing is going to shit before my eyes."

Carlos wasn't sure if the congressman was talking to him or just thinking out loud. "Sir, we need to keep this short."

"Who the heck did he send with my son?"

"I don't have that information."

"Then get it. How am I supposed to assess the level of this threat if I don't know who's out there headed toward my family?"

"I'll work on it. In the meantime, you might try to contact the security detail traveling with your families. They need to keep their eyes open. Now I have to go."

"Contact me again tomorrow," the congressman said.

"If I can."

"Do it!"

Carlos ended the transmission and changed that radio to a different frequency. He pushed his chair back and stood, stretching to shake out the tension. He opened the windows and then the front door, stepping onto the porch for a smoke. There was still a lot of activity around the command pod. The tension was amped up, everyone running around in their full loadout, bristling with weapons.

Carlos considered many of these men to be his friends. It bothered him to feel like he was betraying them. He had to remind himself it was a job. Carlos had been fresh out of the army when he got a job with the Capitol Police. The congressman had put in a good word for him, helping him get an important promotion, yet everything the congressman did came at a price. There were always strings. Always conditions.

The congressman's job recommendation only came with one. Work your way into Arthur Bridges' good graces and buy a position within his compound. Once he'd done so, it was his job to be the man on the inside and keep the congressman apprised of activities on the compound. It was only when the world began falling apart that Carlos realized the significance of his deal with the devil. He was expected to live at the compound and continue his role as the man on the inside. When the time came, he was expected to help overthrow it.

Carlos sat down on the steps and lit up a smoke. He was slouched on the steps when a side-by-side pulled onto the command pod and rolled to a stop. He spotted Brandon rolling out of the passenger side. He was going to flag him down and see if he could press him for information but Brandon shot off toward Arthur's cabin. Then Carlos noticed the driver, an Army combat veteran named Cass, staring at his cigarette.

He held it up toward her. "Want one?"

She let out a sigh and came forward.

"You act like I'm the devil," Carlos joked.

"No, but cigarettes are," she replied. "I'd quit before the crap hit the fan. Now, with all this stress, I'm craving them big time."

Carlos pulled out his makings and rolled her one. She wasted no time snatching it when he was done, taking the lighter he offered. She took a drag off the cigarette, then pulled it out and stared at it, exhaling a cloud of smoke. "How can something so little have such a big hold on people?"

"It's a drug, baby," Carlos said. "You're an addict."

"You are too."

"I own it," Carlos admitted. "I came prepared. I've got cartons. I've got enough rolling papers and loose tobacco to keep me smoking for years."

"Or until you die from it," Cass pointed out.

"Roger that," Carlos laughed. "So what you guys been up to?"

Cass took a look around. It wasn't like she was sworn to secrecy or anything but gossip was frowned upon. It violated Arthur's principles of keeping information compartmentalized for operational security. Still, just like in the military, gossip was what you did. It was what you talked about when you had time to talk.

"With all the enemy at the front, we launched an operation out the back. You hear about it?"

Carlos nodded. "Yeah. A little. I heard they sent the prisoner out with some escorts."

"That's it," she said. "I never did hear what they were supposed to be doing out there."

Carlos sat up and leaned forward conspiratorially. "I think they're supposed to be intercepting the congressman's family so they can keep them from showing up here. I guess they're thinking that may force those assholes to pull off and go away."

Cass shook her head. "If that's the case, with all these skilled soldiers to choose from, you'd think they would have sent some more capable folks on that operation."

This got Carlos's attention. "Why? Who'd they send?"

"The civvies."

"Really?"

Cass nodded. "Robert and Sonyea. They're friends of Arthur's and they seem capable enough, but you have to wonder how much experience they have. None is my guess."

"No doubt," Carlos said. "I don't know those guys."

"The guy is the father of that chick that came with the horse trailer. The soldier in the wheelchair with her is the son of the woman. Those two just had the bad luck to end up getting trapped here when the congressman showed up. Otherwise they'd have been on their way a long time ago."

"If this mission is so important, why did they send those guys? You sure they're not spooks or contractors or something? Kevin and Arthur know some switched-on folks."

Cass laughed. "I know that the guy, Robert, is a writer."

"A writer? What kind of writer?"

"Science fiction."

"Nerd stuff? Really?" Carlos was incredulous. Of all the people to send on a critical mission.

Cass nodded. "Apocalyptic, end of the world, nerd stuff."

Carlos shook his head. "They gonna die. They gonna die *so* bad."

"Arthur says his books are pretty good but I've never read one. Been thinking about it though. There's a couple of them floating around the bunkhouse right now."

"I don't read squat," Carlos said. "Cereal boxes and texts. That's about it."

"Caveman."

Carlos shrugged. "I am what I am. People can take it or leave it. So what's this guy's last name?"

"Why, you writing a book, too?"

"No," Carlos said. "Just curious. I get bored enough, I might start reading."

"Yeah, right."

The sound of footsteps caught their attention and they both turned to find Brandon running in their direction. Cass tossed her cigarette butt into a five-gallon bucket half-full of nasty water. "Guess it's back to work for me. Thanks for the smoke."

"No problem," Carlos said, getting to his feet. "I got to get back on duty too."

"Hey, Brandon," Cass called. "What's that writer guy's name?"

"Why?"

"Carlos was asking," Cass said. "Says he wants to read one of his books."

Brandon gave Carlos a look like he wasn't buying it. Brandon read a lot and had never seen Carlos with a book. It would have been the kind of thing he would have noticed. "Robert Hardwick."

Carlos nodded at Brandon. "Thanks, man. You guys be safe."

Cass and Brandon piled into the side-by-side, did a U-turn, and accelerated back in the direction they'd come from.

Carlos took a final draw off his smoke then tossed the butt into the bucket. He climbed back up toward the commo shack.

Robert Hardwick.

20

Back at the compound, they'd determined that Highway 64 in North Carolina's Nantahala National Forest would be the best spot to intercept the convoy of families. The destination wasn't significant in terms of miles but it was hard terrain. The mountains were steep and there were treacherous creek crossings. They ran into numerous pipe gates and steel cables intended to keep folks from doing exactly what they were doing. They used bolt cutters, a sledgehammer, and the bumper winch to bypass them.

As the day wore on, Sonyea and Robert became more comfortable, assuming they were finally out of range of any pursuers. They could breathe easier. They'd taken so many turns on the mountain roads by this point it was unlikely anyone could be following them. Even Jeff, radiating anger and frustration like a solar flare, had settled into the ride. Robert's mind wandered forward, hoping the RVs had not already passed them by. Beyond that, he started to strategize on how he was going to stop their progress and turn them around once he found them. There was always something to worry about.

Robert slowed the Razer when Sonyea pointed out his next turn. It was a gravel road that wound over a thousand feet down a mountain in an extensive succession of serpentine switchbacks. The road was clear of fallen trees and there was good visibility as they descended from alpine meadows into mossy forest. The temperature dropped, the moisture in the air increasing from the cold mountain stream that tumbled over rocks and filled the valley with a cool mist. It was almost pleasant, or might have been if circumstances had been different.

When they reached the last switchback it was as if they'd entered a new world. Thick moss in varying shades of green carpeted downed trees and rocks the size of minivans. Lofty poplars and oaks stretched upward, straining toward what limited light reached the deep valley. Sound took on a different quality than it had on their previous stops. The moss created a muffling effect, like they were in a sound studio, the walls covered in sound-dampening foam. The only sound was the tumble of water over rocks, a low and constant roar that was almost calming.

"This was a primitive campground," Sonyea said. "The map shows camping and fishing spots throughout the valley bottom."

"Reminds me of home," Robert said. "This is what Damascus looks like. Trout streams and deep forest."

"Sounds beautiful," Sonyea said.

"It is. Gets a little crowded in the summer when tourists show up."

"You were a tourist there once, weren't you? You said you moved there from somewhere else. You're like one of those reformed smokers who now despises the thing you used to be."

"Yeah, my wife reminds me of that too," Robert said. "Usually when I'm bitching about tourists."

Robert eased into a blind left turn, both the road and the creek following the bend of the valley. Halfway through it, he saw the road ahead was blocked by vehicles. They weren't sideways, like an intentional barricade, but parked. They likely belonged to the people staying in the campers crammed onto the narrow shoulder. They were still a good fifty feet ahead of him but Robert understood instantly there was no way he could get past them. The valley was narrow to begin with and there was a rock cliff just feet from the left of the road. To the right of the parked vehicles, there were campers, trees, and the trout stream. There was one way through and it was completely blocked.

"Why did they have to park in the road?" Robert grumbled. "I'm pretty sure this is probably not one of the approved campsites either."

"You think that really matters anymore?" Jeff asked, looking at Robert like he was idiot. "You've been cutting locks and bypassing gates all day."

"The main road is on the other side of these vehicles, according to the map. That's exactly where we're headed," Sonyea said. "They probably came in from that side and didn't expect people to show up here."

"Is there another road?" Robert asked. "Any way around?"

"There's no other road unless we backtrack a long way."

"Backtracking is wasting fuel," Robert said. "We only have so much and I'm not certain it's even enough to do what we need to do. We have to get around them if we can."

"Then go ask," Sonyea suggested. "Maybe they'll let us slip through. Not everything has to end violently. There's probably still room for some discussion and negotiation in this world."

"I hate to take the chance," Robert said. "We don't know what kind of people they are. It could end badly."

"Guess you're going to find out. Someone's coming this way," Jeff said.

Sonyea and Robert had been distracted mulling over the map and hadn't noticed two men striding toward them. Both had rifles in their hands but not pointed in their direction, more curious than cautious. That was probably a normal reaction to someone showing up at your campsite in a remote area. Almost simultaneously, there were two metallic clicks within the Razer as both Sonyea and Robert released the safeties on their weapons.

Sonyea had a flannel shirt in the back that she'd been wearing earlier in the day. She tossed it into Jeff's lap. "Cover those cuffs. Now!"

"Don't do anything stupid," Jeff hissed. "I'm defenseless here. I'm a sitting duck."

"That goes for you too—nothing stupid," Robert said. "Now sit back and shut up." He threw a hand up and waved at the approaching men. It was a casual wave, like men passing on a country road, but it felt anything but casual.

One of the men waved back, not smiling but not unfriendly. He looked to be in his thirties with long hair and a beard. He was dressed in jeans and a black t-shirt. Despite the normality of that outfit, it looked odd to Robert after seeing nothing but camo, military, and tactical clothing for the last few days. The other man, wearing jeans and a NASCAR shirt, hung back and didn't approach the vehicle.

The man coming up on Robert's side appeared more interested in the Razer than Robert. "I always wanted one of these," he said. "Fast, aren't they?"

Robert nodded. "It'll move along."

"What the hell you doing out here running around the woods? You hunting? And where did you get gas for this thing?"

Robert shrugged. "We haven't been able to get any gas. We're just running on what we had left at the house. We're not hunting. This is my wife and son. We're trying to reach my mother-in-law." It sounded like the best story. Something nearly everyone could relate to, trying to reach family.

The man cast an eye around the vehicle at Robert's "family." "Not sure I'd be running toward my mother-in-law. More likely I'd be running the other way."

Robert forced a laugh. "Family has to pull together in hard times. Even with those family members you don't particularly care for."

The man in the black t-shirt was still examining them in detail. His eyes wandered across the passengers, their clothing, and the items sitting around them. Then his gaze wandered to the packs, the plastic totes of gear, and the multiple jerry cans of fuel. He pointed at the fuel cans. "Any of those full? We'd pay good money for a can of gas. We got fish and meat to trade."

"I appreciate the offer but I can't spare any," Robert said. "I'm not even sure I have enough to get to my mother-in-law's house. It's going to be tight."

The man looked more disappointed than angry. His eyes wandered to take in the wooded valley, his expression that of a man regarding a dream home that's turned into a money pit. "We decided to come up here where the game was better until things get back to normal. Thought we'd have a better chance getting by. Figured we could at least put food on the table. I ain't so sure now that it was the best move."

"Why's that?" Robert asked.

"We burned up what fuel we had looking for game trails. Now we're doing it all on foot and it's a lot harder. This is big country out here and it'll wear a man down traipsing these hills all day long. Something like this Razer would make it a lot easier."

As the man said it, Robert could see an idea take shape in his eyes. He'd put together that he could probably take this vehicle from these strangers and turn them out on foot. Who was there to stop him? What could they do about it? So pleasing was the vision unveiling itself in his mind's eye that he couldn't keep a faint smile from curling the edges of his mouth. That was when Robert understood he had a short window in which to get this back on track before it got ugly.

"We were hoping to get by those vehicles of yours and be on our way," Robert said, trying to redirect the man. "This is kind of an emergency. We have people waiting on us. So if you could just help us out here and get those out of the way, we'll get out of your hair."

"Those people of yours might be waiting a long time," the man replied.

Robert's chest tightened and his blood ran cold. "Why do you say that?"

The man gave a smile that bore no sincerity. "Those vehicles won't move without gas. Now if you'd traded us some, I might could have moved them. Things being what they are, I reckon we'll just leave them be."

Robert frowned and looked around the windshield toward the vehicles. "Can't you push them?"

The man's expression revealed what he thought of that suggestion. "Probably could but I think I like them right where they are. I push them somewhere else, I have to walk farther if I need something out of them. That inconveniences me, you see. But maybe if you were to pay a toll—like a can of gas—we might be inclined to help you out. What do you say?"

Robert tried to gauge the man. It was a standoff now. As much as the idea burned his ass, should he go along with it? There was an inherent risk in it. They still might be surrounded and all their fuel taken. If he gave up anything at all, where did it stop? They might be killed for their vehicle or for the totes of food. He needed to get out of here. All of this talk was going nowhere. Negotiation was a waste of time.

"I think we'll just be on our way," Robert said. "Thanks and good luck to you."

The man at Robert's side still had his hand on the roll cage and Robert noticed the grip tightening, as if the man was so desperate to keep them there that he thought he could hold the vehicle in place. He was searching for words, looking for a new angle, for anything he could say to get Robert out of the vehicle, when a third man emerged from between two of the campers.

"Who the hell is that?" the man snarled.

It was at this point that Jeff did something completely unexpected. He shrugged the flannel shirt from his lap and yanked his handcuffed hands up as far as his bonds would allow. He showed them to the man at Robert's door.

"Please help me," he begged. "I'm not his son. These people kidnapped me. They're going to kill me."

Robert was taken by surprise. He'd lost control of the situation. Everything began moving in slow motion. He whipped his head from Jeff's direction toward the man at his side of the vehicle. He saw horror and surprise on the man's face. Then the stranger's eyes rolled down to catch his and a decision was made. The man began hauling his rifle up toward his shoulder.

"Noooo!" Robert roared. His AR pistol was laying across his lap with the safety off, pointed right toward the door and toward the man on the other side of it. Without even raising the weapon, he squeezed off three rounds, shooting right through the plastic door. At least one of the rounds found flesh because the man screamed and back-stepped, collapsing on the deep moss behind him. The man writhed on the ground, trying to staunch the flow of blood from his bleeding thigh and groin.

The sound of gunfire exploded in the peaceful valley. NASCAR man, standing just ahead of the vehicle, was desperately working the bolt-action of his own rifle when Sonyea fired a hastily-aimed shotgun blast over the roll cage. It was not a direct hit but staggered the man, forcing him to drop the rifle as he fell to the ground.

There were shouts and screams from people around the campers that they couldn't see. In seconds there could be dozens of weapons on them. Robert was paralyzed with fear and frustration.

"Go! Go!" Sonyea yelled. "Get us out of here!"

Robert shifted to reverse and punched the throttle. The racks and gear blocked his vision, forcing him to hang his head out the door to get a clear view behind them. A sound of warning from Sonyea made him glance forward and he saw two men at the campsite raising rifles in their direction.

Still reversing, he raised the AR pistol with one hand, resting it on the roll cage above the windshield, and pulled off three hasty shots. They were nowhere close to hitting anyone but they scattered the men.

Sonyea knew they were still sitting ducks. "Give me that," she said, unfastening her seatbelt and leaning forward to grab Robert's AR pistol.

"Safety is OFF!" Robert warned her, but she was already shooting before he was finished with the sentence.

Standing in the back seat, Sonyea dumped rounds at the riflemen, trying to force them behind cover so they couldn't get a decent shot at the Razer. Backing up this straight, narrow road, it wouldn't take any skill at all for a shooter to put a couple of rounds through the windshield. She couldn't let anyone get that shot.

Finally hitting a wide spot in the road, Robert spun the wheel hard to the left, making a sharp bootlegger turn. He'd failed to warn Sonyea and she went flying, hitting the roll cage, and sagging to the floor. She was still healing from the injuries she'd sustained fighting Gamma Ray at her farm and the pain took her breath. She collapsed in the back seat, holding her ribs, the AR pistol clattering to the floor.

Sonyea was crying and cursing, struggling for breath, but Robert couldn't focus on her. He shifted to Forward and hit the gas, wheels spinning as the vehicle sought traction on the damp ground. He threw a quick glance at the rearview mirror, trying to spot his friend but she was not in his view, curled in the floor.

"Sonyea! You okay?"

When she didn't respond, he spun in his seat, wanting to see how she was doing but not wanting to take his eyes from the road long enough that they might run up a tree. He found her red-faced, eyes filled with tears, struggling to catch a breath.

"You okay?" he repeated, turning back around just in time to slide around the first of the switchbacks taking them back up the mountain from which they'd just come.

"Eyes on the road!" Jeff screamed. "You're going too fast and there's no guardrail. You go over, we're dead."

Robert hit the brakes and skidded to a stop. He could see the road beneath them and there were no pursuers yet. He looked behind him. "Are you okay, Sonyea?"

She nodded, her eyes closed. When he turned back to the road, Robert caught Jeff out of the corner of his eye. This was all his fault. Before he could stop himself, he backhanded Jeff with a hammer fist, catching him below the left eye socket.

"What the hell, dude?" Jeff cried, bending over and cradling his face.

"This is your fault," Robert hissed through clenched teeth. "You're lucky I don't kill you right now. Do you think I won't? Do you think I'm playing around?"

When Jeff didn't answer, Robert fired another fist at the side of the man's head, causing him to cry out and flinch away from him.

"I don't think you're playing!" Jeff yelled. "I don't. Quit hitting me. I'm sorry."

Robert grabbed Jeff by the hair. "You get one of us hurt again and I'll drag you behind this vehicle until there's nothing left of you. I swear to God I will."

"I hear you!" Jeff sobbed.

A hand on Robert's shoulder got his attention. It was Sonyea. He caught her eyes.

"Drive," she whispered. "Keep moving. We can deal with him later."

THEY STOPPED at a natural clearing high on the mountain with vistas that went for hundreds of miles in all directions. In the distance, power line right-of-ways traced wide swaths across rolling hills, the towers bearing useless wiring that provided nothing now but a resting place for birds. They were perhaps only five miles from where the shootout occurred but they'd followed a convoluted path in their retreat. Hopefully the men they'd run into were being honest about not having gas and would be unable to search for them. Without vehicles, it was unlikely anyone would hike those steep switchbacks just to track them down.

Sonyea lay on the ground beside the Razer, stretched out on a sleeping bag. She'd taken acetaminophen and was waiting for the pain to subside to a tolerable level before they got on the road again. Robert was drinking water from a Nalgene bottle and studying the map. With their planned route to Highway 64 blocked by the vehicles they'd just encountered, he needed to find an alternative route as soon as possible. Every minute they were delayed, he imagined the caravan of families bypassing them and driving into what would soon be a battle for possession of Arthur's compound.

As much as he hated himself for it, the idea had entered his mind that he could just keep going and drive in the direction of home. He had no idea how far this fuel would get him but any movement north would be progress. He wouldn't do it, though. He was determined to help his friends and be a better person. Still, it was hard to force the idea from his head. The more he tried to *not* think about home, the more he found himself thinking about it.

"Hey, I need to take a bathroom break," Jeff said.

Robert glared at him. At Sonyea's prompting, he'd reluctantly given the young man a bottle of water. His preference was leaning toward just killing Jeff and being done with it. Robert still felt like he could have talked his way through the situation on the road if Jeff hadn't whipped out his cuffs and claimed to be a kidnap victim. While technically he *was* a kidnap victim, hadn't he agreed to this? Hadn't he come along willingly to help save his family?

An idea hit Robert like a bad smell. It was an utterly disgusting revelation. To some extent, he and Jeff were alike. They were both struggling with trying to do the right thing. They were both weighing selfishness against selflessness. They were weighing what they wanted to be against what they needed to do. Both of them were regularly coming up short. It reminded Robert of that old saying that the things that bothered you most in other people were sometimes the things that reminded you of yourself. The thought that he and Jeff were similar was disturbing to him. If anything, it should encourage him to strive harder to be a better man. He hoped that was true.

"I just gave you that water," Robert said. "It go right through you or something?"

"I don't need to pee," Jeff said, lowering his voice and throwing an embarrassed look in Sonyea's direction. "Must be all this bouncing around or something. I'm not sure how long I can wait."

"Geez," Robert groaned. He folded the map and dropped it in the driver's seat, then pulled a twelve foot length of chain from a bag strapped into the back of the Razer.

Before unhooking Jeff's cuffs from the grab handles, he fastened the chain to the cuffs with a padlock, and then released them from the grab handle. Robert drew his gun and stepped away from the passenger door. "You're going to walk over there to that poplar tree. I'm going to wrap this chain around the tree and secure it with a padlock. Then you can take care of your business. Holler when you're done."

Jeff eased out of the vehicle and scanned his surroundings. "Which tree?"

Robert pointed. "That one."

Jeff started in that direction and Robert hung back, ready to do whatever had to be done if Jeff tried to make a break for it. When they got to the tree, Robert ordered Jeff to stand about eight feet away while he padlocked the chain around the tree. When Robert was done, Jeff extended his cuffed hands toward Robert.

Robert shook his head. "No way, man."

Jeff looked disappointed. "Dude, really?"

"Really."

"How am I supposed to do what needs to be done?"

"You'll figure it out."

"TP?"

"Nature will provide."

"Dude, that's messed up," Jeff said, revolted. "We're men, not animals."

"Animals don't use anything. Grass is a step above the animals."

"Well, it's one hell of a step down from Charmin."

Robert walked off. "Deal with it or use your sock," he called back. "Not my problem."

He could hear grumbling behind him as he went back to the Razer. He got the map and sat down in the grass, leaning back against the plastic door. He looked over at Sonyea and saw her eyes were open. "You doing any better?"

"A little," she said. "I should be fine in a few. The Tylenol is taking the edge off."

"You're a tough woman."

"Don't feel so tough now."

"You know, he could have got us killed."

"A lot of things could have killed us," Sonyea said. "He's just one of them. But we're still here."

"Here we are having to go the long way around, thanks to him."

"Those guys wouldn't have moved those vehicles anyway," Sonyea said. "Even if Jeff hadn't blown it, there would have been a standoff over fuel or the Razer."

"I didn't peg those guys as killers."

"I wouldn't peg you for a killer either, but you are. It's the times, not the people."

Robert hated to admit it but she was probably right. It made him feel better to blame Jeff, though. It reminded him not to trust the kid and not to let his guard down around him. This thought made him realize that he should probably check on the kid. He should be done by now. He got to his feet.

"I'm going to get him moving. You about ready to hit it again?"

Sonyea sat up and rubbed her eyes. "I guess so. A cup of coffee would be nice. I was getting a little sluggish."

"No time for that now but I have some caffeinated jelly beans if you want a pack."

She shook her head. "Sorry, just not the same."

"Suit yourself," Robert replied, moving around to the front of the Razer. "You done over there, kid?"

There was no response.

"Jeff?"

"He not answering?" Sonyea asked.

"No," Robert replied, heading toward the tree where he'd left Jeff.

The chain was still visible, cinched and padlocked around the tree at about waist height. Robert drew his pistol and kept his distance from the tree, moving left to gradually reveal what lay on the other side of it. He didn't want to get too close in case the kid had some attack planned. Once he'd moved far enough laterally, he found the kid squatting at the far reach of his chain but his pants were still around his waist. Whatever he was doing was something other than he was supposed to be doing.

Robert's brow furrowed, trying to figure out what was going on. Then he saw a white wire extending from the kid's ear to a device cradled in front of his mouth. He heard the low whispering and figured it out. It was a radio. The son-of-a-bitch had a radio.

Robert charged and lashed out with his foot, kicking Jeff over to his side. The radio flew from his hands but was stopped in its flight by the cord connecting it to his ears. While Jeff lay stunned, Robert snatched up the radio, yanking it free, and unplugging the earbuds. A man's voice was barely audible through static. In fact, he could barely understand the voice at all. Robert hit the volume key and the voice grew louder.

"Can you repeat that?" the voice said.

Robert glared at Jeff, still lying on the ground, not meeting Robert's eye.

"Please repeat that last transmission," the voice said. *"We've lost you."*

Robert jumped on Jeff, sitting on his upper body, and throwing a punch at the younger man's head. "Who the hell was that? Who were you talking to?"

Jeff squirmed, tried to dislodge his attacker, tried to get a hand up to shield his face, but he didn't answer.

"I asked you a question," Robert repeated, punching the man again, then grabbing him by the collar and screaming in his face. "Are you setting us up? Where did you get the radio?"

As Robert shook him, a scrap of paper fell from Jeff's balled fist. Robert stared at it a second, then picked it up. Jeff scrambled, trying to take it back, but couldn't reach it. He recoiled when Robert drew his fist back to strike him again.

Robert got to his feet and backed away from Jeff. He could smell the paper in his hand. It smelled like mint. Like mint gum. Then it hit him. He remembered finding Carlos at Jeff's cell in the hay barn, the piece of gum he'd given him, and the wrapper that Jeff slipped into his pocket. Robert unfolded the paper: *This radio will reach your dad. Don't worry. You have friends on the inside.*

"Is that who you were talking to?" Robert demanded. "Your dad? The men back at the compound? You trying to direct them to us?"

Jeff shook his head.

Robert yanked his pistol from the holster and leveled it at Jeff. "I will kill you. Who were you talking to? You have one chance."

"My family!" Jeff spluttered. "And the men escorting my family. They're apparently on the same frequency. They heard me and started talking to me."

Robert holstered his gun and drew back his arm, his frustration driving him to throw the radio as far as he could. Just before he could throw it, a hand closed around his forearm. He whipped his head around and found the hand belonged to Sonyea.

"What the hell?"

"We can use that," she said. "If it picks up the families, we can listen in to what they're saying to each other. They have to be close if he's picking them up with that handheld."

Robert realized she was right. Throwing the radio was a stupid idea. He relaxed his arm and Sonyea released him. He shoved it in a pocket.

Sonyea faced the prisoner. "Did he hurt you?"

"A little," Jeff said, sensing she was the more compassionate of the two. He was wrong.

"Good," she said. "You deserved it. This is the second attempt you've made to sabotage us today. It better be the last. What did you say to them?"

"Nothing," Jeff said. "I was trying to get my dad. When that guy gave me the radio, he didn't know anything about me coming out here. He thought I could use it for talking to my dad from the cell. I thought I'd try it and see if it would still reach my dad's camp but it didn't. One of the men escorting the families heard me say my dad's name and they asked me to identify myself. We were just starting to talk when that asshole knocked me down."

Robert glared at Jeff. "He's probably lying. He's trying to set us up."

"I'm not lying."

"What else did Carlos give you?"

"Carlos?" Sonyea asked. "I'm confused."

Robert held up the scrap of paper. "I saw Carlos giving him this note in the hay barn. I didn't think anything about Carlos being in there at the time. I guess I should have said something about it. He must have given him the radio too."

"What else did he give you, Jeff?" Sonyea asked.

Jeff shrugged. "Nothing."

"He could have a weapon," Robert said. "Cover me. I'm going to find out."

With Sonyea holding her pistol on Jeff, Robert thoroughly searched him, looking for anything that might be used as a weapon. In the small of Jeff's back, he found a thin knife clipped to the inside of his waistband. He held it up for Sonyea to see.

"What was that for, Jeff?" she asked.

"Nothing," he said. "I wasn't going to use it unless I had to."

Robert pulled the knife from its sheath and tested the blade with a thumb. Jeff watched him with wide eyes. "I should cut you right now. Just enough to make a point."

"No!" Jeff wailed.

"Don't do it, Robert," Sonyea said.

Robert shoved the knife in the sheath and stood, tucking it in a pocket. "You're going to run out of chances, kid. I can see it already."

"Can I finish my business now?" Jeff asked. "I've still got to go."

"You've got to be kidding. We gave you plenty of time for that already," Robert said.

"I'm sorry," Jeff said. "I never got to it because of the radio."

Robert looked at Sonyea.

She shrugged. "What choice do we have?"

"You better make it quick," Robert ordered. "And I'm not leaving you alone this time."

Sonyea returned to the vehicle to repack her sleeping bag. Robert dug in his pocket to find the key to the padlock fastening Jeff's chain to the tree.

While Robert was distracted with unlocking the chain, Jeff raised his cuffed hands to swipe a grimy forearm across his runny nose. As he did, he casually spat a handcuff key into the palm of his hand. When he turned away from Robert to unzip his fly, he slipped it into the watch pocket on his jeans, and casually went about the mission at hand.

When he was done, he zipped up and turned back to Robert. "I'm ready."

Roberttook up the slack in the leash and nodded toward the vehicle.

Jeff walked by and took a seat in the Razer. Sonyea was already in the back, the shotgun laying across her lap.

"You ready?" Robert asked, cuffing Jeff to the grab handles with the second pair of cuffs.

"Yeah," Sonyea said. "I guess."

Robert settled into the driver's seat and fastened his seatbelt. "If I'm reading the map right, we have to drop down over the southeast side of this mountain now, pick up a different road, and try to make it to Highway 64 before those families do."

"What are you going to do to them?" Jeff asked. His tone implied a serious concern about their well-being.

"I haven't thought out all the details," Robert said.

"Will anyone be hurt?"

"A lot of that depends on you, Jeff," Sonyea said. "If you can't keep your head in the game, if you keep withholding stuff from us, we might not be able to assure their safety. Whatever the plan ends up being, you need to go along with it. You need to do your part. That's the only way you keep your family from getting hurt."

"They're at a campground," Jeff mumbled.

Robert, who'd already started the Razer, turned it back off again. "Excuse me? What did you say?"

"They're at a campground. It's near some town called Marble. The Cozy Creek Campground."

"And you know this *how*?" Robert asked.

"They told me just before you pounced on me, dude," Jeff said.

"They said they were supposed to wait there until they received word from Dad."

"Why should we believe you?" Sonyea asked.

Jeff looked at her like the answer was obvious. "Because I don't want my family to die. I know I probably can't save my dad but maybe I can save the rest of them."

Robert restarted the vehicle. "Maybe you can."

21

U nder a heightened state of alert at the compound, everyone had assigned tasks or stations. This was one of the things they drilled on during the training sessions conducted a couple of times a year during normal times. Carlos was supposed to be glued to the radio while other residents of the compound patrolled the grounds, sat in sniper nests, or tended to various support duties. Carlos also needed to satisfy his other bene- factor. He needed to check back in with the congressman. He wanted to pass on Robert's name and the information he'd gotten from Cass, but he wanted a little more.

Finding a moment when things were quiet around the command pod, Carlos slipped out the door of the commo shack and headed for one of the outhouses located nearby. He paused at the door, made sure no one was looking, then bypassed the outhouse and disap- peared into the woods. He caught a cleared footpath and accelerated to a jogging pace. He needed to make this quick and get back to his station.

It took him several minutes to get to the first of the bunkhouses located at the core of the property. This wasn't his bunkhouse but he hadn't noticed any paperback books laying around the one he was staying in. This unit, where both Brandon and Cass had bunks, was the place to start.

He slowed and looked around, feeling like a spy as he crept up the steps. He peered through the glass panel in the door and didn't see anyone inside. He was relieved to find the door unlocked. The bunkhouse he stayed in was never locked either, so he'd anticipated this. Living together in these conditions required a certain degree of trust. After all, everyone had been vetted. They'd all gone through background screenings and been cleared. Even Carlos.

With one last glance at his surroundings, he opened the door and slipped inside. The bunkhouses were long, simple cabins but were designed to provide comfortable year-round living quarters. They were insulated but had bare plywood walls with a minimum level of trim. They were neat without being extravagant. There were windows for light and ventilation, with a woodstove at one end to provide heat when required.

Bunkbeds provided the sleeping accommodations. Both the top and bottom bunks had privacy curtains. To the side of each bunk there were personal lockers for storage of weapons and gear. A solar setup provided illumination by way of a few twelve-volt LED bulbs. At each end of the bunkhouse, an odd assortment of yard sale furniture provided a place for people to hang out. There were no showers or bathrooms within the quarters. A gravity-fed, solar-heated shower facility was located centrally to all the residences. An outhouse was located just outside, and downwind, of each bunkhouse.

Carlos walked the length of the room, headed straight for the sitting area at the far end of the space. He checked the coffee and end tables. There were gun, fitness, and off-roading magazines, as well as several paperbacks. Carlos flipped through the stack but none were by Robert Hardwick. He frowned. Somebody must be reading it at night. It had to be in someone's personal pile.

During the day, with the bunkhouse abandoned, the facility was dim, the only light coming from the stray illumination filtering its way down through the tree cover. Carlos pulled a Streamlight flashlight from his pocket, thumbed the switch on the butt, and began scanning nightstands. Despite the fact that he working for the enemy of these folks, despite the fact that he was trying to get them all evicted for the convenience of a greedy congressman, this simple act felt like a violation. It was odd how morality worked sometimes, kicking in when one least expected it. He pushed that feeling to the side and did what he had to do.

Halfway up the narrow aisle he saw a battered paperback dangling off a bedside table. The cover showed a heavily-muscled man in tactical gear. He was shirtless but wore a plate carrier. He held his rifle in such a way that his bicep flexed and showed off tattoos. On his arm was a buxom woman, scantily-clad in shredded clothing. She'd obviously just been rescued by the hero. Carlos considered the cover, thinking this book might be pretty good after all. He stared at the title. *Angels of Armageddon* by Robert Hardwick. He'd found what he was looking for.

Carlos shoved it inside his shirt and slipped out the door. When he was certain there was no one around to see him, he started running again. He returned by the same route he'd used earlier, slipping by the outhouse like he was returning from using the facilities. He slowed at that point, making his way casually across the open command pod.

He didn't start to relax until he was climbing the steps to the commo shack. He would go in, get the congressman on the horn, and tell him what he'd found. He was already digging the book out of his shirt when he tugged open the screen door and went inside. He stopped in his tracks when he found Kevin waiting on him.

The contractor was sitting in Carlos's chair, fiddling with the dials on the radio. Carlos froze. He already had the book out in the open. It was too late to put it back in his shirt, too awkward to whip it around behind his back.

"Where have you been?" Kevin asked, accusation and disapproval in his voice.

"Taking a dump, man," Carlos said, holding the book up in the air. "Guess I got sucked into this book I'm reading."

"There's a lot going on right now," Kevin said. "You should request somebody to cover your station if you're going to be out of action. You know how this works."

Carlos shrugged. "Sorry, man. Didn't think I was going to be that long. Things were quiet. Didn't think it would be a big deal."

"Maybe it is, maybe it isn't," Kevin said. "But you don't know because you were out of action. You have no idea what might have been transmitted in your absence. What if we missed an important transmission? What if one of our guys was in trouble and depending on you to relay a request for assistance?"

"I'm sorry," Carlos said. "It won't happen again." He strived to sound apologetic, though he hated being reprimanded like this.

Kevin got up from the chair and walked by Carlos. "It better not happen again. This isn't the military but your duties here are serious. If you don't understand that, you don't belong here."

Carlos flushed, embarrassed at the dressing-down. Kevin pushed out the door and headed down the steps.

Carlos realized something and stuck his head out the door. "You never did say what you needed."

"Forget it," Kevin said, waving him off.

Carlos crumpled his face in concern. What had Kevin wanted? Had he been compromised somehow? Had he given himself away? He went to his desk and slipped his headphones on. He put the book on the desk in front of him. After staring at it for a moment, he powered up one of the secondary radios and switched it to the memorized frequency.

"Green for White. Green for White."

It took several minutes of repeating the transmission before there was a response.

"Go for White," Bradshaw said.

"I have more information," Carlos said.

"One second."

Shortly, the gruff voice of Congressman Honaker barked into the radio, *"What have you got for me?"*

"Robert Hardwick," Carlos said, reading the name from the cover of the book despite having memorized it.

"Who's that?"

"The guy who took off with your son. The writer."

"You got any background?"

"Only from the back cover of his book."

"What does it say?"

"'Robert Hardwick writes from his fortress of solitude deep in the mountains of Damascus, Virginia. He spends each day looking for new ways to destroy the world so he can enjoy writing about it.'"

"Robert Hardwick, Damascus, Virginia," the congressman repeated, scribbling the information on a piece of paper. *"And the woman?"*

"Nobody famous," Carlos said. "She owns a riding school for people with disabilities. Sonyea Brady is her name. Took some asking around to get that."

"Riding school for the disabled. How noble," the congressman drawled, his voice oozing sarcasm. *"Anything else?"*

"That's all I got. I couldn't ask much without raising suspicion. Things around here are on a need to know basis."

"Let us know if you hear anything else, especially any information about what this mission of theirs entails."

"Got it," Carlos said. "If you don't mind me asking, how much longer do you think this is going to take? I'm getting a little edgy. I'd like to get across the wire and link up with you guys."

There was a delay before the congressman responded and Carlos could imagine him on the other end scowling at the radio. *"You need to grow a set and focus on your job. You'll stay within the walls of that compound for as long as we need you to stay. That's all I have to say about that right now."*

Overwhelmed by a wave of rage, Carlos had to bite his tongue to stay cool. "Roger that. Green out."

He changed the frequency on that radio and turned it off. Even though he'd just had a break, he returned to the porch, sat down on his favorite step, and lit up a smoke. Across the command pod, Kevin and Brandon were talking at the rear of a side-by-side. Carlos could have sworn that he saw them looking in his direction several times.

What were they talking about? Him? Maybe he was just being paranoid.

What if he wasn't?

22

"So no one has heard from the families today?" Congressman Honaker asked after getting off the radio with Carlos.

"You know I'd have told you if I heard anything. I've babysat that radio all day," Bradshaw said. "They were supposed to reach the campground yesterday and check in with us today. I wasn't all that surprised when we didn't hear from them last night. I figured they might need time to rig up an antenna or something. That can be a big operation in these mountains. They'll have to get up high."

The congressman took a healthy bite of his freeze-dried lasagna, his eyes distant, his mind calculating. As much as he hated to admit it, the food was showing improvement since they'd replaced Jeff with someone who had more aptitude for the job. Jeff had only been doing it because the congressman had promised his wife he wouldn't put Jeff in danger. Cook was the only safe job they had. "You think those people that escaped Arthur's compound have caught up with them yet? Maybe done something to them?"

Bradshaw twirled a fork around his own plate, chasing down entrails of pasta. "I don't know. I doubt they've reached them yet. Travel takes longer when you're not on the main roads. Besides, it's not like they know where to look. There will have to be an element of luck involved. It might not be that easy."

"I have a file on all the shareholders in Arthur's little corporation, though it doesn't cover those visitors. I'm pretty sure Robert Hardwick and Sonyea Brady weren't in my intelligence reports. In fact, I don't recall them ever showing up on my radar before. They must have never visited when Carlos was onsite. When he visited the compound to work or train he always sent me detailed lists of everyone he ran into. It was part of his job."

"Intelligence is never foolproof," Bradshaw said. "It's always the unexpected variables that throw a wrench in things. I've heard of international espionage operations going awry because a maid came home early or because someone ran out of gas. Shit happens."

"I'm not sure what to do. Do we pull off and go help our families or do we keep fighting here?"

"I don't know. Maybe after dinner I'll walk up and check our antenna," Bradshaw said. "Perhaps a tree branch fell on it and pulled the wires loose or something. If it's down, we won't hear the families even if they are transmitting."

"We need to let them know they have people headed in their direction. They need to be on the lookout," Congressman Honaker said. "I've got to come up with a plan for us too. We can't just sit here forever. The families aren't carrying a lot of supplies. Staying in campers on the road isn't sustainable. We need to get inside that compound."

"Or give up on it and find a different spot," Bradshaw suggested.

"I don't like the idea of giving up. I believe in sticking to a plan. You don't concede defeat. That's what separates the winners from the losers in this world."

"Then I don't know what to tell you. Negotiation has failed, threats have failed, and a direct assault would be suicide. I don't know what you have left in your bag of tricks but I'm not seeing a path to victory here."

The congressman got up and threw his paper plate into the trash can. He paced the narrow aisle of the RV, wracking his brain. "There has to be some angle we haven't tried."

"How long do you think the disaster will last?" Bradshaw asked.

"Projections say a year or two before things are back up and running. Could be as long as five years before things are what we consider normal again. Everything I've read, everything we've been told in congressional briefings, makes it clear that the next year or two could be very dark times for the country. We'll lose a lot of people. To survive, you have to be dug in. You have to have supplies."

"Then maybe we need to consider a new plan," Bradshaw said. "Maybe we need an easier target. Someplace we can actually get into and hole up before things get really bad, even if it's someplace different than you originally intended. This place may not be worth the loss of life."

The congressman shook his head. "This was the place I always planned on coming. I built everything on taking it and I didn't get where I am by accepting defeat. Or accepting *no* as an answer. I got where I am by getting the things I wanted, even if I had to take them by force. Even if I had to step on a few people along the way."

"Is winning worth the cost?" Bradshaw said. "If you lose half your men, who's going to protect this place for you? Who's going to help you run it? Will you be able to defend it from the next guy who comes along?"

The congressman shook his head in frustration, as if trying to shake loose some of the ideas fighting for space. There were too many variables, not to mention the life and death consequences of his decisions. "I need time to think. You check that antenna and let me know what you find. If you hear from the families, track me down."

"Got it," Bradshaw said.

The congressman clambered down the steps and out of the RV. There was a rack of rifles against the wall of the RV and the congressman stared at it. He didn't really understand the fancy military-style rifles but that was all there was to choose from. He grabbed one and slung it over his shoulder, figuring if he was going to be out walking around, he should probably have one, even if it was only for appearances.

"Going somewhere, sir?"

The congressman turned around to find one of his men, a cop named Catron, behind him.

"I need a walk to clear my head."

"I patrol this section," Catron said. "You should probably walk the road away from the compound and stay out of the woods. That would be safest."

"I'll do it. Thank you."

"You're welcome, sir," Catron said, returning to his patrol.

The congressman ambled out of camp, admiring the nice day, and trying to remember how long it had been since he took a walk on a country road. He'd grown up on a dirt road and his first few steps took him back to a different time, to a different place in his life. It made him feel a way he hadn't felt for a very long time.

WHEN THE CONGRESSMAN returned to his RV, he found Jacobs and Bradshaw outside the RV having a heated discussion. That somewhat disappointed the congressman. He'd enjoyed his walk and returning to a conflict was depressing.

"What's going on?" he asked.

"The antenna is destroyed," Bradshaw said.

The congressman sighed, placing his rifle in the rack against the wall. "Is it repairable?"

"No," Jacobs said. "We're not even sure where all the pieces are. They broke the damn thing into tiny pieces and scattered them through the forest on their way out."

The congressman sagged into a camp chair and rested his face in his hands. "Aren't antennas the simple part of the radio? Can't you just build another one?"

Bradshaw threw his hands up. "Well, I guess you can if you have the knowledge and the materials. I don't have either. I don't think anyone here is capable of doing that."

"Where does this leave us?" the congressman asked, still not looking up.

"That's what we were just discussing," Jacobs said. "We can communicate with Bridges' compound and with our own men in the immediate area but that's pretty much it. We're not reaching out of this valley without a more substantial antenna placed higher on the surrounding hills."

"Great," the congressman said, slouching back in his chair, his face red from leaning forward, his expression downcast.

"What do you want to do?" Bradshaw asked.

"Call back a few of the men," the congressman said. "Have them start tearing down the camp. We're pulling out." He gave them a pained smile, which was all he had left to offer.

"What?" the other men asked simultaneously, both of them erupting into a barrage of questions.

The congressman held his hands up, asking for silence. When the men conceded, he continued.

"I have a new plan. I can't reveal it all now. All I can tell you is that the next step is to rendezvous with our families and make sure they're safe. As far as the Bridges compound goes, they've won. Taking the place is not worth the cost to our people."

"I think you're making the right decision," Bradshaw said. "We still have enough fuel to find a new place."

"I think it's a mistake," Colonel Jacobs said, shaking his head. "We could have taken it, given enough time. All I needed was freedom to take the necessary steps. If you'd just allowed me to do my job this would be over already."

The congressman got to his feet. "My word is final. My ship, my rules. You want to stay on my ship, follow them. You want to find your own ship, then help yourself."

Both men nodded somberly and wandered off. They had work to do.

The congressman threw back the screen door and went inside the

RV. He found a bottle of Buffalo Trace bourbon in one of the cabinets, grabbed a glass, and slid into the cramped dinette. He poured a glass of the amber liquid, smiling when the aroma hit his nose. He tipped it back, allowing the shot to work its magic. He folded his arms on the table, lay his head down upon them, and closed his eyes.

23

"This is Bragg. I have unusual activity at the enemy camp."

Arthur was just considering a nap when the transmission broke the silence in his bedroom. He picked up a handheld radio from the nightstand. "This is Bridges. What do you have?"

"Sir, I could swear they're tearing down camp."

That got Arthur's attention. "Can you repeat that?"

"Yes sir. I could swear they're tearing down camp. They've dropped the big tents and have a team stowing gear in vehicles and trailers."

"I'll be right there," Arthur said.

Bragg was in an observation post that had a good view down on the camp. While he couldn't see everything, he could see enough. Arthur couldn't believe this. Either Robert's ploy to lure them off was working or the congressman was up to something.

Arthur stretched and slipped his boots back on, zipping up the sides. He slipped on his plate carrier, his hat, and grabbed a rifle. He was slipping the radio into a pouch on his chest when he heard Carlos on the radio.

"Carlos for Bragg. Can you confirm that last transmission? They're packing up?"

Arthur frowned at this. As far as he was concerned, they were in the midst of an operation and needed to restrict radio traffic. This wasn't the time for idle chatter. Carlos had no critical reason for needing that information. He should be monitoring and waiting for instructions. Arthur yanked the radio back out of the pouch and held it to his mouth.

"Bridges for Carlos. Clear the channel."

"Carlos for Bridges. Roger that. Sorry, sir."

Arthur shook his head in frustration. Kevin was just complaining about the radio operator earlier. Despite his attempts to only allow solid folks into the corporation that operated the compound, sometimes folks didn't show their true colors until the bullets started flying. Even if the kid wasn't cut out for this, what could Arthur do about it now? Carlos had been a member for several years now. They'd trained alongside him, worked alongside him, and broken bread together. The man revealing himself now was wholly unlike the man Arthur had gotten to know over the years.

Arthur headed out the front door and was starting down the porch when Kevin roared up in a side-by-side. "I caught the transmission and had to see this. If it's true, this is an interesting development. It's also a little suspicious."

"No kidding," Arthur said, sliding into the passenger seat. "I'll believe it when I see it."

Kevin punched the gas and spun the vehicle in a circle, accelerating rapidly toward the observation post that overlooked both the compound entrance and the congressman's camp. Arthur had to grab onto the roll cage to keep from sliding around the cab.

"Watch much of that Baja racing when you were a kid?" Arthur asked.

"How could you tell?"

"Oh, no reason," Arthur replied.

Kevin skidded to a stop near the observation post and both men piled out of the vehicle.

"Whatcha got, Bragg?" Arthur asked.

Bragg was in a bunker of sorts, made of old logs and brush. It looked more like a pile of logging debris than a manmade structure, which was exactly the point. He leaned away from a spotting scope and gestured the men inside. "See for yourself."

Arthur slipped in behind the Leupold spotting scope. He observed in silence, then adjusted the tripod to allow him to pan the scope around the congressman's camp. "I'll be damned. I think you're right."

Arthur moved out of the way and let Kevin take a gander.

"It's not exactly a hasty retreat," Kevin said after a moment, "but it does look like they're pulling up stakes. You know if they're dropping the dining tent they're not sticking around for long. That bunch hates to miss a meal."

"Roger that," Bragg agreed. "It happened quickly. A couple of men double-timed in from their stations and started tearing stuff down. As far as I can tell, the congressman is in the command RV. There are still snipers and patrols active. They haven't pulled everyone in yet. They're not letting down their guard."

"Maybe I should get on the horn and tell them we'll let them go peaceably," Arthur said. "They can stop patrolling. We're not going to attack them if they're trying to leave. That's what we've wanted all along."

"You could try that," Kevin said.

Bragg took over the spotting scope again. "They're rolling up the awning on the command RV."

"Good work, Bragg. Thanks for the heads-up. Keep us updated," Arthur said.

He and Kevin got in the side-by-side and were starting back up the hill when Arthur spotted something in the woods below the road. He smacked Kevin in the arm.

"What?" Kevin asked.

"Stop!"

Kevin laid off the accelerator and the vehicle abruptly slowed on the incline. "What's up?"

Arthur pointed and Kevin saw a man running through the woods toward the observation post. "What the heck?"

"It's Carlos," Arthur grumbled, jumping out of the vehicle. He cupped his hands to his mouth and yelled. "Carlos!"

The man in the woods slowed. He was less than fifty feet from Arthur. He came to a stop but didn't approach.

"What the hell are you doing? Who's on the radio?"

Carlos came closer. "I was just coming to check out what Bragg said. That's good news, right? This whole mess might be over soon."

Arthur was about to lose it. "I don't know what the hell is going on with you. Where's your discipline, man? Get in the back of this vehicle now. I'm returning you to your station. If you leave it unattended again, you're out. We were clear in the training about emergency procedures. I swear to God I'll send you packing."

"What about my money?" Carlos asked.

"What money?" Arthur asked.

"The money I paid to buy into the corporation," Carlos said. "Do I get that back if you throw me out?"

Arthur's face darkened. "Not right now you don't. We're in a state of emergency and aren't issuing refunds at the moment. Especially if you're leaving for failing to hold up your end of the agreement. You're in dangerous territory right now, son. I'd advise you to just shut the hell up."

Grumbling, Carlos climbed into the cargo area of the side-by-side. Arthur shook his head in frustration. Kevin gave him a knowing glance, a reminder that they'd just talked about this very thing earlier today, about Carlos's inability to manage the pressure and responsibility. Kevin restarted the machine and shot up the hill. He enjoyed driving just as fast as he had earlier, knowing it forced Carlos to scramble for handholds. The kid would be a little banged up when he got back to his station and it would serve him right. Maybe he'd think twice before abandoning it again.

At the commo shack, Kevin killed the engine and Carlos hopped out, jogging up the steps before Arthur could start in on him again. That didn't sit well with Kevin.

"Hey, Carlos!" he called.

Carlos stopped at the top step. When Kevin didn't continue, he turned around. Kevin caught his eye.

"Don't leave that radio again without permission. I can't give orders here but I can make threats. Consider that a threat. We need to be able to depend on you. If we can't, you're just *dead* weight that might get someone killed. You understand me?"

Carlos glared at the man for a moment before turning and going inside.

"Good thing we don't have a human resources department," Arthur said. "He'd probably be filing a complaint that you triggered him."

"If I trigger him, it'll be with a real trigger."

Arthur laughed at that for a good long time. He was still chuckling when Kevin drove him back the short distance across the command pod. As he exited the vehicle, he slung his rifle over his shoulder and glanced back toward the commo shack. "You know, maybe I should get on the radio and check in with the congressman. Perhaps he'll tell me what he's up to. If he doesn't, I still get the fun of badgering him a little."

"Worth a try," Kevin said, climbing out of the driver's seat.

The two climbed the wooden steps of the commo shack. About halfway up Kevin froze in his tracks and shot an arm out to halt Arthur. When Arthur looked at his friend questioningly, he saw Kevin's head cocked to the side, listening.

"What is it?" Arthur asked.

Kevin held a hand up to silence him. When Arthur focused, he could hear Carlos speaking inside in a raised voice but he couldn't decipher a word of it through the insulated walls and closed doors. Kevin wasn't having any better luck.

"I can't hear any of it," Kevin said, shaking his head in frustration. "I wonder who he's talking to."

"My handheld is on and I can't hear a damn thing," Arthur replied. "Maybe he's talking to himself. Maybe he's cracking up. The kid could have PTSD. He had combat time, and perhaps the transition from civilian life back to these conditions is too much for him."

"What do you want to do?"

Arthur was contemplating this when the door to the commo shack swung open and Carlos was standing before them, a startled look on his face.

"What the heck?" Carlos asked.

"What's wrong?" Arthur asked. "Why so jumpy?"

"No reason," Carlos replied nervously. "I was just going to grab a quick smoke."

"Who were you talking to in there?" Kevin asked.

"Talking to?"

"Don't play dumb with me. We heard you talking to someone," Kevin said. "It sounded like you were arguing with someone."

"No," Carlos said. "I was talking to myself. I was pissed at myself for screwing up earlier and leaving my station. I was reminding myself to stay focused. Sometimes it helps if I talk things out, even if it's just with myself." His eyes flitted around the entire time he was speaking. He was obviously making the story up as he went.

"I've heard people talking to themselves before," Arthur said. "If you're arguing with yourself, it's a little concerning."

"I'm good," Carlos said. "Really I am." He lit his smoke and took a deep drag. He leaned against the railing and looked off into the woods. He was done with the conversation.

Arthur continued up the steps and stepped around him. "We need to borrow the radio a minute."

"I can help," Carlos offered, trying to slide back into the room.

Kevin shot a hand out against the doorframe and barred Carlos from going inside and shook his head, the message a clear *not happening*.

"You just enjoy your smoke and give us some privacy," Arthur said.

"No prob, whatever you say, boss." Carlos looked at the ground.

Arthur let the sarcasm in Carlos's voice slide and went inside.

Kevin closed the door behind them. "It's sweltering in here," he said, raising a window on the back, away from where Carlos was smoking. "Why aren't these open?"

"Who knows? I don't have any better answer for that than for any of the rest of it." Arthur dropped into the desk chair and confirmed that the radio was on the same frequency they'd been using to reach the congressman, then slipped on the headset. He dropped the volume on the external speakers that Carlos had clearly planned on using to monitor radio traffic from the porch.

"Bridges for Congressman Honaker. Bridges for Congressman Honaker."

The congressman fired back nearly immediately, as if he'd been sitting there waiting on the transmission. *"What is it, Arthur?"* He sounded frustrated, with less theatrics and bluster than on previous transmissions. He sounded like hearing from Arthur was just one more bad part of an already crappy day.

"Looks like you're packing up over there. What's going on?"

"You think we really have a choice?"

"No, you never had a choice," Arthur replied. "I made that clear to you from the beginning and you just weren't interested in listening."

"Well, I never expected you to go after our families," the congressman shot back. *"What kind of man are you?"*

Arthur didn't reply. He was staring at Kevin in surprise. The plan was that Robert would attempt to lead the families in the wrong direction and then disable them somehow so that they couldn't make their way to the compound. Arthur had no intention of letting the congressman in on the plan until the families were already stuck. Hopefully, that would increase his sense of desperation and force him to pull out quickly to save them. There was no way the congressman should already know that they were en route to the families. Even if he'd surmised that they got a vehicle out of the compound during the fiasco with Bob the training dummy, there was no way they should have known where that vehicle was headed.

Unless someone told him.

Arthur dropped the headphones, letting the last question from the congressman go unanswered.

What kind of man was he?

The kind who killed a traitor when he found them.

Kevin was a step ahead of him, yanking the door open, and exiting with pistol drawn. Carlos was nowhere to be seen. "You think it was him?" he asked.

"Has to be," Arthur said. "Why else would he be acting this way?"

"He'll be trying to get to them. He can't afford to let them get away without him. He'd be stuck. His only chance of surviving is with them."

"I want his butt back here," Arthur said. "We need to confirm that he's the spy and that he's the only one."

Arthur went back inside and put the headset on. He switched to the frequency his men used for their own internal communication. "Bridges for all hands. If anyone spots Carlos Munoz I need him detained. Please consider him armed and dangerous. Use utmost caution but try to take him alive."

He slipped the headset off his head and leaned back in the chair. He'd considered a lot of scenarios but this wasn't one that had even crossed his mind. He never expected to find a rat within their walls. He started to get up, then noticed a paperback book on top of one of the radios. It looked familiar. Arthur flipped it over and saw it was one of Robert's books. It was unlikely Carlos was reading the book. He'd never seen the man with a book before or heard him express an interest in reading. Was he researching Robert? If so, why? It was just one more question begging for an answer.

"We need to find him," Arthur repeated to Kevin.

Kevin pulled out his handheld radio. "Kevin for Brandon. Kevin for Brandon."

"Go for Brandon."

"I need you at the commo shack in full load-out ASAP. We're going hunting."

24

"So you were just going to pull out and leave me?" Carlos hissed through clenched teeth, trying to speak into the handheld radio while desperately running for his quarters.

"The idea that you are somehow a central part of this operation is a misperception," the congressman replied. *"Certainly you were an asset important to this phase of the operation but you've become obsolete."*

"Obsolete?" Carlos barked. "What the hell is that supposed to mean?"

"The compound is no longer our objective. Your role in this operation was only relevant toward helping us reach that particular goal. Toting you around now would be like hanging on to a spare oil filter for a car you no longer own. What's the purpose?"

"The purpose...is that...you got me into this and...you have to...get me out!" Carlos was speaking louder now, his labored breathing making it difficult to hold a conversation.

"I have to do no such thing. Was there ever any discussion of me accepting responsibility for you if this mission failed? No, there wasn't. There was only one discussion: help me get into that compound and you're welcome to stay on and reap the benefits with the rest of us. You failed to help us get the compound. In fact, you were a faulty component from the

start. You did nothing to further this operation. If we ever conduct any post-game analysis, we may find that your failure to provide useful intel doomed this mission from the start. So don't bother coming over here. You're not welcome."

"I will...*kill* you!" Carlos snarled.

The congressman chuckled. *"You'll do no such thing. In fact, I doubt you'll even escape that compound. If you're compromised, they're probably coming for you right now. I expect they'll be torturing you for information here pretty soon and you don't even have anything useful you can give up."*

"Please? I'll beg...if I have to. I have...family at home waiting...to hear from me."

"I just checked my list and that's not my problem," the congressman said, the smug humor in his voice driving Carlos into a rage.

"You better hope I never find you," Carlos warned. "If I do, I'll be the last...thing you ever...see."

"Oooh, I'm terrified," the congressman replied, his voice quavering theatrically.

Carlos choked back a cry of rage and hurled the radio with all his might, shattering it against a tree by the side of the trail. He buried his head and dug in, running as fast as he could. He should have been smarter about this. He should have had a bug-out bag hidden in the woods near the commo shack. He should have considered the possibility of being compromised a long time ago, but it never occurred to him. The congressman had been so certain they could take this camp that Carlos just assumed it was a matter of time until it belonged to them.

Now the mission was a total failure. Carlos was a total failure. His family hadn't wanted him to leave them alone in the suburbs of Northern Virginia but Carlos told them he had no choice, that he was leaving them behind to secure their future. Now he had no idea how he was going to get home or what he might find when he got there.

His only hope was to stow away in one of the vehicles belonging to the congressman's party. Perhaps one of the other guys would help hide him. There were other vehicles besides the congressman's. If he could reach those guys and lay his cards on the table, maybe one of them would help him. Soldier to soldier. Father to father. Man to man.

Carlos was running so hard when he reached his bunkhouse that he leapt the two stairs to the porch. He threw out his arms to catch himself when he hit the wall, then slung the screen door open and raced inside. He went straight to his bunk and began throwing on gear. He dropped on his plate carrier, strapped on his belt, and pulled a backpack from beneath his bed.

He slung open his locker, the steel door swinging wide and smacking against the cabin wall. He raked out things he thought he'd need and shoved them in the bag. Snacks, ammo, survival gear, headlamp, and poncho. Basically everything but spare clothes was crammed into the pack before it was fastened and slung over his back. He grabbed up his rifle, slammed in a mag, chambered a round, and headed for the door.

The weight of the gear felt awkward. As a stockholder in the compound, he'd taken weapons and survival training on a regular basis, but he hadn't operated with a heavy pack on his back since leaving the military. Part of it had to be the weight of the ammo but he'd just shoved in all of it. It was too late now. There was no time to repack or jettison gear. To stop now was to die.

He lumbered back out the screen door and down the steps, taking them more carefully now as his body adjusted to the weight of the pack. He paused a moment to take his bearings. The most direct route to the congressman's camp was to return to the command pod and then angle toward the gate but that was out of the question. There were too many people there and a greater concentration of sentries. He would be spotted. They may have even alerted folks to be on the lookout for him. He didn't know.

After bolting from the steps of the commo shack, it might have been smart to monitor the compound's channel rather than ranting at the congressman but he couldn't stop himself. He had to try, he had to make another attempt at swaying the congressman, who had remained immoveable.

Carlos was new to the ways of espionage and was only realizing at this belated stage of the game that he should have established a better contingency plan. Though he'd studied the compound maps numerous times, he'd never paid any attention to the terrain around his bunkhouse and how it related to the perimeter of the property. He had few options and had to get moving. He picked a direction, did some dead reckoning, and started running. It was all he had.

There were no trails going where he wanted to go. He jogged through an ankle-high carpet of forest debris. Rotting leaves, small branches, and low briars tugged at his feet as he fought the terrain. He hadn't taken the time to properly strap on the pack and the heavy burden swayed on his shoulders, threatening to make him lose his balance. He'd gone less than a hundred yards when he tripped in a hole left by a rotting stump. The hole was buried beneath the leaves and he never did see it.

He face-planted hard, the heavy pack grinding him into the forest floor. He recovered quickly and forced himself back to his feet but there was a nagging pain in the side of his knee. He remembered that particular pain from before, from a long run in boot camp. The doc said it was his iliotibial band. He recalled the knife-sharp sting and the fact that it took so long to heal. He would have to tough it out.

The pain was made worse by the uneven terrain. He ran along a hillside, one leg higher, the other lower, and the pack swaying. His feet slid continually, losing purchase on the damp mulch of rotting leaves and moss. He'd gone nearly a mile before he started to breathe easier, thinking he'd gone deep enough in the forest that he was safe. Then he heard the rhythmic plodding of steps tearing through the leaves.

Carlos froze, hoping he might be able to sink down and blend into the terrain. He hadn't located the source of the noise yet. Maybe it was a deer or one of the free-range hogs?

It wasn't. It was that idiot Kevin Cole. He must have placed himself between the congressman's camp and the bunkhouse, then started working his way back. He'd anticipated Carlos's move. Worse yet, he'd already spotted Carlos and was headed straight for him. His only hope was to move quickly and keep trees between him and Kevin's weapon.

Carlos propped his rifle against a tree and dumped his pack. It hurt to do so but it was the only way he even had a chance. It was too damn heavy and awkward. The pack hit the ground and started rolling down the slope away from him. Carlos grabbed his rifle and turned to run. When he did, he found Brandon mere feet away from him, honed in like a ballistic missile.

Carlos cried out in panic, trying to get his rifle up, and get a shot off. There was not enough time, not enough space, between him and the speeding man. Brandon went airborne, striking Carlos with a flying Superman punch that knocked his lights out.

Brandon fell on top of Carlos and was prepared to restrain him but there was no resistance in the limp, unconscious man. Brandon was just climbing off him when Kevin closed on them, his weapon at the ready.

"He's out," Brandon said.

"Good job," Kevin said. "How did you get here so fast? You had a lot of ground to cover."

"I ran," Brandon said, like it was the most obvious thing in the world.

"I ran too. Your running and my running are apparently different," Kevin replied. "You search and secure him, then we'll retrieve his gear."

Brandon went into action, carrying out Kevin's request. While Kevin covered him with his weapon, he hit the mic on his radio and called for a side-by-side to pick them up nearby. Brandon retrieved Carlos's pack and rifle, slinging it over his own back.

"Where to now?" Brandon asked.

"We haul his sorry ass up to the bunkhouse trail, then we take him to the hay barn. Arthur has a few questions for him. Wants to have a private talk."

"You want to carry him or carry this pack?" Brandon asked. "Not sure I can do both."

"I'll take the pack," Kevin replied.

"I figured that's what you would say," Brandon said, unslinging the pack and dropping it to the ground. "But you're going to have to help me get him onto my back. If I ranger roll him on this hill, we may both roll all the way to the bottom."

Kevin helped Brandon shoulder the stocky Carlos, then followed behind while Brandon carefully negotiated the climb to the trail.

"You're a better man than I am, Brandon," Kevin said.

The only response he got was the steady, forced breaths of a man concentrating on managing a heavy load without dropping it.

25

T he national forest where Georgia met North Carolina was beautiful country. It would have been an amazing opportunity to see it by ATV if not for the distraction of all that had happened that day. It made it impossible for Sonyea and Robert to let down their guard at all. They were wary of strangers and of riding into a trap. They were wary that Jeff was lying to them and all of this time spent trying to find this campground was a waste. If this was a trick and he was taking them in the wrong direction, the families would probably slip by them on the road and all of this would have been for nothing.

As if they weren't nervous enough already, things got hairy when they approached the general area of Murphy, North Carolina, where a lake limited their trail options. They had to take more public roads and traverse neighborhoods where they were exposed and vulnerable. Robert was deathly afraid they'd encounter a roadblock or someone would open fire on them. He skirted the actual town, and ran into no problems. He maintained enough speed that he was gone before people really had time to process what was going on.

They re-entered the woods near a casino, following a winding road to the top of a mountain. Robert killed the engine in an empty clearing. The sun was setting, throwing a brilliant orange light on the world around them.

"We stop for the show?" Jeff asked, nodding toward the sunset.

"We're close to that campground you were talking about," Robert said. "As long as you were telling the truth."

"I am telling the truth!"

"It's just down the mountain from us. I want to refuel the vehicle and grab a bite to eat. Once we start this ball rolling, it's hard to say when the next opportunity for a meal might come along."

"How are we going to start the ball rolling?" Sonyea asked.

"Depends on what we find," Robert replied. "No idea, really."

Robert and Sonyea climbed out, leaving Jeff cuffed in the vehicle.

"I need to stretch my legs," he whined.

"You'll have plenty of opportunity for that later," Robert assured him. "We'll probably walk from here."

"It's that close?" Sonyea asked.

Robert nodded. "The sound of this machine will echo a pretty good distance in these valleys. I don't want to put anyone on guard and give them any reason to be expecting something."

They unpacked a plastic tote with food and bottled water. Sonyea set Jeff up with food and a drink, uncuffing one of his hands so he could reach his mouth. Robert checked weapons and topped off magazines. He double-checked the battery levels in flashlights, optics, and night vision, as well as making sure they each had spare batteries.

They ate foil pouches of tuna, crackers, and string cheese. While they ate, Robert separated out some food, splitting it into two stacks.

"Put that in your pack," he told Sonyea.

"We're taking packs?"

"I'm damn sure not leaving my pack behind," he said. "What if this thing goes sideways and we get separated from each other? What if someone finds our gear while we're gone? I don't want to be stuck out here with nothing. It's like I told Grace, the bag always goes with you, otherwise it's useless."

"Don't get preachy on me, Robert Hardwick. I know what I'm doing. I just want to make sure we're on the same page."

Robert paused his hurried movements. "I'm sorry. I just get focused. I forget to be patient."

"Clearly," Sonyea said. "Your wife must be a saint."

"My entire family is pretty patient with me. I'm a lucky man."

They fell silent at the talk of family, both of them feeling incredibly distant from where they wanted to be right then, missing their loved ones terribly. If they could just wrap this up, get the congressman to pull off the compound, maybe they could all go home.

"How's the fuel holding out?" Sonyea asked, hoping to change the subject.

"Probably a good time to fuel up." Robert unstrapped one of the full jerry cans from the improvised cargo rack and set it off to the side of the vehicle. "I'll take care of it once I've got this gear dealt with."

"How far do we have to walk?" Sonyea asked. "It's getting dark fast."

Robert unfolded the map from his pocket, finding their position and squinting to see it. "It's hard to estimate with all the switchbacks, but a mile or two, I think."

"Then we better get on the move."

"We have night vision devices," Robert reminded her.

"Yeah, but Jeff doesn't. It's hard to do a lot of walking in them if you're new to it. We're going to sound like a herd of cattle coming down the mountain, stumbling all over the place. The farther we can get in natural light the better."

"You're right," Robert agreed. "Let's button this up and get on our way."

"Where are we going to leave the Razer?"

Robert glanced around. "How about at the edge of the woods over there? I don't think anyone will come along but you never know."

While they were strapping on gear, Sonyea asked, "What are we going to do with the key?"

Robert hesitated. "You're probably right. We shouldn't leave it in the ignition."

"I agree, but neither of us should carry it."

"Why not?"

Sonyea looked at him matter-of-factly. "We don't know who's coming back and who isn't. What if one of us dies down there? We need to leave the key so the survivor isn't stranded if things go badly."

It was a sobering thought but a very realistic scenario. If he got killed, she shouldn't have to retrieve his body to be able to make her escape. "Let's move it now and we'll hide the key together."

They securely stowed the food and gear totes, then climbed back in. Their own packs and plate carriers went into the back seat beside Sonyea since they couldn't sit in the vehicle fully loaded-out. Distracted by the reminder of their own mortality, the fact that one of them could possibly die out here, neither noticed that Robert forgot to fuel the Razer, leaving one of the spare fuel cans sitting in the tall grass.

When they had the vehicle repositioned, Robert placed the key behind the rear driver side tire. He forced Jeff out of the vehicle to reduce the weight, then he and Sonyea rolled the vehicle back far enough that the key was sitting immediately beneath the tire.

"If I go down, put it in neutral and roll it forward," Robert said. "Just tell my family...you know."

Sonyea nodded. "I know. Same here. Tell Tom I love him."

THE FADING EVENING light had been sufficient in the high clearing but lost most of its effectiveness as they entered the forest. The thick pines and hemlocks kept the forest cool and dark on the sunniest days. Now it shielded out nearly every bit of ambient light. They were on a national forest road, red dirt that was sporadically-maintained. Once every few years, depending on the budget, a dozer and one extremely bored equipment operator would pass through, scraping out the worst of the ruts.

They travelled at the fastest walk they could manage, taking long strides to maximize the distance covered with each step. Occasionally their momentum led to slips as small stones rolled beneath their feet. Jeff stewed and fumed behind them, towed along on a length of chain like a dog refusing to take that last pee before bedtime on a cold night. He cursed and complained, unable to use his hands to maintain his balance.

"Just drag me, will you."

"Quit your bellyaching," Robert said. "This could be over soon."

"Seeing as how I don't know what that means yet, excuse me for not feeling comforted," Jeff shot back. "*Over* could mean *dead*."

"He has a point," Sonyea remarked.

Robert stopped for a moment, using the red bulb of his headlamp to examine the map. He traced a line with his finger. "There's a hiking trail that connects straight to the campground where Jeff says they're staying."

"Where they *are* staying," Jeff corrected.

"Where they *better be* staying," Sonyea clarified.

Jeff scowled and backed away from the circle of red light, mumbling angrily. When he reached the full length of the chain it tugged against Robert, who yanked it back hard.

"Stand still," he grumbled. "I'm trying to read this map."

Jeff complained but did as he was told.

"Those little hiking trails are hard to catch in the dark," Sonyea warned. "We'll have to watch carefully."

"I can use GPS if we have to. It's more precise but the brightness of the display screws up your night sight."

"Last resort," Sonyea said.

Not long after checking the map, they had to go to night vision. They were beginning to stumble in the fading light and had lost the ability to see the road in front of them. Robert's device was attached to a mount on a bump helmet, allowing the optic to fold down into place. Sonyea had what was referred to as a "skull crusher", plastic headgear that ratcheted tight and held the optic in front of one eye. Regardless of which setup you had, it could be awkward and there was an adjustment period during which you could expect to make a few missteps.

Despite the awkwardness of their headgear, the optics always worked like a miracle. They turned their switches and a green glow swelled to life, bringing a clarity to the darkness that was both unnatural and amazing. It also allowed them to find the trail to the campground in short order, clearly marked with a primitive wooden sign that read "Cozy Creek Campground."

Sonyea and Robert, noticing the sign around the same time, turned to the left and started down the trail. Ten feet behind them, at the end of the chain, Jeff was now stumbling along totally blind. He could see nothing and failed to sense the change in direction until the chain caught on the sign, yanking both he and Robert to a stop.

"What the...?" Jeff growled.

"We turned!" Robert hissed. "We found the trail. What are you doing?"

"How am I supposed to know that?" Jeff shot back. "I can't see anything."

Robert realized it was true but there was nothing he could do about it. They didn't have another device and flashlights were out of the question. "You're just going to have to stay closer to us until we get there. I'm going to shorten your leash. We'll try to warn you if we come on hazards."

"Please do," Jeff moaned. "I don't want to be blinded by a branch or sprain my ankle on a root."

"I'm not concerned about your injuries," Robert said.

"Oh, you want to carry me?" Jeff asked. "I'm no use to you if you don't get me down this mountain in one piece so I'd advise you to take good care of me."

Robert sighed loudly, the only sound in the vast darkness. "We're wasting time."

From that point, Robert took the lead, pulling Jeff along. Sonyea stayed behind Jeff, where she could see if he started to go astray. They moved along this way nearly an hour before Robert stopped. He failed to signal this change in pace and Jeff ran into him before Sonyea could stop it.

Robert mumbled and cursed.

"He can't see you," Sonyea reminded him. "You have to say something."

"Shhhhh!" Robert hissed. "Listen."

They fell silent. They heard night insects and the occasional bird. In the distance, a dog barked. Then, beneath it all, singing. Two voices singing in stark harmony over the percussive strumming of an acoustic guitar.

"Sounds like a party," Sonyea whispered.

"Sound like your people?" Robert asked Jeff, watching his reaction in the green glow of his night vision.

"I don't know," Jeff said. "I only know my family. I don't know any of the others. It might be them, it might not."

"What's the plan?" Sonyea asked.

"We get as close as we safely can and find a place to stop. I'll chain Rover here to a tree with you. I'll leave you my AR pistol and I'll take your shotgun. I'll try to get closer and confirm that these people are who we think they are. You provide cover in case anything goes sideways."

"Sounds good," Sonyea said.

"Rover?" Jeff asked. "You're an asshole."

Keeping his voice low, Robert said, "I hope I don't have to remind you of our little talk earlier, Jeff. You compromise us in any way and people down there will get killed. Is that what you want?"

"No."

"So you keep your mouth shut and do what you're told. You don't make any noise. In fact, you don't say a word unless Sonyea asks you a question. Got it?"

"I got it," Jeff said with the tone of someone resigned to an unpleasant but inescapable fate.

"Then let's find our overwatch position. Sound carries so move slowly and use caution."

26

Carlos regained consciousness face down in the grimy cargo bed of a side-by-side ATV. Mulch and rotting bark were embedded in his throbbing face. Some had worked its way into his mouth, creating a muddy, foul-tasting grit that he was too parched to spit out. He tried to move his arms beneath him to push over onto his back but found his arms restrained. The cutting sensation in his wrists told him it was flex-cuffs. He was screwed.

He tried to wriggle around, to use momentum to roll himself into a more comfortable position, but that attempt was quickly shut down by a boot pressing down on the small of his back. He twisted his head around and saw Brandon standing above him, clinging to the roll cage with both hands while the vehicle tore down a gravel path.

"Don't move, traitor," Brandon growled, his face a mask of contempt.

It wasn't like he could move a lot anyway. Defeated, Carlos rested his head back down on the dirty cargo bed and relaxed his muscles. It was all be could do, other than dwell on how much trouble he was in. It was probably a considerable amount. This was serious. His failure to read the situation properly, his failure to escape, would likely have fatal consequences.

The driver slammed on the brakes and momentum compressed Carlos face-first against the front rail of the cargo bed. If he had a hand free he could have arrested some of that momentum but he didn't. His face pressed hard into the plastic ridges of the bed liner. There was a ratcheting sound as the parking brake was set. The foot lifted off his back and Carlos heard Brandon hop to the ground. Levers were released and the short tailgate dropped, allowing Carlos to straighten out his legs.

The relief was short-lived. Two sets of strong hands latched onto his ankles. Before he could say anything, they yanked hard, pulling him backwards. His face scrubbed across the cargo bed and then he was momentarily floating before he dropped to the ground face-first.

He emitted an *oof* sound as he hit, the wind knocked out of him. His face impacted sharp gravel and at least one tooth chipped. He could feel the fragment at the tip of his tongue like an ice chip. All this felt less critical than his inability to breathe. Before he could recover, hands latched onto his ankles again, dragging him face-down into the hay barn. He tried to arch his back to keep his face from abrading against the ground but he couldn't do it. He felt a deep burning on his chin, cheek, and forehead as the skin ground away.

Once he was inside the barn they released his legs, clouds of dust rising when his heavy limbs hit the ground. Someone grabbed him and rolled him over onto his back. His eyes watered and it was hard to open them with dirt caked on his face. When he finally blinked enough to clear them he made out the cloudy visage of Arthur standing astride him, his face a mask of fury. He knelt over Carlos and leaned close, his breath warm against Carlos's injured face.

"I need to know everything," Arthur hissed. "Everything."

Carlos tried to talk but dirt clung to his tongue. He sucked some into his airway and choked, launching into a coughing fit.

"Get me some water!" Arthur demanded.

Kevin stuck a five-gallon bucket under a barn hydrant and raised the handle. A thumb-sized stream of gravity-fed water poured into the bucket.

"That's enough," Arthur said after a moment.

Kevin lifted the bucket and delivered it to Arthur, who dumped it on Carlos's face. When he was done, he flipped the bucket over and took a seat on it.

"I need everything. I need to know how far this goes. I need to know what you've told them. I need to know why you did this, and I need to know if there are any more of you people inside my walls. You've been here long enough to know how serious I am about this. I will get my answers no matter what I have to do to you."

Carlos knew he was telling the truth. This compound was all that Arthur and the other men here had or cared about. They would stop at nothing to keep it safe. He had violated their trust in a way they would find totally unacceptable. He had no doubt that he was going to die. The only question was the manner in which he died. He knew those would be Arthur's next words.

"I can't tolerate what you've done here, Carlos," Arthur said. "It's not just me. Your betrayal is a crime against every man in this compound. You have to pay for that. The only thing you can control is how it happens. There's *easy* dying and *hard* dying. You get to pick."

Carlos didn't immediately respond. He thought about the congressman and his group. By the time Arthur was done interrogating him, those men would be gone. They would have left without him. He was disposable. He was their garbage, left behind on the side of the road. How could anyone remain loyal under those circumstances?

"I'll talk," Carlos croaked.

Arthur nodded at Brandon. "Help me set him up."

The two men sat Carlos up, leaning him back against a nearby round bale. His face was a mess. There were raw abrasions still caked with dirt despite the bucket of water. There were bruises and a pronounced knot on his forehead. His dirty face was streaked by the tears pouring from his irritated eyes. No one made an effort to clean him up. It didn't matter. He probably wouldn't be alive much longer.

"From the beginning," Arthur said. "Start talking."

"Can I rinse my mouth out?" Carlos asked, screwing his face up as if tasting something bitter. "It's hard to talk."

Arthur pulled a bottle of water from his belt, opened it, and held it for Carlos to rinse his mouth out. Carlos swished the water around, spit it out, and repeated the process. When he was done, he sagged back against the bale and sighed with the resolve of a man who had lost everything.

"I'm waiting," Arthur said, retaking his seat on the bucket.

"When I came back from Iraq, I got a job with the Capitol Police. The congressman's buddy Bradshaw was my boss. I ran into the congressman a lot. He always liked to think he was a regular guy, a man of the people, so he would talk to everyone. Didn't matter who you were — cook, doorman, bathroom attendant, cop — he would stop and BS with you. One day he asked what was going on in my life and I told him I was up for a promotion. He took it upon himself to speak to Bradshaw and got me that promotion. He liked to have people in a position where they owed him, but I didn't understand that at the time."

Arthur nodded. He was familiar with that aspect of the congressman's personality. It was the same way the congressman had played up the roots he and Arthur shared as country boys both living in Washington, D.C. Arthur knew now, just as Carlos did, that it was all part of an elaborate manipulation. It was part of a con the congressman used to disarm and relax those around him — those he might need one day.

"Three years ago he reminded me of that favor and said he needed something from me. Of course I was glad to do him any favor, him being a congressman and all. I had no idea what he was going to ask for but he said it was very important. In fact, it was so important that he didn't want to talk about it there in the Capitol. He took me out on his boat with him one day. Just the two of us. While we were out there, he said he needed me to join a survival group. There was a cost to buy-in but he would cover that. I would just have to come down here and do the regular trainings that you required from members. For doing that, I got a thousand bucks a month in cash. I had a wife and a kid so I needed the money. I didn't think I was doing anything wrong at the time. He just said he wanted me to keep an eye on you guys."

Arthur looked at him with surprise. "You have a wife and kid?"

Carlos nodded. "I know. I lied. I told you I didn't have any family. The congressman told me to say that."

"Where are they now?"

"Northern Virginia," Carlos said. "Waiting on me to come for them."

Arthur shrugged. "I hate to tell you this, buddy, but that's probably not happening. While I feel bad for your family you know how this works. You know what you've done and what the consequences are."

Carlos nodded, his irritated face growing even redder as he started to sob. "I filed reports with the congressman every time I got back home from visiting your compound. Sometimes after he got those reports he would call back with questions. Eventually, he told me that if the time ever came that the grid went down, I would be expected to show up here and operate as a mole from the inside. I was supposed to feed them intel that would help them take the compound without losing the supplies."

"So you've been feeding them information the whole time?" Kevin asked, a look of disgust on his face.

Carlos nodded.

Kevin cursed and paced, shaking his head.

"Is your family not en route here with the other families?" Arthur asked. "Are they not part of the entourage making their way here now?"

"No. He told me I could bring them down later, once we took the compound. That was my only motivation for sticking to the promise I made them. It was hard to leave my family with all this scary stuff going on in the world. I told Honaker that but he assured me everything would be okay if I kept my end of the bargain."

"What is the congressman up to now?" Arthur asked. "All this work and he just gives up?"

"They're pulling out and heading somewhere else is all I know.

He wouldn't tell me much. He said I'd failed and they had no need for me anymore."

Arthur winced. "That has to suck after all the effort you've put into this. You put your life and your family's lives at risk for this plan of his."

Carlos nodded but choked up and couldn't speak.

"Did the congressman say anything to you leading up to the decision to leave? Anything that might give you a clue of what's going on in his head?"

"I told him what had really happened to his son, the whole diversion and all that. He asked who was with his son. When I told him, he asked some details about the writer guy, Robert."

"Why?" Kevin asked. "Why would he give a damn about Robert?"

"No idea. He just asked who he was. I read him the guy's bio off the back of one of his books. He seemed real interested in it and made me read it to him a couple of times. It sounded like he was writing it down."

Arthur looked at Kevin, then back at Carlos. "Why would Robert's bio be so interesting to the congressman?"

Carlos shrugged. He didn't have an answer for that.

"Where is that book now?" Kevin asked. "The one with the bio you read to the congressman?"

"It's in the commo shack, I guess. That's the last place I saw it. Sitting on the desk with the radios."

Kevin made a mental note that they would need to find the book and read the bio. Maybe there was a clue in there as to what the congressman was thinking.

"I've got one more question for you, Carlos. It's very important that you're truthful with me," Arthur said. "Does he have anyone else in here? Are there any more men on the inside?"

Carlos did not hesitate. "Not as far as I know."

"As far as you *know*?" Kevin interjected, not satisfied with that answer.

"I have no knowledge of him having anyone else on the inside. I was never told that he did. I thought I was it, though I can't guarantee that he didn't pull the same crap on someone else that he pulled on me. He has a long reach. He could have got to one of your other guys."

Arthur nodded, fully familiar with both the congressman's reach and overreach. Coming to some conclusion, he looked at Kevin and got confirmation in a cold, detached nod. "You've left us no choice here, Carlos. You've betrayed all of us. I need to send a message that this is unacceptable. Perhaps it will also serve as a warning to anyone else that the congressman may have reached out to."

"What...what does that mean?" Carlos asked, desperation in his cracking voice.

"You'll be executed, son," Arthur said, rising from his bucket and stretching.

Carlos started crying. "How? How will you do it?"

"You'll be hung."

"Can I ask a favor?" Carlos choked out.

Kevin frowned. "You've got a lot of damn nerve."

"Let him ask," Arthur said. "But if you're going to beg for your life, there's no point. My decision is final."

Carlos cleared his throat. "I'm not going to beg but can I write a letter to my family?"

"Sure. We can let you do that," Arthur replied. "I'm not sure when the mail will be running again, though."

"I understand that," Carlos said. "But when it does, all I ask is that you stick it in the mail for me. I just don't want my family thinking... that I ran out on them. That I forgot about them."

"Brandon, can you fetch some paper and a pen for this young man? I believe there's a clipboard hanging on the wall near the stalls in the back."

Brandon jogged off and returned shortly with the clipboard and an ink pen. He set them down on the bucket and stepped away while Arthur drew a folding knife from his pocket. He slipped it inside one cuff and tugged the blade through the plastic. Carlos pulled his hands in front of him and extended them while Arthur cut off the second cuff. Arthur pocketed his knife, then leaned to the left to retrieve the clipboard and pen from the upturned bucket.

Arthur's moment of inattention was all Carlos needed. His hand flew out to Arthur's holster. There was no retention system so the handgun yanked free. Carlos leaned back, shoving Arthur with his foot, knocking him off-balance and out of the way. From his back, Carlos raised the gun.

The second he saw Carlos go for Arthur's pistol, Brandon yelled a warning and drew his own pistol. Kevin saw it too, and was already drawing at the same time. He and Brandon fired simultaneously, putting four rounds in Carlos's chest. He slumped back, arched, and then died, dropping the gun to his side. Arthur staggered to his feet, stunned at the turn of events.

"Why the hell did he kick me?" Arthur asked between rapid breaths. "He could have just shot me or taken me as a hostage?"

Kevin looked at Brandon. "Was he aiming at you?"

Brandon shook his head, his gun still aimed, like Kevin's, at the inert body in front of them. "No, I thought he was aiming at you."

"I think he was aiming between us," Kevin said.

Arthur shook his head bitterly. "He wanted us to kill him."

"Do you think he really had a family?" Brandon asked. "He made us kill him before he even wrote them a letter."

Arthur stared at the body. "We'll never know, son. We'll never know."

———————

27

The hiking trail switchbacked down the mountain for another half-mile before Robert found what he thought was the optimal spot to stop. It was close enough to the singing that they could monitor them with a monocular but far enough away that any small noises made by their movements might not be detected by the camp.

"Sit down at the base of this tree," Robert whispered in Jeff's ear, easing him back against the rough bark. "I'm chaining you here with very little slack. If you move, the sound will carry and you know the consequences of that. So sit here, be quiet, and don't move."

Jeff didn't reply but cooperated with Robert. What other choice did he have?

Sonyea removed her pack and laid it on the ground. Her upper body was propped up on the pack, staring through a monocular at the camp. When he was done with Jeff, Robert joined her.

"What do you see?"

"Oddly enough, it just looks like a bunch of folks camping and having a good time. There's some people singing and drinking out of cups. There are kids roasting hot dogs over a fire. They have a propane lantern going. I'm not sure if these people even know the world fell apart or not."

"Maybe they've been insulated from it," Robert said. "If they've had an armed escort this whole time they may not have had to deal with the same crap most travelers have faced."

"Speaking of which, I don't see any sign of armed folks yet. No weapons. Nobody that looks like a cop or soldier. We've also been listening to the radio we took from Jeff and there's been no radio traffic at all. Something seems off."

"I don't have any answers yet," Robert said. "Hopefully I can get close enough to find a few."

"I don't know about this," Sonyea said. "They're a little carefree for me. It's hard to imagine anyone being this happy with all the stuff going on in the world."

"Maybe it's for the kids," Robert said. "They have a way of pushing the troubles of the world aside. They might just be trying to keep things normal for the kids."

"Perhaps. So what now?"

"I'm going to leave my AR pistol with you. It's got more range than the shotgun, even with the red dot. If things get weird, lay down some cover fire so I can get away."

"Got it."

"Don't wait on me if things go bad. Just plan on meeting back at the Razer. If I don't show up within a reasonable amount of time, go on back to the compound without me."

Sonyea didn't respond.

"You heard that, right?" Robert asked.

"Yeah, but I'll make my own call on when it's the right time to do that," Sonyea said. "If I leave you out here it's only because I don't feel like I have a choice."

"Fair enough." Robert got to his feet. "Back in a few."

"Be careful," Sonyea whispered.

In the green glow of her PVS-14, she saw him nod, looking like some agreeable space marine in his helmet, protruding optic, and web gear. Then he eased off down the trail and was gone.

Robert moved slowly and cautiously, fully aware of the fear that could be generated by a stick cracking in the dark. One errant step, one bump in the night, and this peaceful party of campfire crooners might go on alert. The hiking trail ended at a grassy meadow and Robert was glad to get out of the woods. Grass was perfect for concealing his footsteps. There was a gravel road bisecting the meadow but he would avoid that. Crunching gravel carried a good distance.

The campground was extensive and spread out, possessing a lot of the same features that all campgrounds had. There were large directional signs and maps telling campers how to find the various features around the property. There were bear-proof garbage cans to keep spoiled bears from looting the trash, and shower houses for folks not staying in campers. There were also lots and lots of trees, all of which provided excellent cover for a man hoping to make his way through the dark undetected and do a little spying.

Robert slouched against one of the bear-proof cans. He killed his night vision, folded it up out of the way, and withdrew a pair of low-powered binoculars from a pouch on his plate carrier. From the point where he and Sonyea observed this encampment a few minutes ago it was difficult to determine the size of it. From here, with a better view of the folks gathered around the single fire, it wasn't nearly as large as what he expected to find—as it *should* have been.

If it were later at night, he could pass it off to people having gone to bed early. Surely that wasn't the case now, though. It was still fairly early and they were making a lot of noise. The group he was looking for was supposed to contain multiple families. He was expecting dozens of people, a fleet of RVs, and several support vehicles with armed guards. This looked nothing like his expectation.

He scanned the area beyond the campfire and could only make out the dimmest outline of three campers. If there were other folks here, it didn't make sense that they would split up into different areas of the campground. Even if they wanted privacy, wouldn't they stick together for security? This didn't seem right. Maybe Jeff, despite his assurances to the contrary, was lying to them. Robert could imagine that Jeff, clearly understanding the consequences of failure, would take such a chance.

He needed to see more of the campground and confirm there weren't other enclaves containing the rest of the families. Might it be as simple as that? Perhaps they just wanted privacy and were controlling the entrance, limiting access to the campground, so they felt comfortable spreading out. There were too many unknowns for Robert's taste.

He turned away from the fire and stowed the binoculars in the pouch. He would make a pass through the entire campground before concluding that the worst case scenario was true. If they had indeed been misled, Jeff would pay. He might leave him chained to a tree in the woods somewhere to die a slow miserable death, or perhaps put a bullet in his head and end things quickly. He would come up with something.

Robert flipped his night vision back into position and turned the switch. He immediately caught movement in the distance before him. A man. No, more than one. Four men closing on his position with rifles raised. They were still nearly sixty yards away but appeared to have helmets with similar night vision setups. With his one advantage neutralized—the ability to see in the dark—they were on an equal playing field, except he was outnumbered. He was screwed if he didn't come up with a plan fast.

Desperate, Robert pulled the one-thousand lumen Fenix flashlight from his belt, covered the tube of his night vision, and swept the bright light across the approaching men. The singing stopped when his beam cut the night, catching the attention of the campers. Screams erupted as the families gathered around the campfire took in the terrifying sight of the armed men closing in. Those screams told Robert that these armed men were not expected. These were not men familiar to them.

The approaching men cursed as the intensifier tubes of their devices overloaded and blinked out as result of being hit with the bright light. It was only a momentary effect and Robert knew he didn't have long. He fired a hasty shot in the general direction of the men and went right, running as fast as he could. With the night vision, it was like trying to run while looking through binoculars. You couldn't see your feet. He paid the price for his haste, stumbling over a root and banging his knee hard as he tumbled to the ground.

Dirt sprayed him when one round, then another, thumped the ground near him. He scrambled on all fours, taking cover behind a tree. He fired off two rounds of buckshot at the men and heard a scream. With the short shotgun, he didn't have to be as accurate as they did. The buckshot cut a swath of destruction and death.

Knowing they had a man hit would cause his attackers to pause, even if only for a moment. Robert took that opportunity to sweep the men with his flashlight again, praying that their devices weren't so new that they would be immune to bursts of light. Crossing his fingers that he'd bought himself another second of safety, he bolted again, trying to put the cinderblock shower house between him and the shooters. He knew exactly when their devices reset because the bullets started flying again. Shots pinged around him, ricocheting off the cinderblock structure as he cut behind it.

His instinctive reaction was to angle away into the darkness, keeping the cinderblock building between him and his pursuers. As soon as he passed the building he saw that this plan wasn't going to work. There were more men coming, flashlight beams cutting the night as they charged toward the gunfire. Robert cut his night vision off and backed into the blind spot between the two groups of men, a pocket of darkness alongside the shower house. His back hit the edge of something and he turned to find he was at the fish cleaning station. He couldn't see it but the smell and feel of the place gave it away.

An idea hit him and he scooted up onto the counter top. It was rickety from being exposed to the weather all the time and got to his feet, standing on it. He was a big man, probably pushing two hundred and fifty pounds with all his gear and full plates. When the counter quit swaying beneath him, Robert pushed off onto the flat roof of the shower house. The surface was covered in rolled asphalt roofing and scratched his fingertips as he clawed his way up. It reminded him of why an old instructor said to always wear gloves in combat situations.

Once on the roof, he pulled off his pack and rolled toward the center of the structure, flattening himself out. He felt trapped and his breathing was rushed. He fought to contain his panic. He'd never been pinned down like this and it was frustrating. He had no idea what would happen if they caught him. Would they kill him? Interrogate him? Torture him?

He shook those thoughts from his head. He couldn't think like that. Submitting to that loop of fear was a downward spiral that didn't end anywhere good. The shootout with the RV folks was over and there were men shouting orders now. Vehicles were rolling in with more men, more loud voices, and more lights.

As he replayed things in his head, wishing he'd been able to make it to the woods, he began to wonder where his cover fire was? There was no guarantee it would have helped him escape but he'd still expected it. Sonya had been watching when he left. She must have seen what was happening.

Unless she'd been captured.

Robert cautiously flipped to his stomach and tried to raise his head enough to see what was going on. Men were combing the woods alongside the grassy field. They had to be looking for him. Other men were tending to the wounded from the camp. Wailing prisoners were corralled off to one side under the eye of a man with a light and a gun. Stark vehicle lights now illuminated the scene. If they'd shown up earlier, there would have been no way they could have missed him.

But they hadn't. It was almost as if they were waiting on him. Like he'd walked into a trap. There was only one person he knew of who could have told them anything. Robert wanted to get his hands on him. He'd kill him this time.

Men cleared the interior of the shower house, checking the showers and toilet stalls but no one thought to check the roof. Robert lay still, ready to bolt and run if someone got smart, but no one did. They didn't show any signs of clearing out anytime soon. Robert laid back down and tried to relax, to wait it out. It would be over soon. The men would pull out and he could clear out of here.

Where would he go next? What did this mean for his big plan of forcing the congressman to pull off the compound and come to rescue the families? Robert had no idea.

28

Chained to a tree in the darkness, Jeff could see very little of what was taking place around him. To his front, Sonyea was silhouetted against the distant firelight, laying with a monocular braced against her pack, intently focused on what was taking place around the fire. Robert's AR pistol lay close at hand, ready for her to lay down cover fire if he needed it. Jeff was determined she wouldn't have that opportunity.

His hands were cuffed in front of him. A padlock secured his cuffs to a length of chain. A second padlock secured the chain around the tree at Jeff's back. He had just enough slack to sit with his back against the tree and his hands in his lap. It was probably enough to do what he needed to do but he wouldn't know until he got started. Without producing a rattle that might give him away, he shifted his body enough to reach the watch pocket on his jeans.

He crept his thumb and finger toward the pocket, easing them in, and fishing for the warm steel of the handcuff key Carlos had given him. He retracted it most of the way, then paused to make sure he had a good grip on it. Millimeter by millimeter he extracted the key. When it was safely in his hand, he stopped and let his breathing return to normal. He watched Sonyea and saw nothing to indicate that she was suspicious.

He cupped the key in his hand and slipped it into the first keyhole, hoping his hand might soften the mechanical noise. He turned the key slowly, circling it until he felt resistance. A little further and there was a faint click. He used his other hand to gently extract the free half of the cuff from the lock. When his hand was free, he allowed the empty cuff to settle between his thighs where it wouldn't rattle against the chain.

Then, much as he did the first, he released the second cuff. He eased the key back into his pocket, just in case he might need it again, and allowed his breathing to return to normal. He found he'd been holding it the entire time and was lightheaded from the oxygen deprivation. As he allowed his breathing to relax, he groped around in the dark for a weapon he might be able to use. There probably wasn't a lot of weight difference between him and the woman. She may also have some type of martial arts training. His only combat experience was in video games.

His hand closed around a damp, rotting stick about as big around as a shovel handle. He wondered how long it was, or if it was connected to another bigger branch, but he didn't dare pull on it yet. If his actions rustled leaves or made any noise at all she'd be on him. She might shoot or stab him. After all, she had real weapons and all he had was a rotting stick of questionable integrity. Even a rock would have made him feel more comfortable, but there were none at hand.

"Oh God," Sonyea said in a low voice.

"What is it?" Jeff asked, afraid not to answer.

BOOM!

It was a gun blast from somewhere down below them. Sonyea hastily shoved the monocular in a pocket and was transitioning to Robert's AR pistol when Jeff saw his opportunity. With Sonyea distracted, this was the time to take action. It might be his only chance.

He sprang forward, the branch in his hand. It was shorter than he'd hoped but it was what he had. Sonyea was less than five feet away and Jeff closed most of that distance before she detected anything. She swung her head back to look at him, ready to issue a sharp rebuke, and could tell something was wrong. She tried to swing the AR around but couldn't do it in time.

Jeff had the stick raised high over his head and brought it down on her with all his might. It caught her high, between the shoulder and neck. While the heavy plate carrier absorbed some of the blow, the stick landed squarely on her collarbone. She was paralyzed for a second, trying to balance the pain with the need to both breathe and defend herself.

Before she could do either, he dropped onto her. Her back plate dissipated the blow but the pressure on her still-healing wounds was painful. Too stunned to fight back, she lay there on her stomach, trying to pull herself together, trying to mount a defense. Then he started beating her with the stick. Kneeling so high on her body left only her head as a target. Jeff hit her with several blows until the stick crumbled into pulp. When he was done, she was no longer moving.

Jeff rolled to the side, winded and shaking from the adrenaline dump. Then he realized he had to bind Sonyea before she recovered and began yelling or fighting back. He went to retrieve the handcuffs but found that the padlocks prevented him from getting them loose from the chain. He didn't have a key for those padlocks.

"Damnit!" he hissed, slinging the chain away.

He went back to Sonyea and searched her for anything he might use to secure her. He found a flashlight in a pouch on her plate carrier and clicked it on. Using the light, he rifled through her pockets, coming up with two heavy zip ties. He tightened one around a wrist, slipped the other through it, then tightened it around the other wrist.

With her hands secured, he rolled her over and searched her for weapons, removing several knives and a handgun, as well as Robert's AR pistol. He tucked the handgun in his belt and shoved the knives in his pocket. The AR pistol had a stretchy sling and he draped that over his neck. He got the radio out of her pocket and turned it on. It was alive with chatter now. The radio silence had been part of the plan, part of the trap, and it seemed to have worked perfectly from what he could tell. Now, with the trap sprung, everyone was talking.

Jeff raised the radio to his mouth and hit the transmit button. His part of the plan, as determined in those scant minutes he had on the radio before Robert caught him, had been accomplished. He'd led them into a trap. Now he needed to radio the security detail that he'd subdued the woman and would be bringing her down.

He released the talk button on the radio and sat back down. Was he doing the right thing? Not for Sonyea and Robert, of course. He didn't care if he was doing the right thing by them or not, but he did wonder if he was doing the right thing for himself. His dad had never respected him. He'd given him a crappy job with no responsibility because he thought that was all he was capable of. The security detail for the families had reflected that same attitude in talking to him on the radio when he was supposed to be taking a bathroom break. They gave him orders and talked to him like an idiot. Why did every male in his life treat him that way?

Thinking back over the past few days, he'd liked the idea of being a hero. He'd liked the idea of being the one that made a personal sacrifice that would save all of the families. If he handed Sonyea over, he wouldn't be the hero. According to the rushed plan, the security detail with the families would use Sonyea and Robert as leverage to force Arthur to leave the compound. But he wouldn't be the hero. It would be the security detail who'd get all the credit. He'd be in the background, again, with the women and children. He'd be a nobody again with all the perks that brought, which was exactly *no* perks at all.

Why should he give that to them? Why should he give them the glory, the prestige, *he* was supposed to get? Why should he allow them to turn Sonyea and Robert over to his dad when he could just as easily do that himself? His dad would be so impressed. He could imagine him looking at his command team with a look of pride.

"Look what my boy did," he'd say. "Brought them back here all by himself."

He wasn't even sure he would be capable of that, taking both of them back. Robert seemed a little unstable, volatile. Could he take the woman, Sonyea, back by himself? Could he safely deliver her to his dad? That should bring Arthur to his knees. If they threatened to kill this woman right on his doorstep, could Arthur allow that to happen? Probably not.

Jeff stood and looked down at Sonyea. She was starting to stir, stretching and moaning. He drew back his arm and threw the radio deep into the darkness, just like Robert had started to do when he found Jeff using it. He had to cut that tie. If the security team tried to reach him, he might feel compelled to answer them. He might be unable to maintain his determination to do this on his own. He didn't want to crumble and give in.

He wanted to be the hero.

He bent down and grabbed Sonyea by the straps of her plate carrier, dragging her to her feet. She swayed and staggered.

"You'll be fine," he said. "It was just a rotten stick. It couldn't have done any real damage."

He clicked the little flashlight back on. Sonyea's night vision was cockeyed, the headgear knocked askew. Jeff pulled it from her head, the abrupt gesture pulling out hair and causing Sonyea to cry out.

"Toughen up, buttercup. I don't see any blood."

Sonyea squinted against the light in her face, trying to focus. "I'll show you buttercup when I get out of this. I promise you that. I'll make you pray for death."

Jeff shrugged, adjusting the headgear on Sonyea's night vision and slipping it on his own head. He turned the flashlight off and switched on the night vision. "Wow! This stuff is amazing. Now I know what all the fuss is about."

"Don't break—"

"Don't talk," Jeff ordered, latching onto Sonyea and tugging her back up the trail.

Her disorientation from the blows to her head was compounded by moving in the dark and being unable to see where she was going.

She started to say something again and Jeff clouted her on the head with his fist. When she cried out, he apologized.

"Sorry, I forgot about the beating with the stick," he said. "If you'll shut up, I won't have to hit you again."

He got ahead of her, holding a bound wrist and practically dragging her.

"I can't do this," she said. "I can't see."

"I couldn't see either, and no one cared," he spat back.

Angered by the recollection of his treatment, he surged ahead, yanking Sonyea along. She tripped and went down.

"On your feet!" he growled, pulling her up and shoving her ahead of him. In the green glow of the night vision he could see her swaying, trying to get her bearings. He gave her no time to formulate a plan, grabbing her again and charging up the hill.

"Where are we going?"

"None of your business."

Sonyea gulped in a deep breath and he knew what she was going to do. She was going to scream. He charged her, wrapping an arm around her, and flattening his other hand over her mouth.

"Shhhhh!" he hissed. "I will tape your mouth shut if you keep this up."

Without warning, she kneed him in the groin so hard he was certain she'd popped his testicles like crushing a fistful of grapes. He cried out but didn't release her. She struggled, trying to get away. When he felt her slipping from his fingers he knew he had to do something. He grabbed the rifle and swung it like a bat.

The act was as much a product of his rage as anything else. She'd hurt him and he wanted her to pay for it. Had it not been for the fact he needed her, he could see himself killing her just to appease the injured parts of himself, continuing to beat her with the rifle until life left her entirely.

The blow staggered Sonyea and she started to go down. He let her fall, taking the moment to cradle his delicate injury. He paced back and forth, his body hunched in pain. "You ever do anything like that again and I'll kill you," he said, teeth clenched.

Sonyea was crying now, her zip-tied hands pressed hard against her injured head. When he felt able to walk again, Jeff yanked Sonyea to her feet and the pair limped up the trail. Jeff wasn't used to hiking and the walk wore on him. Added to that, his testicles were now swollen to the size of eggs and hurt with each step.

He was carrying Sonyea's pack, gun, and dragging her along, all of which required a monumental effort. Yet he was afraid to stop, worried that any rest break might allow someone to catch up with him. He didn't know if it would be the security force guarding his family or Robert, if he'd been able to escape capture. Either way, he wanted no part of either scenario. He was in charge now. This was his show.

Jeff was relieved when the grade eased and they broke from the forest. The night was muggy and he was soaked in sweat, his clothes sticking to him, his jeans heavy. When they entered the meadow the sky opened above him and Jeff was enthralled, temporarily forgetting all the pains that assaulted him. With the night vision he could see the most minute stars, including those that didn't register on the human eye. It stopped him in his tracks.

"You can let me go," she said.

Her voice broke the spell and Jeff yanked her arm. "Shut up."

Unable to locate the Razer with only the night vision, Jeff got out a flashlight and started waving it around. "Whoa! What happened?"

"It blanks out the night vision. You need to turn it off. There's a dial."

She started to point it out to him but he yanked away from her. He flipped it up out of the way instead and played the light around until he caught sign of the Razer.

"Let's go." He tugged her to it, tossing her pack in the back seat. "Get in."

"Just leave me here," she said. "I'll only slow you down."

Jeff snatched the door open and put a hand on Sonyea's head, shoving her in like a perp on a cop show. "You slow me down and you'll wish you hadn't."

She cried out at his rough treatment, her head already bruised and banged up. She lay across the seat, whimpering, while Jeff dug the handcuff key out of his pocket. The second set of cuffs was still fastened to the roll bar. Jeff had the light in his mouth, fumbling with the key, when Sonyea lashed out with her boot, catching him in the groin a second time.

The blow stunned him and he doubled over, dropping the key. The pain was explosive. Even worse than the last time, which he hadn't imagined was possible. He didn't think he'd be able to stay conscious, didn't think he'd ever draw another breath.

Sonyea threw her leg over his body and locked her feet together, trapping him between her legs. Had she been higher, she might have been able to get them around his neck and try to choke him but she wasn't in position for that. They were around his waist with one arm trapped in her grip and one raised above his head.

She tried for some kind of arm lock but he was too sweaty and she couldn't get a grip. He was injured but not disabled, still fighting her. As he regained strength, overcoming her groin strike, she became more desperate and began raining down blows with her two bound hands. She dropped an elbow on his head, then another. Jeff yelled at her, trying to fight his way loose.

Sonyea was yelling now too, cursing Jeff and grunting with exertion. She wanted him dead now. For all she'd wanted Robert to go easy on the kid, she hated him now and did not want to be his prisoner. It wasn't working. She was not winning this fight. Her blows were not having the desired effect. He was on his knees and the pull of gravity was allowing him to slip from her grasp. Her legs, already tired from the long walk up the mountain, were quivering. She couldn't keep him in the hold much longer.

The flashlight lay on the floor shining upward. In the glare of the stark beam she could see the reflection of the slowly spinning open handcuff. Jeff had managed to open the one side not attached to the roll cage before she kicked him. She grabbed his extended arm, trying with all her might to pull that wrist toward the cuff. More intent on working his body loose from the grip of her legs, he paid little attention to what she was doing with his wrist. He couldn't see the cuff, couldn't see her intention. She could do this.

As she pulled harder, her actions got his attention. He twisted his head and in the beam of the light she saw his forehead beaded with sweat and oil, his angry eyes, and his twisted mouth. He yelled and twisted his other arm free of her failing legs. Then he had her by the wrist and before she even knew what was going on, he'd fastened the cuff around her bound wrist.

She sagged into the seat, spent and exhausted. She'd given it all she had and it wasn't good enough. He had her now. She was not escaping. She began to cry.

Jeff pushed himself up from her, his grimace underlit and terrifying. His chest heaved as he caught his breath. He seemed not to know what to do, then he lashed out with a hard fist and Sonyea's world went black.

29

R obert lay on the dark roof for over an hour, trying to piece together what was happening around him. He heard snatches of conversation, the squawk of radio traffic, and men shouting. Occasionally, he would raise his head like an alligator rising from the murky water of a swamp to try to catch a glimpse of what was taking place. He wondered about Sonyea and Jeff. Why hadn't she laid down cover fire? Had something happened to her? Had she been captured by the men who sprang this trap on them? He wondered if it even *was* a trap. Perhaps he'd just wandered into someone else's mess.

The only way he was going to get any answers was to get off the roof. When the activity around him began to slow, Robert slid his gear to the edge. He bobbed up again, checking his surroundings. There were men at the campers, but most of the vehicles were turned around and leaving. He assumed they'd only come for him and were forced to leave empty-handed. That small detail gave him a degree of satisfaction.

He slipped from the roof, carefully planting his feet on the unstable surface of the fish-cleaning table. He lifted his gear and gently set it down onto the table. With each movement, the table swayed through a greater range of motion, the joints weakening, a sure sign that collapse was imminent. Afraid to hesitate any longer lest the table crack loudly under him, he jumped to the ground. When he hit, he paused to make sure the sound hadn't brought unwanted attention. When he was certain no one had heard him, he pulled his pack on and took up the shotgun.

His first order of business was to bolt for the woods and get some concealment from the men still moving around. Once shielded in the woods, he crept toward the campers and attempted to eavesdrop on their conversations. With one of the men talking loudly, as if volume alone lent credibility and authority to his words, Robert was able to hear parts of his conversation with the terrified campers.

It sounded like a typical story pasted together when someone official screwed something up. The security detail couldn't exactly come out and admit they'd used the campers for bait, but Robert was fairly certain that's what they'd done. He'd had plenty of time to think that out while he was laying on the roof. They were spinning a tale about dangerous fugitives active in the area who were part of a terrorist operation, perhaps even part of the same group who'd attacked the United States and caused this whole disaster. They'd simply been caught in the crossfire as the security detail, who described themselves to the campers with the generic term "government agents," intercepted the dangerous man.

The security detail was painting a horrible picture of him to cover for the danger they'd put the family in. Robert was practically painted as being evil incarnate, so he realized he'd better hope he didn't cross paths with any of those campers tonight. If he did, it was likely they'd shoot him on sight. After what they'd been through, he would be public enemy number one.

When things began to wrap up, Robert retreated from the campers. He wasn't entirely sure what to do. He wanted to run back up the trail and see if Sonyea and Jeff were where he left them but couldn't imagine they were. If that was the case, Sonyea would have let him know somehow. She certainly would have given him the cover fire he needed. If he hadn't been in such a hurry they could have set up a radio protocol before they split up and kept in touch. He hadn't bothered, thinking there was no point. Little details like that were what separated the amateurs from the professionals. What separated those who survived from those did not. Right now, he was among that group not likely to survive, and it was not a comforting feeling.

He needed to find where the families and the security detail had set up their camp. If they'd captured Sonyea, that was probably where they'd taken her. Jeff was likely there now, gloating over turning the tables on them. Wherever these armed men were going when they left, wherever the other trucks had already gone, was where he needed to be. While the men from the security detail finished with the unfortunate campers, Robert made a beeline for the spot where they'd parked their trucks.

He thought of jumping into the back of one of them. That was how folks always did it in the movies. They jumped in the back and there just happened to be a stray tarp in there to pull over them. Everything worked out perfectly. His luck was different. Things never worked out that well. What if some of this group had ridden out here in the back of one of these trucks? What if he hid in there only to be discovered by boarding passengers? He'd probably end up dead and would be no good to anyone—not Sonyea, not the folks back at the compound, and not his family in Damascus.

In the distance, the remaining security detail was backing away from the folks at the campers, guns still on them. They had traded in their night vision for glaring headlamps now, the need for stealth unnecessary now that the trap was sprung. They played bright flashlights around the hillside as they walked, hoping for some last break that would reveal their quarry. Fortunately for Robert, luck was not on their side tonight.

Six men returned to the two trucks. There was a brief argument over who was riding in the back and no one gave in. All insisted on riding up front despite the bulky tactical gear. No one gave in and the grumbling men piled into the trucks with lots of cursing and complaining. Robert was trying to plan how to most effectively hitch a ride aboard the nearest truck bed when he noticed that the distant truck had a mesh cargo carrier extending from the trailer hitch. He'd seen those before on the highway, often on an SUV, usually holding a big cooler that the driver didn't want to haul inside. This one only held a red metal jerry can strapped down with bungee cords.

When the trucks started he had little time to think about this. All efforts to get his courage up were failing. He needed the mental equivalent of giving a rebel yell and smashing a beer can on his head, something to spur him into action. The truck nearest him pulled forward and headed down the road. The second, nosed up against a fence, had to back away before turning. When it backed in his direction, he acted without thinking because that was only slowing him down. Thinking was telling him that this was a stupid idea and it was going to get him killed, not what he needed to hear right now.

He waited for the back-up lights to go off, afraid they'd illuminate him in the rearview mirror. When the backup lights, then the brake lights, went off, he sprang into motion, lunging from behind the laurel bush and running in a crouch directly toward the bed of the truck. A thousand dissenting voices erupted in his head, telling him this was a stupid thing to do, the wrong thing to do, and he was only going to get himself killed. He blocked all of them, running on pure adrenaline.

The truck was easing forward under idle, the driver not yet applying the gas pedal. Robert hooked his right hand over the tailgate and put one foot on the mesh platform. It was nearly as wide as the tailgate and gave him plenty of room to climb on. It was hard to perform this action and not rock the truck but that was exactly what he tried to do. Had it been a light-duty truck, the suspension might have responded to the additional load of his weight. This was a heavy-duty truck, a three-quarter or one-ton pickup, and the stiff suspension didn't react to his presence at all.

Robert greatly overestimated his physical prowess most days. He'd visualized performing this task with much more fluidity and grace than he was actually able to bring to the task. Once he had both feet on the platform, he was immediately forced to latch his other hand onto the tailgate because maintaining his balance was proving more of a challenge than expected. It was like doing a squat on top of a big exercise ball and expecting a single hand touching the wall was going to stop you from rolling off onto your head. Add to it the fact that his knees were protesting since he had to remain in a squatting position to keep low. His plate carrier was compressing his torso and restricting his breathing. They weren't even out of this section of the campground before Robert was struggling. It occurred to him that the most comfortable position for riding on this platform might be to approach it as if he were in fact riding on the tailgate of a pickup. The only question was how to change to that position now that the vehicle was in motion. The gravel road was fairly smooth and the truck wasn't going fast. Perhaps he could pull it off.

He was unable to arrive at an efficient way to make the transition. He decided to release his left hand from the tailgate and try to turn in a circle until he was facing rearward. Then, hopefully, he could hold on to the platform with both hands and sit down, letting his legs dangle off the back. He didn't have a lot of time to plan for it. His legs were going numb from his current stance and he could imagine them going out at any time with no warning.

Desperate, he released his left hand and began turning while in his squat position. It was going well until the driver hit the brake for a speedbump. Robert lost his balance. His free hand waved in the air, trying to find something to hold onto. All he could reach was the platform at his feet and he latched onto the edge of the steel frame. That threw his balance too far to the rear. He was beyond his tipping point and, worst of all, he could feel his strong hand slipping from the tailgate.

There wasn't even time to look for a new handhold. One moment his brain registered the slipping hand, the next it registered the impact with the gravel. While the face plant from a moving vehicle stunned him, he was aware that he needed to make sure the truck didn't stop. Maybe the driver had seen his graceful dismount? He rolled to a position where he could see the departing truck but the driver made no sign of stopping, continuing on down the road without a care in the world.

Feeling safer now, Robert slumped flat on his back. What the hell was he doing? He should be home with his family, looking after them, not here in the middle of nowhere doing whatever the heck it was he was doing now. He wrote this stuff, he didn't live it.

He took a deep breath and sat up. The truck had been going slow and he hadn't fallen far. He was also wearing thick clothes and a plate carrier that absorbed part of the blow. For the second time that night, he wished he'd been wearing tactical gloves. His palms, knuckles, and elbows stung with road rash. The pants he was wearing had built-in pockets for knee pads but he'd left them out because they felt awkward when he walked. He touched his knees, finding holes in the pants there and burning, raw flesh beneath it. Once he started walking and sweating again, those skinned knees would feel a lot more awkward than the kneepads ever felt. While his injuries were not life threatening, the nagging pain would do nothing to improve his already dark state of mind.

He got up and took a look around. There was no sign of people anywhere so he risked using a flashlight to check the ground around him to make sure he hadn't lost anything. He checked the Kel-Tec KSG. No clogs in the barrel, no deformations, and no broken parts. That was good. He checked his Glock 19 and found it to be in good shape, mostly protected by the holster.

He clicked the light off and shoved it back in the pouch. He went to drop his night vision back into place and found that the bracket didn't want to swing back into position. He applied more pressure and it snapped off into his hand. He got his light back out and examined the mount. It was broken and the PVS14 was dinged up a little.

He had an immediate *old world* reaction, thinking about how much money the thing cost. His second, more appropriate, reaction was along the lines of how much he needed the device, how he couldn't get the device repaired, and how it better work because he darn sure couldn't just go out and buy another. He turned the flashlight off, turned the knob on the night vision, and it glowed to life.

"Thank God for small blessings," he mumbled.

He might not be able to wear it but he could at least look through it. After a moment's consideration Robert decided to dig out the weapon mount for the night vision and mount it to the shotgun. It wasn't ideal but it was a far sight better than having to shoot with one hand while holding the device in front of his eye with the other.

When he had everything situated, he took a drink of water, not sure when he'd taken his last sip. He dug a protein bar out of a pouch and ate that while he started off in the direction the trucks had gone. His knees and elbows hurt. He had a bit of a headache, which he attributed to dehydration. He was tired and he missed his family. Worst of all, he was certain this night was a long way from being over.

ROBERT WALKED for about twenty minutes before he spotted a bonfire and several illuminated houses in the distance. He crouched by the road and examined the scene through binoculars. The families and their security detail had apparently opted to stay around the cluster of ranger cabins rather than at a campsite. The reason why was obvious. The houses were all lit, not by lanterns, but by electricity. At this remote location, with government money paying for it, these ranger houses probably had propane-powered generators.

Some of these houses would have been full-time residences for campground staff. If these families were occupying those houses now it made Robert wonder what had happened to the rangers and their families. They'd probably been evicted by the security detail, just as the congressman hoped to do with Arthur and his compound. Robert hoped they'd been ordered out rather than killed and their bodies dragged out.

He went back to night vision and scanned the area surrounding the house. He was paranoid about sentries but saw no one outside of the group sitting around a campfire in the yard. There were no women and children. Robert checked his watch and saw that it was late enough they'd probably retired for the night. The men were winding down by the fire in the way men typically did, with a strong drink. There were several bottles passing around. He saw a few cans of beer, too, and wondered if the families had brought them or if they'd been confiscated from the residents of the cabins. Robert thought he might kill for one of those cold beers right now, or at least lay down some serious threats.

He looked for an avenue of approach. The men were armed, but their long guns were propped against trees, vehicles, and odd pieces of outdoor furniture. There were still sidearms in holsters for sure, but he hoped to not give anyone a reason to draw on him. He was so vastly outnumbered that stealth was the name of the game. He was one guy and there were over a dozen of them. Some looked older, with gear and skills. Some were younger and a little green, perhaps younger men from the families or sons of the men among the security detail.

Robert eased in closer, going structure to structure and trying to stay on the mowed lawn, which was more likely to be free of noisy sticks and leaves. The closer he got, the clearer the voices became. He flattened himself against one of the dark campers and eased along its length. When he peered between it and the truck towing it, he had a decent view of the campfire.

"I'd say he's dead," one of the men said. He was overweight, dressed in expensive tactical clothing, and had a beer cooling on his thigh.

"Not so loud," another man, wearing a camo t-shirt and jeans, warned. "You want his mom to hear you?"

"The facts is the facts," the overweight man said.

"Then I'll let your fat ass explain to the congressman that *facts is facts*. I'm sure he'll be completely understanding," camo guy replied.

"All I'm saying is Jeff said he'd take the woman as soon as the guy left. The guy must have left because we saw him in the field near the campers. Either the woman killed Jeff when he tried to overpower her or the guy we saw in the field caught up with Jeff and killed him. Either way, I don't think we're going to find him. And speaking of the congressman, I'm starting to worry about him a little too. We were supposed to hear from him today. You ever think he might be dead also? Are we just supposed to wait here and hope he calls? I'm starting to wonder if we might need another plan."

Camo t-shirt guy shook his head, exasperated. He apparently didn't have much luck with getting the overweight guy to shut up.

"I didn't hear any shots," said another man, older, with a gray buzz cut. "Just the rounds we exchanged. I don't think anyone shot Jeff."

"They could have used a silencer. These guys are pros," camo guy replied. "Jeff said so when we talked to him. He said the whole camp was nothing but mercenaries. They'd be too smart to do something that would give their location away. They could have even knifed the poor kid."

Robert couldn't help but smile at that. Mercenary? Pro? He was anything but. While there were certain areas where he felt proficient, this was not one of them. He felt like he was in over his head, always a single move from utter disaster.

Beyond that entertaining tidbit, what was the rest of their conversation about? Jeff had played a role in setting this up? He obviously had more time on the radio and said more than Robert thought. The whole bit about being a better person, about helping save lives by leading Robert and Sonyea to the families, was a lie. He was leading them into a trap the whole time. A trap devised by him and the security detail.

Clearly, though, these people had been expecting to find Jeff and hadn't. Part of the plan seemed to be that he was going to overpower Sonyea and deliver her to this camp while the family's security detail took down Robert. What had happened? Jeff hadn't shown up here, yet Sonyea hadn't laid down cover fire either. Was she laying up there mortally wounded? Had she and Jeff wounded each other? There was only one way he was going to find out. He was going to have to get back up the trail, then get the hell out of here.

He slipped back into the night, hoping the popping of the fire and the animated conversation covered any accidental sounds he made. He ran on night vision, retracing his steps, walking as quickly as he could while still watching his foot placement. At the end of the driveway, he got on the main campground road and headed back the way he came.

Shortly after getting on the road, Robert saw a sign he'd missed on the way in. Probably because he'd spotted lights and was focused in on them. The sign was brown with white lettering, like all the other signs in the place. It said *Maintenance: Authorized Personnel Only.*

The sign stopped Robert in his tracks. He wasn't even sure why at first. Something about the sign was tickling the back of his brain but he didn't get it. Whatever thought was being stirred never floated to the forefront. He started to continue on past it but stopped again. He'd always told his daughter Grace that intuition was a valid sense and should not be ignored. Whether intuition was *real* or *valid* in scientific circles was completely irrelevant. When you were in a situation where your senses were keeping you alive—where you were on alert—it should not be ignored.

Was he going to take his own advice?

He turned around and headed down the gravel lane. Leaves formed a tunnel that glowed pale white in the perpetual green of his night vision. He moved slowly, not knowing what was at the end of the road. He emerged in a wide gravel lot with several structures. There was a tractor in an open shed, a grading blade attached to the rear. A D3 dozer was parked beside it, looking much cleaner than any bulldozer Robert had ever seen before.

A cinderblock garage with a corrugated steel roof and doors of the same material sat off to one end of the lot. In front of the garage, firewood was in various stages of processing, from round logs to split lengths waiting to be stacked. A gas-powered log splitter stood in the middle of a circle of firewood.

One door of the garage hung asunder. Robert walked closer and saw the hasp had been pried loose with some type of tool. The frame was splintered and barbs of thin steel curled around empty bolt holes. He couldn't leave without looking inside, though he already suspected what had been taken. Inside, he lost the ambient light provided by stars and had to turn on the infrared illuminator on his night vision.

The illuminator glared off reflective surfaces, giving the room a surreal atmosphere reminiscent of a science fiction or horror movie. He expected at any moment to see a scientist in a hazmat suit or a toothy, clawed alien. All he found was a rather sparse shed housing a side-by-side ATV with a large bed for collecting firewood. A rack mounted behind the cab held a chainsaw, saw gas, and an ax.

Robert lowered his shotgun-mounted night vision and drew a flashlight from his plate carrier. He closed his fingers around the beam to limit its reach while he played it around the room. There was a hook with old chainsaw chains, a bench with a disassembled chainsaw, and a specialized grinder for sharpening old chains. A yellow steel cabinet against the wall caught Robert's attention. The labelling indicated it was for storage of flammable liquids. In other words, *gas*.

He rushed to the cabinet, threw open the doors and found it empty. Someone had been there and cleaned it out. It was probably why they'd broken in there to begin with. Maybe if they'd found cans of gas they didn't bother siphoning the side-by-side. Robert slipped into the driver's seat and looked for the key. He felt a wave of frustration when he found the ignition empty. Then he remembered he was dealing with a government-operated campground.

Robert played his light around the wall until he found a steel key box. Sure enough, there was one mounted on the cinderblock wall. He tried it and found that it was unlocked. When he opened it, there were several hinged racks holding tiny hooks, many filled with labelled keys. It took him a matter of seconds to find the correct one.

It slipped smoothly into the ignition, bringing a smile to Robert's face. The digital gauge showed around half a tank of fuel. That was fine. All he needed was enough to get up the trail and see what had taken place with Sonyea. If she was injured, he could use the vehicle to deliver her back up the trail to their own Razer. He turned the key off and thought for a moment. He needed to make sure he covered all the angles.

The sound of the engine would likely bring the security detail running. He could use the lights on the side-by-side but he would be easily trackable, even when he raced up the trail, and into the woods.

They might not have vehicles that could pursue him off-road but they could still shoot at him. With lights glaring he would present a clear target even at a distance. He needed to remove the night vision from his shotgun and use that to navigate. They could still hear him but hopefully the lack of headlights would delay them long enough that he could put some distance between them.

Holding the night vision was awkward and would limit him to driving with one hand. There might be complications with that if the side-by-side didn't have power steering. He definitely didn't need to use the headlights though, because he might have to pause for a moment at the spot where he'd left Sonyea and Jeff. Sitting there with headlights would be like sending a beacon out to anyone pursuing him.

He decided he'd thought this out long enough. Like boarding the moving truck earlier, there was a time you just had to quit thinking and act. This was the time. He released his night vision device from the rail on the shotgun and stowed it in the vehicle. He hooked the weapon sling over the gear shift since he wouldn't be able to hold it during his evac.

The last detail was swinging the double doors open so he could drive the vehicle out. He needed both hands so he worked by feel. He gently lifted the door that had been damaged in the break-in. It had a broken top hinge and was resting on the ground. He moved it as gently as possible but the wood framing shifted with his movement, producing a squeaking sound when it rubbed against the corrugated steel. It sounded deafeningly loud to him but he didn't imagine it would actually carry that far through the dense foliage around the maintenance shed.

The second door swung freely. At the end of its arc, it emitted a groan from the rusty hinges that brought a wave of nausea to Robert. He might as well be announcing his plans over a loudspeaker. When he had that door resting solidly at the full swing of its hinges he returned to the side-by-side. He relaxed and cleared his head. Once he started the vehicle, it was on. There was no backing down.

He turned the night vision on, started the engine, then raised the night vision to his eye. His heart nearly stopped when he found two men standing directly in front of him, just outside the door. It was so unexpected, so startling, that he was paralyzed for a moment and simply stared at them. When one of them shouted at Robert, ordering him out of the vehicle, it broke the spell, and it registered that they were wearing night vision too. That was how they'd managed to get so close without him picking up their lights.

Robert slammed a palm against the rocker switches that controlled the headlights. An array of lighting burst to life on the front of the vehicle, overwhelming their optics, forcing both men to turn away and shield their eyes. Robert dropped a hand to his holster and drew his Glock. He leaned to the left, cleared the windshield, and double-tapped the leftmost man. The first round hit armor. The second caught him in the neck and a dark geyser erupted.

The man to the right was panicking. He'd flipped his night vision out of the way and tried to line up a shot but was still blinded by the headlights. Robert stomped the gas pedal. The side-by-side spun, then caught traction and slewed forward. The driver scrambled for cover but was in the center of a gravel lot with nowhere to go. Robert aimed for him, forcing the man to dive to the side at the last minute.

Robert groped for his night vision, grateful he'd taken the time to hook the lanyard to the webbing of his plate carrier. He got it in front of his eye, then used his steering hand to kill all the lighting. Another man charged into the road from the side, trying to get a look at what was going on, clearly not expecting to find himself in the path of a charging vehicle that he couldn't see. Robert's immediate reaction was to go for his gun but he had no free hand with which to shoot.

Instead he used the only weapon he had, slewing toward the man. Even though he couldn't see the vehicle bearing down on him, the man honed in on the growing whine and knew he was the target. He dropped his gun and leaped backward into the brush, his arms clawing and flailing as he tried to escape the onrushing vehicle.

Robert cut it close but avoided hitting the man, even though he could have. Despite the vehicles being tough, crashing into something the weight of a man might bend the bumper back into the tire or cause the plexiglass windshield to come crashing in on him. Better to avoid it if he could. Behind him, there were lights, flashlights searching for him, their beams cutting swaths through the dense trees to either side of him.

There was a burst of gunfire. He didn't hear anything hit the vehicle but he began weaving back and forth, making himself a hard target just in case. It sounded like a single rifle dumping a mag one round at a time. Robert dropped an eye to the speedometer and saw he was only going twenty-five miles per hour, already hitting the maximum capability of this particular vehicle. It definitely wasn't a Razer, made for work instead of fun. It should be fast enough as long as he was only trying to escape men on foot. If they got a truck on the road, he was screwed.

As if that very thought manifested it, the trees around him were suddenly illuminated in the high beams of very bright headlights. Robert cursed. He would have slammed the steering wheel with his fist but he didn't have a free one. To his horror, the headlights were getting closer. Caught squarely in the lights, there was no use wasting time with the night vision any longer. He let it drop on the retention lanyard and slammed the dash again, turning on the banks of lighting.

There was a gunshot. This one was different, probably a shotgun. He had a hard time telling anything over the scream of his engine. The glow of headlights was growing in the cab of the side-by-side. It was now bright enough that he could have read a book, or even a set of annoyingly small Chinese instructions. The truck tailing him was getting too close for comfort. If they opened fire on him, he was a sitting duck.

Robert grabbed up his shotgun, shoved the safety button, and aimed it out the door behind him. He was unable to aim but he pulled the trigger and the weapon boomed. He couldn't tell if the shot produced any effect or not. He pulled the weapon back into the cab and pumped the action, then fired again. The erratic jerk of the headlights illuminating the cab told him that this shot did something.

He racked the slide again, preparing for yet another shot, then realized he was at the turn to the campground. He whipped the wheel to the left, the vehicle going into a four wheel slide. He stayed on the gas, trying to keep that momentum pushing forward. The motion forced him to grab the wheel with both hands and he lost hold of the shotgun. It clattered to the floor but stayed inside the cab. Fortunately, the trigger did not snag on anything and fire inside the cab.

His pursuers were still on him, his maneuver having given them advance warning of the upcoming turn. He chanced a look behind him and saw them straightening out. They were on the gas now, accelerating hard after him and closing fast. If the shotgun was handy, he'd have sent more rounds in their direction, though he didn't dare risk fishing around for it. Piling into a tree wouldn't have helped anything.

He knew his next turn had to be coming up soon but everything looked different at this speed. He hit the open grassy field and knew it was here somewhere. He whipped the wheel again and the vehicle slewed, losing traction momentarily in the grass. His pursuers were still behind him, gaining, and, in his mind, lining up what would be a fatal shot.

Then he saw the yellow pipe gate that closed off the trail from the campground. Knowing that pipe gates were not always enough of a deterrent, the Forest Service had dumped several backhoe loads of dirt in front of the gate. That was okay. Robert was certain he could get around it.

At the gate, he eased around the dirt pile and steered the narrow vehicle onto the hiking trail. The Razer might not have been able to make this narrow gauntlet but the smaller trail-width vehicle had no problem. It occurred to Robert that the ability to get onto this trail probably wasn't simply good fortune. The rangers might take this very vehicle this way to collect firewood from downed trees.

By cutting his speed to negotiate getting around the gate, Robert allowed his pursuers to close on him. He waited for them to get out and open fire on him. He was on the trail and accelerating uphill. He didn't feel like he was moving quickly enough. No speed would have been fast enough. The men on his tail were not thinking clearly, though. They'd become so laser-focused on catching him that they didn't take the opportunity to stop and shoot at him. Instead they were intent on running him down like a wild boar. They'd lost clarity and were making bad decisions.

They swerved their Toyota pickup around the dirt pile and the pipe gate. On a muddy slope, they punched the gas and all four wheels spun. The driver was determined to make the Toyota fit through an opening that was at least two feet narrower than his vehicle. It was physically impossible. When he couldn't make it, he tried to reverse and look for another opening, but the vehicle slid broadside into a tree, pinning the passenger door closed. They were stuck.

Robert couldn't see all this but noticed that the headlights were no longer gaining on him. Realizing they'd either stopped or been stopped, he waited for the shots to come. It was then he realized that he was still running with headlights, presenting a nice bright target for anyone wanting to shoot at him. Panicked, he shoved the rocker switches to the off position, groped for his lanyard, and got back on his night vision.

Ahead he saw the first switchback. He spun around, not even slowing, knowing that this would not only put physical distance between him and his pursuers, but dirt too. There would be a physical barrier they could not shoot through.

With this brief joy came a wave of recognition. He dropped off the gas pedal and coasted to a stop, hit the parking brake, and got out. He lowered his night vision and came back up with a flashlight. He tapped the switch on the base of the light and stared at the road behind him.

This was the switchback where he'd left Sonyea and Jeff. This was where he'd expected to find something.

There was no one there.

30

R obert fought against panic. Far below him, he could hear the crunching of metal as the Toyota's driver fought to free the vehicle from where it was pinned. As long as they were engaged in trying to get the vehicle loose from the tree they weren't firing at him. He scrambled around, shining his light over the ground, looking for any clue of what had happened here. Was this even the right spot?

He saw a flattened area, the leaf litter scraped to the side. When he stood there it seemed vaguely familiar. Was it the spot where he'd watched the campers before turning his post over to Sonyea? He could see nothing on the ground. No signs of struggle, no lost gear.

No blood.

He threw the beam of the light up against the tree where he thought he'd left Jeff. The chain was still there. This was definitely the right spot. He hurried over and found the cuffs hanging open, still padlocked to the chain. Robert shook his head. Had someone let the kid loose? Sonyea didn't have a key. Maybe Jeff had one? It would have been easy to miss the tiny key in the tentative search he'd made of Jeff's person. He'd been looking for a gun or a knife. Something big and dangerous, yet a tiny key was perhaps the most dangerous thing of all.

Before he left, he had one more place to check. He returned to the spot he'd left Sonyea and shined his light down over the hill. He was looking for a body, confirming that Jeff had not killed Sonyea and disposed of her. He breathed a small sigh of relief when he didn't find a body. If Jeff had killed her, he hadn't left her here.

There was a shot in the distance and bark exploded from a tree near Robert's head. He hadn't even noticed that the sounds from the stuck Toyota had quit. The men must be on foot now. Running in his direction. Coming for him. He clicked off the light and ran for the side-by-side.

The engine kicked to life when he turned the key. He opted for driving by night vision, not sure how vulnerable the next switchback would leave him. Even at its slow utility vehicle speed, the machine was way faster than anyone could walk or run up this incline. With each minute, Robert felt a degree of relief, a little less worried that he would take a bullet to the back.

In short order, he was topping out on the forest road and entering the vast mountain meadow cleared at the top. The light of billions of stars trickled down on him, brightly illuminating the field for anyone wearing night vision. He paused to orient himself, trying to remember where he'd left the much faster Razer. Determining that it was along the tree line to his left, Robert punched the gas and the vehicle spun in that direction.

When he failed to spot anything with his night vision, he turned it off and used the vehicle's bright headlights. He figured he'd put enough distance between him and his pursuers that he had a little window of time. His anxiety was still through the roof. Then he found what he was looking for–a wide area of beaten down grass told him he'd found the right spot, but the Razer was gone.

Robert slammed the dash with his fist. "Dammit!"

After stewing for a moment, he killed the engine and got out, walking around in a circle. Four points of compressed grass and a path of beaten down weeds confirmed he was in the exact spot where he'd parked the machine earlier. Playing his flashlight around, looking for any clues, he caught the reflection of shiny plastic in the grass.

It was a pair of zip ties. They were used but had been cut loose with a sharp knife. Robert got a sick feeling in his stomach. There was no reason Sonyea would have done this. It had to be Jeff. But it made no sense. Why would he have not turned her over to the families? There were plenty of armed men ready to take her. If Jeff had done that, it was unlikely Robert could do anything to get her back on his own. So what was Jeff doing? What was going on in his head?

He raised the flashlight, examining the path the machine had taken. It was going back in the direction from which they'd come. Robert considered this. Was that just coincidence? Maybe Jeff had some other location he was going. Perhaps he was just tired of it all and was going to head back home and put all of this behind him.

That was how Robert felt at the moment too. Tired of it all and ready to go home. All this time and effort he'd spent, yet he was no closer to being home than he was a week ago. If anything, his situation was more dire, depressing, and perilous than ever before. He didn't have the folks at the compound to help him. He didn't even have Sonyea to cover his back and complain to. He had nobody but himself. He had never felt so alone and desperate in his entire life.

The feeling made him want to get in the side-by-side and head home. He could call it quits on everybody and everything outside of his immediate family. Just the thought of his family conjured a desperate longing for them. He wasn't the most affectionate man in the world sometimes. Maybe he wasn't the best father either, but he loved them with a fierce loyalty that made him nearly crazy to be home.

What was waiting on him back at the compound? More of the same? There was nothing attractive in that. Could he even make it back to the compound? If he chose the other option, running away, could he even make it home from here or would he die in a ditch somewhere, shot by some roadside bandit?

"Get out of your head, Robert," he chastised himself. Speaking out loud carried more authority. "Get out of your *head!*" It was a command this time and it spurred him into action. He had to move. Activity would pull him back to where he needed to be. He had to do something.

He returned to his vehicle and turned the ignition on, staring at the gauges. There was fuel, though not nearly enough. He didn't want to think about it. He couldn't allow himself to get bogged down like that again. He couldn't worry about fuel, family, or his fate. He needed to find Sonyea. That was the immediate task. If he continued to stand here pondering life, the security detail would eventually catch up with him. He'd be killed or captured and it would truly be over then.

He retook the driver's seat and started the engine. The headlights burst to life. He decided to use them for a while to make driving easier. He'd put some distance between him and his pursuers so he wasn't too concerned about them now. The headlights would allow him to make better time. He hit the gas and crept forward, paying attention to follow the trail beat into the grass by the fleeing Razer.

As he picked up speed, he immediately felt better. It was much better to be doing something than to stand there feeling sorry for himself. For him, activity freed the mind and relaxed the soul.

From out of nowhere, a thought entered his mind and he stomped on the brakes, sliding to a stop in the grass. He yanked on the parking brake and jumped from the cab, pulling his flashlight from his pocket.

He ran back in the direction he'd come from, veering off into the weeds. He scanned frantically, searching with his light, and then he saw it. He couldn't help but smile. It was the jerry can of fuel he'd removed from the Razer sitting there like a gift. He'd intended to add it to the tank before they parked the Razer but he'd forgotten about it when he moved the machine, failing to notice the can in the waist high grass. He picked it up, ecstatic to find it still full. He could have hugged it.

He returned to the side-by-side and killed the engine. He carefully poured all five gallons into the vehicle's fuel tank, then secured the can in the cargo bed. When he got back in and restarted the engine, the LED gauge rose to full.

Sometimes in the darkest, most despairing moments, life tosses you a bone. Providence graces you with a nod and a smile. Perhaps this blessing was intended to string him along until the next dark moment, but he'd gladly take it. He floored the gas and shot forward in the dark. While Jeff had a good head start and a faster vehicle, Robert was determined. This was his mission and he would not stop until he found them.

31

Sonyea stirred to consciousness and pitched forward to vomit between her feet. When she looked up, the sky was gray around them. It was perhaps early morning but she wasn't sure. Her head was splitting and she felt dehydrated. With all the blows she'd taken to her head, she'd have never been allowed to remain unconscious if she was in the care of people who cared about her. As it was, she was in the care of a pathetic younger man who apparently had something to prove to the world.

When she was done, she spat out the window, wanting to wipe her mouth but unable to raise a hand high enough. She cocked her head to the side, scraping her mouth against the coarse webbing of her body armor. It didn't help. She threw a harsh glance at her captor. She had trouble focusing, but he appeared torn between sympathy and joining her in throwing up.

"I've got to get out of here," he said, gagging as a wave of nausea hit him.

"I'm sorry," she said, sounding anything but. "Maybe you shouldn't have hit me so hard. I've probably got a concussion. You'll be lucky if I survive the trip."

Sonyea felt weak. Putting those words together into a sentence required a tremendous amount of effort. She may well have a concussion but she didn't feel like she was in imminent danger. She'd probably live, or at least survive this to die in some other equally disturbing fashion.

Jeff shoved open the plastic driver's side door. He wasn't two steps from the vehicle when he began spewing acidic vomit onto his shoes. He stood hunched over, hands on his knees, strings of gelatinous fluid hanging all the way to the ground.

Sonyea felt no sympathy. In fact, if she could get to the ESEE Izula hanging around her neck, and if she could get free from her handcuffs, she'd plant that knife in his back with very little hesitation. Right now, though, the knife was buried beneath her body armor where it did her no good at all. That was a lesson for the future.

"Excuse me for not holding your hair back, asshole," she growled. "Guess you have a weak stomach."

He didn't respond, which told her he was still in distress. That was good. She couldn't strike back but making him miserable gave her a small degree of satisfaction. She could tell he was emotionally unstable and that his stomach wasn't the only weak thing about him. If she could create an opportunity for herself, she could probably take him. She needed to be more certain of her chances next time. She didn't need another beating. If she lashed out again, he needed to die.

"I guess it's a good thing I didn't actually throw up on you," she said. "That would be gross. Imagine it. Vomit in your lap, on your neck, your hair. Maybe even on your face if it spewed out hard enough."

The sound of more vomit hitting the ground made her smile. Mission accomplished, but smiling hurt in a dozen different ways.

"Shut up!" he barked. "I'll hurt you!"

"You've already hurt me, Jeffrey. You hurt me any worse and you might kill me. What will you have then? Nothing. Of course, there are ways to beat people and make them hurt without endangering them. You obviously don't know how to do that. You're an amateur here.

You're in over your head. You need to just let me go and cut your losses."

She decided to use *Jeffrey*, wondering if the name might harken back to his childhood. Maybe it was a name that authority figures used with him, or what he was called when he was in trouble. It couldn't hurt.

Talking so much had made her lip split open again. It had to be from one of his punches. There was a burning sensation. The handcuffs rattled as she went to touch her lip but her movement was restrained before she made it. She touched her dry tongue against it instead.

"Stop talking or I'll hurt you worse. Right now, I don't care if you make it or not. All I want is to stop throwing up."

She decided it might be wise to stop there and not push him any further in that direction. She changed tactics. "Why don't you get us both some water? I think that would settle our stomachs. I'm pretty sure I have some Pepto Bismol in my pack. It would help."

Jeff straightened up, wiping his mouth with the back of his hand. He wandered in a circle, sucking in deep breaths, trying to steady himself. "This is your people's fault. If you'd just left like we asked you to, this would all be over now. I wouldn't be out here in the middle of nowhere puking my guts out in the weeds like a sick dog."

"That's ridiculous, Jeffrey. That's like criminals getting mad when a robbery goes wrong. I think it shows low intelligence on the part of the criminal, this idea that people should just roll over and agree to be victimized. Besides, I don't even live at the compound. I'm merely a visitor caught in the crossfire. I'm the one who should be mad. So if you want to look at it that way, we're both victims here."

Jeff made a grunt of some sort, then went to the back of the vehicle and started digging around in the supplies she and Robert brought with them. He appeared at her door with a bottle of water and extended it to her.

She turned her wrists to him, nodding at the cuffs. "Could you?"

He shook his head. "I'm not letting you go. I don't trust you."

"Just take one off and fasten it to the grab handle," she said. "If you just free one it would help. I could drink on my own."

Jeff pulled her pistol from his waistband. He put it against her head, then fished the handcuff key from his pocket. "Anything funny and I pull the trigger. Got it?"

She looked him in the eye, not expecting this level of callousness. It made him seem less amateurish, but perhaps it was only fear talking. "I won't try anything."

He extended the key, placed it in the keyhole, and turned it. She tugged on her wrist and the cuff fell free. While he placed the key back in his pocket, she locked the free cuff around the passenger grab handle and ratcheted it closed.

She gestured to her work. "Good enough?"

Jeff grabbed the cuff and tugged. When he was satisfied, he picked up the water bottle and handed it over. She sucked it down greedily, gasping for air when she pulled it away. Jeff rinsed his mouth out, then drank sparingly, not yet sure he could keep it down.

"You should let me go, Jeffrey. Just leave my pack with me. You don't have to take me anywhere. Just let me go."

Jeff took another sip of his water. "Can't do it."

"If you don't, something bad is going to happen, Jeffrey. You'll get back to the compound and Arthur's people will kill you. Or Robert will catch up with us first and he'll kill you."

Jeff huffed. "Robert is not hurting anyone. My guess is that idiot is chained up to a tree right now, just like he left me."

"You seem awful sure of yourself."

Jeff shook his head like she just wasn't getting it, like she'd missed something so obvious. "It was a trap. I set it up before you guys caught me with the radio. He walked right into it. They were waiting on him."

"You what?"

"I. Set. Him. Up."

Sonyea shook her head. She was having trouble believing it. Jeff didn't seem capable of hatching some complicated plan. "What about me? If you had this big plan in place, then why are we out here in the middle of nowhere?"

"That wasn't part of the plan," Jeff admitted. "I improvised."

"Oh, you improvised," Sonyea said, nodding, eyes wide. "Got it."

Jeff appeared insulted. "I have my own plan and you don't need to know everything."

"That's fine. I feel much more comfortable knowing you have a plan."

Jeff's lips tightened. "We need to get back on the road." He marched around the back of the vehicle and climbed back into his seat.

"What about this?" Sonyea asked, gesturing to the puddle of vomit on the floor.

Jeff scowled and looked around the vehicle. He saw Sonyea's sweatshirt in the back. He leaned over and shoved the sweatshirt in the vomit, swabbing it around the floor, and then leaving it laying there. "That'll soak it up."

"Appreciate that."

He smiled at her. "No problem." He turned the key and started the engine.

"Jeff..."

He sagged as if losing patience. "What!"

"If you let me out now, I won't have to kill you."

Jeff spun on her and she could see in his eyes that he was considering hitting her again. He turned his burning gaze back to the windshield and accelerated into the gloomy morning.

THE DRIVE WAS MISERABLE. Besides how bad she felt physically, Jeff was a poor navigator, having paid little attention to the route they took when he was in the passenger seat. He tried reading the map but was from a generation raised on GPS and voice navigation so he was unfamiliar with the basics of route-finding with a map. Every time he consulted the map he became frustrated and ended up crumpling it up with a few choice words.

At first, Sonyea struggled with whether she should help him or not. If she didn't, or if she intentionally misdirected him, they could find themselves caught in some roadblock where she'd be unable to defend herself or even escape. She decided her best chance, if Jeff was intent on returning to his father at the compound, was to guide him there to the best of her ability and hope that Arthur's men could rescue her.

However, familiarity with the route gave no assurances that they would get there in one piece. Jeff was turning out to be a pretty poor driver. Sonyea had no idea how he managed in a car but he'd clearly had no off-highway experience before. He evidently did not understand the basics of crossing a tree branch, negotiating steep grades, or getting the vehicle unstuck. Several times she found herself having to talk him through maneuvers. He became very volatile at those moments, having apparent issues with people telling him how to do things.

It was like the navigation issue; she didn't like doing it, but what choice did she have? If he got them stuck out here, they were both in trouble.

They crossed a public road near the Georgia state line, easing off the pavement and through a creek before continuing their trek through the woods. Heavily travelled this close to a public access point, the forest road was wide and well-maintained. Jeff was comfortable here and accelerated to faster than his customary speed. Sonyea watched him out of the corner of her eye, noting that he actually seemed to be enjoying himself. Then the vehicle lurched, the engine sputtered, and the Razer decelerated rapidly.

Jeff raised his hands from the steering wheel, staring at the gauges as if trying to determine what magical force propelling the vehicle had failed them.

Sonyea shook her head. "Fuel, Jeffrey. We're out of gas."

"Gas?" he echoed, panicked. "We have gas, right?"

"There are cans in the rack, Jeffrey. You'll have to check them."

He set the brake, climbed out of the vehicle, and unfastened the first jerry can from the rack. When he picked it up, he froze. He replaced it, then went to the next can. He shook it in the rack. The can clattered within the confines of its steel rack, also empty. "They're *empty!*"

"We must have used it all on the way out," Sonyea said. "I don't remember how many times we filled up."

Jeff roared in frustration and slung the gas can as far as he could. It went about twenty feet before impacting a tree with a hollow thud.

Sonyea shook her head. "You might as well go get that. If we find gas we won't have anything to put it in without cans."

"How are we supposed to get there now?"

"You're in charge of this mission, Jeffrey. You said you have a plan. The details are up to you."

Jeff's face turned red and he stabbed an angry finger at Sonyea. "I've about had it with that *Jeffrey* crap! You need to lay off!"

"Let me see the map."

"Get it yourself."

"I can't reach it, Jeffrey...Jeff."

Jeff stalked to the vehicle, snatched up the crumpled map, and threw it at Sonyea. It bounced off the side of her face. It wasn't painful but irritating. She cut him a look before attempting to unfold the map.

"This would be easier with two hands," she said.

"This would all be easier with you dead!" Jeff spat back. "Keep that in mind."

She awkwardly unfolded the map with her teeth and free hand. When she had it mostly unfolded, she smoothed it across her lap and began searching it, using her finger as a cursor. "This is the road we just crossed."

Sonyea laid her finger along the scale of the map, then estimated the distance from the compound. "I bet we're only about seventeen or eighteen miles from the compound. In these mountains it might take a day and a half to get there on foot. If we put in a good effort the rest of the day, we could be there by lunch tomorrow."

Jeff came to the door and stared in at Sonyea. She pointed at the map.

"See?"

Jeff grabbed the map and balled it up in his fist. When it fell to the ground, he kicked it, sending it sailing into the weeds. "I don't want to walk! We've got a perfectly good vehicle there. It just needs gas."

Sonyea sighed loudly. "It's not going to be that easy to find gas. We're in a remote area. If you find vehicles on the road we just crossed, it's likely they've already had the gas siphoned from them. You could spend all afternoon looking for gas or we could spend the afternoon making progress toward the compound. You could see your dad tomorrow."

The mention of his dad stopped him in his tracks. Was that really what he wanted? He'd come all this way to prove something to his dad, but that wasn't the same as being excited to see him. The knot in his gut reminded him of how much anxiety was provoked by being around his father. If anything excited him, it was the idea of proving his dad wrong, showing him that he was capable and not the worthless loser his dad always portrayed him to be. He was starting to wish there was some way to prove that to his father without actually having to confront him, but he couldn't think of one. He was too far in now. There was no backing up.

"What's it going to be?" Sonyea asked. "Either way, we need to do something. Sitting here isn't an option."

Jeff took both hands and pressed on his forehead, then ran them through his hair. "What do we need to walk to the compound?"

"Well, I need to be unhooked from this vehicle, first of all. I'll need my pack. You'll need something for carrying gear. We'll need food and water. That's probably it."

Jeff looked at the sky. "It looks like it's going to rain. What do we do then?"

Sonyea looked at him like he was an idiot. "We get wet."

"Do you have a raincoat?"

She nodded.

"Do you have two?"

"Hell no. Why would I carry two?"

"Do we stop if it rains?"

"No. There's a tarp in there. You can make a poncho out of it if you need to."

"Show me what to get."

"You'll have to let me out of here," Sonyea said. "I can't do it from here."

"I'll have to cuff your hands back together."

Sonyea hesitated. When he'd freed one of her hands to drink the water earlier, it had given her the ability to draw her neck knife. With her hands cuffed, she couldn't get a hand behind her body armor to reach it. With him behind the vehicle, rifling through the gear like a scavenging bear, she pulled the short ESEE knife from its sheath and tucked it in the tourniquet pouch on her belt. He'd already searched her earlier and she felt he was unlikely to do it again. With the knife there, she could reach it if she had to. She hoped it didn't come to that. She didn't like this kid, but murdering him was something she hoped to avoid.

"That's fine," she said. "Cuff me if you need to but let me get my pack on first. You'll need me to carry some of the load."

"You might carry all the load," Jeff said.

She couldn't tell if he was joking or not. Maybe the sympathy she afforded him was misplaced. She had no response; anything she was likely to say would be cutting, demeaning, and unlikely to earn her anything but another beating, so she kept her mouth shut.

Jeff appeared at her door again, her handgun in his hand and pointed directly at her face. Sonyea noticed with some concern that his finger was curled dangerously around the trigger. While she briefly considered whether she should take the time to correct him on his gun handling, perhaps she'd already pushed her luck too far.

"I won't try anything," she said.

"Please don't. I would have to shoot you and I don't really want to." He fished out the handcuff key, uncuffed her from the grab bar, and stepped away from the door. "Get out, slip your pack on, and cuff yourself back up."

She opened the Razer's doors and slid out, the dangling loose cuff rattling and banging on different surfaces. She stretched, doing it carefully to avoid alarming him with any sudden movements, then reached into the back seat. Jeff was standing about eight feet from her, obviously terrified she was going to manifest a weapon from thin air and gun him down. She came out with her backpack, a three-day pack in coyote brown. She slipped the straps over her hands and shouldered it.

"Anything in there I need to be worried about?" Jeff asked.

"Not sure why it matters. It's not like I can reach any of it."

"You could find a way."

"Check if you want to."

"Lock the cuffs back."

She did as she was told and Jeff relaxed a little, returning the gun to his waistband.

"There's a duffel bag in there you can throw over your shoulder," she pointed out. "The food is stored in that white five-gallon bucket. Make sure we each have a couple of bottles of water and food."

Jeff dumped the contents of the bag onto the ground and added the suggested items. He unzipped her pack and made room by tossing her spare clothing out, leaving just enough room for four bottles of water and a couple of MREs.

She stared down at her clean clothes discarded on the ground. "Did you have to do that?"

He shrugged. "You'll never be back here again. What does it matter? Would you have preferred I fold them?"

She didn't answer.

He nudged her pack. "Get moving."

She made note of the fact that he didn't take the map. Either he remembered the way from here or thought that she did. She didn't ask. If he was relying on her, maybe she could use that to her advantage. She would see if the opportunity presented itself.

32

R obert drove his side-by-side leaning forward in the seat, as if his posture might urge the machine forward. He looked like a kid trying to get a little more downhill speed out of his Big Wheel. The Razer had been a lot faster, designed for speed, handling, and recreational off-roading. Robert's current ride only operated at about one-third the speed and was something a farmer might ride around to check the fences or spray weeds. The only positive of this machine was that the smaller engine increased fuel economy. It was a feature that would get Robert further on a tank of gas but would be totally pointless if he couldn't catch up with Jeff.

He navigated by handheld GPS, taking shortcuts when he could find them. When he saw a turn that might save him a few minutes, he took it, hoping those few minutes extra might help him gain ground. He pressed the machine hard, pushing it over banks, rocks, and downed trees. Despite its more utilitarian design, it was just as tough as the Razer. Then it overheated.

He wasn't sure what happened at first. He'd been on a long incline, ready to top a hill when the engine just quit, the machine coasting to a stop. The simple dash didn't have a tachometer but it was probable that he'd been close to that red line. Robert pulled a bandana from his pocket and scrubbed at the grimy dash, trying to reveal what the various dirt-encrusted gauges said. The one with the flashing red light, when cleaned up, displayed a thermometer icon.

Robert groaned, then smacked the dash with his fist. He climbed out and stomped around, agitated and angry with the world in general. They were likely hours ahead of him anyway. Every moment that he sat here idle they were putting even more distance between them. He would never catch up at this rate.

He yanked his GPS from its pouch and examined the screen. The topographic lines on the display showed that his route was mostly downhill for the next short distance. He would be going down the other side of the hill he'd just climbed. Perhaps he could coast for a while. He wouldn't have power steering with the engine off but he could manage as long as there were no steep turns. The air flowing over the engine may even assist the engine in cooling down.

He climbed in the cab, the seat pressing his clammy body armor against his back. It was so tempting to take it off but he wouldn't do it. With his luck, taking it off would inevitably lead to taking a bullet. He released the parking brake and dropped the shifter to neutral. The heavy side-by-side rolled forward a few inches, then stopped.

Robert stuck a foot out the door and pushed like he was on a scooter. He'd apparently overestimated his own strength, because his first efforts accomplished nothing except painfully straining his groin muscle. He climbed out and braced his shoulder against the roll cage. He dug in and shoved hard, gaining several inches with each wave of effort. He could see a point ahead where there was an obvious change in grade. Soon he was there and the machine gained momentum until he was hardly pushing at all.

He hopped back in the seat and the vehicle rolled faster. Exactly as promised by his GPS, he soon hit a steeper grade and the machine picked up even more speed. He felt confident. He remembered this section from the trip out. It was mostly gentle turns for a little over a mile, then the trail crossed a wide creek. Hopefully, by that point, the vehicle would have cooled sufficiently that he could start it and continue his journey. He could do this. He just needed to keep calm.

The vehicle coasted with no more assistance from him, although at a much slower speed. In an effort to distract himself from his waves of frustration, he got his handheld radio out and began experimenting with different frequencies. He tried raising Sonyea but got nothing. He tried the frequencies monitored by Arthur's compound with the same results.

He exhaled violently, rage making him want to bash the radio to bits. He had no right to expect anything from it, though. Deep in this forest, blocked in by surrounding mountains, there was probably no one in range. His anger was merely a symptom of his frustration with everything and all of it went back to a single cause—he wasn't home with his family. He was trying hard to do the right thing and the world was erecting barriers in front of him at every turn.

He tried to push those thoughts from his head as the decline increased and the machine picked up speed. Now he was making good time. He turned the key enough to activate the gauges, glanced at the indicator lights, and found the temperature gauge was no longer flashing. That was good. The wind running over the engine was helping. If he could leave the engine off until he reached the bottom of this hill it might save him a little fuel. It was probably a ridiculous thought, reminding him of old people he'd known in his youth who insisted on turning their cars off or shifting into neutral on long descents to save gas.

By the time he hit the creek, he was coasting way faster than the twenty-five miles per hour top speed of the machine. He thought he might be going as fast as forty. The machine was bouncing and jostling at the edge of control. Before he thought any better of it, he hit the wide creek at the bottom of the hill at full speed, hoping that momentum would carry him across and up the opposite bank. The water was deeper than he remembered and cascaded over the top of the vehicle, high plumes spraying from the tires and skid plate.

He couldn't see out the windshield through the wall of water in front of him. It sprayed in the cab from all directions, soaking him and all his gear. It felt good with the muggy heat and put a smile on his face. The momentum hadn't fully carried him across the creek though. The water bogged him down like hitting a deep mud hole and he came to a stop near the center of the forty foot wide creek.

The exhilaration of his joyride dissipated quickly. The sense of impending doom, the weight of responsibility, bore down on him with a crushing weight. He turned the key. He needed to get on with things. The machine, which had always started right up, didn't catch. Robert adjusted his foot on the brake, making sure he was pressing hard enough to engage the safety switch there beneath the pedal, and tried again.

Nothing.

He tried several more times to no effect. He put it in gear, then out of gear. He let it rest for a minute then tried again. Nothing worked. He sighed aloud and climbed out into the knee-deep water. It felt good for a few seconds, then quickly became numbing cold as Robert removed gear from the cargo bed and pitched it into the cab. He tilted the cargo bed back and examined the engine. It was completely soaked.

He unsnapped the air filter housing and found water inside it. He held the black plastic cover up, tilted it, and creek water poured into the stream. He yanked the sodden air filter out of place and tried once again to no avail. He'd killed his ride.

How could be so stupid? What else had he killed, or at least doomed, in the process? Sonyea? His family? His own chance of survival?

He shouldered his pack, grabbed his rifle, and waded to the shore. He sat down hard in the damp soil and considered his options. The vehicle had a winch. Should he winch it to shore and wait for it to dry out or should he proceed on foot? There was no guarantee that sitting for even a couple of hours was enough to make the engine start. Meanwhile, what was he going to do during that time? He was too wound up to just sit patiently or take a nap. He would go stir crazy.

Walking meant moving at a slower speed but at least he'd be moving. He got out his GPS and checked his location. Just beyond the creek there was a state road. From that road, it was probably about eighteen miles to the compound. Robert checked his watch. It was 4

PM. While it was getting late, he still had hours of daylight. In the five hours up until dark, he could cut that distance in half. If he chose to sit around and wait for the engine to dry out, he might still find himself having to walk out of here but having lost hours of time. It was no decision for him.

He would walk.

He got to his feet, double-checked that he had all his gear, and climbed the short stretch of trail leading to the paved two-lane road. He stopped in the middle of the road, standing directly on the center line. Easier walking lay to both his left and right. Paved. Flat.

To either side of him were fresh prints. Two muddy tracks made by knobby off-road tires such as those on his disabled side-by-side. It was also the type used by the Razer he was pursuing. What were the odds that two such vehicles recently came by here? Probably very slim.

Dropping to his knee, Robert touched one of the muddy prints, running his finger across it. It was dry as chalk. He looked at an area where the mud was thicker, where perhaps the tire had discharged a clump of mud as the tire flexed. He squeezed that clump between his fingers and it was moist beneath the drier shell. He decided it was probably from today. Any longer in this heat and it would be completely dried through, baked by the hot pavement.

The tracks led across the road and up the trail access. It was the way they'd come. At least now he knew for certain that he was on the right track. For whatever reason, Jeff was headed back to the compound. He started walking, using the same long strides that he used on backpacking trips when he wanted to get as much distance as he could from each step. Still, it was hard not to be aware that he was probably travelling up this incline at two miles per hour and they were able to travel it at highway speeds as long as they had clear trail in front of them.

"Focus," he told himself. "Don't waste time thinking about variables you can't control."

When the trail flattened out, he began running. He knew he couldn't keep that pace up forever but he often ran with a light pack.

He would do this for a while, walk until his breathing stabilized, and then turn the pace back up.

He'd covered only a quarter mile of trail when a bend in the trail revealed the Razer stopped before him. Robert froze, then angled off-trail and took cover. For a moment, he did nothing but watch. He carefully examined the vehicle and all of the area around it, watching for movement, scanning for dead bodies. He found nothing.

As quietly as he could, he broke cover and eased forward like he was stalking game. He watched each step, aiming for greenery or moss over twigs or anything crunchy. His shotgun was at high ready, safety off. By the time he reached the vehicle, he'd still seen no signs of movement. He eased around the driver's side looking for bodies, or a trap.

No bodies. No blood.

The packs were gone, as were Sonyea's weapons. Robert checked through the rest of the supplies and found some of the food missing. The key was in the Razer and he tried to start it. It turned over but wouldn't start. Had they taken on water too? He didn't think that was likely. This vehicle was better protected against problems like that. It had to be fuel.

He recalled that he'd started to fill the Razer up before they descended on the campground. The can of gas he'd forgot to put in the Razer was the can that allowed him enough fuel to escape in his own vehicle. There had been no more full cans aboard the Razer so all they'd had was what remained in the tank. Apparently, that was enough to get them this far but no further.

Robert considered his options. He could keep running or he could try to fuel up the Razer and continue in it. They'd come prepared to siphon fuel if they ran short. They had empty cans and a length of tubing in the Razer. Robert grabbed them and headed back the way he'd just come, moving a little less quickly but with a smile on his face. If this worked, it would be a game changer.

~

Robert threw both hands in the air and cheered when the Razer started up. He'd managed to get a little over two gallons from his last ride, though he didn't think that would get him very far in this more powerful vehicle. Although he promised himself he'd take it easy and not have a lead foot, it was hard to resist the rush of exhilaration from being in a motored vehicle again.

He didn't know how far Jeff and Sonyea could have gotten. When he placed his hand against the Razer's oil pan, it was warm to the touch but not hot. He didn't have any science behind his estimate but he imagined they'd probably put a couple of miles in on foot by this point. Even in the worst scenario, as long as they stayed on this trail he'd find them by nightfall.

That thought raised its own set of questions. How would he find them? If they heard the vehicle approaching, they'd surely not throw a thumb up and ask for a ride. He imagined Jeff would scurry for the shoulder like a rat ducking a flashlight and they'd wait for him to pass. They would also be leaving more subtle signs as they moved through the forest. If he was following them on foot, even a tracker as unskilled as he might have the occasional chance of finding a clue. At the speeds this vehicle travelled he would not see anything but the road ahead.

Did that mean he should abandon the vehicle and proceed on foot? He didn't like the idea of that. Should he stop occasionally and get out to scout on foot? If so, how often should be do that? What would be the point? The sound of the approaching Razer would travel so far ahead of him that they'd hear him coming.

It was frustrating to think he'd come across such an advantage to only find that it put him at a disadvantage. He decided there was no way Jeff, and hopefully Sonyea, were going to make it back to the compound by tonight. He would allow himself fifteen miles and then he'd stop and wait on them. Hopefully if he passed them, they'd assume he went on to the compound and wouldn't be concerned about him lying in wait for them.

He would cruise along at roughly ten miles per hour. That would put him in a position of gaining ground on them but would hopefully still be slow enough that he could observe his surroundings. This eased his mind a bit. He was still a long way from home, he was still missing his family, and he was still searching for a missing friend, but this was the first time in over twenty-four hours where he felt like he had a plan.

He should have seen that as a warning sign.

33

When Sonyea heard the first rumblings of an approaching engine, she did her best to try to cover for the sound. While she wasn't certain it was Robert, it was possible. She hoped it was him, anyway. She needed it to be him. She scuffed her feet as she walked. When the volume of the engine rose over the level of disturbance she was creating, she took to humming, then to singing.

Finally, Jeff could stand it no longer and lost it. He yanked the rope tied to her handcuffs, stopping her in her tracks. "What the hell are you doing? Shut up!"

In the pause between his outburst and her reaction, he heard it. His eyes grew wide and he immediately understood she'd been trying to distract him, to cover for the possible approach of a vehicle.

"Off the road!" he shouted, jabbing his finger toward the shoulder.

"What?" she asked. "They might not even be coming this way." She needed to delay him. If she could slow this down, Robert might show up and save her. He might come around the bend in the road at any moment and this ordeal would be over.

To Sonyea's surprise, Jeff charged her, shoving her toward the edge of the trail. With her hands cuffed, she was unable to maintain her balance or even catch herself. She fell hard, crying out before she tumbled over the bank and down into the thick trailside brush. She was already hurt from her various scuffles with Jeff and the pain was overwhelming. Her head throbbed and all of her bruised muscles cried out.

She struggled to right herself but her head was lower than her legs. It was like trying to do a sit-up on an incline bench. She tried to channel her pain to rage, digging deep to tap the well of contempt she was feeling for this young man. Before she could get herself straightened out, Jeff scrambled down beside her and hooked a forearm beneath her bicep. He started dragging, pulling her over sharp briars, broken branches, and jagged rocks. She screamed and protested but it had no effect.

"Quit screaming," Jeff said, dumping her to the ground and lashing out with his foot.

The kick caught her in the hip, blinding her with pain. She shut up then, biting her lip, and visualizing what she was going to do to Jeff when she turned the tables on him. Then she remembered the neck knife she'd stashed when she had one hand free. Not only had she forgotten about it in her pain and rage, she'd never wanted to kill him this badly until now. At this moment, she would do it without a second's hesitation if she got the chance.

The whine of the engine was getting closer. Jeff struggled to wrap Sonyea's leash around a downed tree then abandoned the effort. Any knot he could tie, she could untie. He resorted to intimidation instead. "You move and I'll kill you!"

She didn't really think he would but she glared back venomously.

Jeff scrambled toward the bank they'd just come down, leaping and stumbling over the debris he'd dragged her through. He flattened himself against the bank where he could peer over the edge and watch for the approaching vehicle. She was probably a dozen feet from him now, watching him as he watched for Robert.

Then the ATV was upon then, the sound was no longer buffered by the forest. Sonyea couldn't see it from her position but knew it would soon be past them. As fast as the sound rose, it would disappear, leaving her in the hands of this jerk. She could almost sense Robert up there, searching for her, watching for any clues along the road, any sign she was alive. She tried to imagine some way she might flag him down or catch his attention but she was too far below his line of sight. She wasn't even sure she could make it to her feet the way everything hurt.

Through eyes blurry with tears of pain and frustration, she saw Jeff flatten himself against a boulder. If this was Robert, he intended to shoot him. The AR was pressed against his shoulder, his eye dropped to sight through the red dot optic. She didn't know if he turned it on, or if he even knew how. She couldn't say if that would impact his ability to hit a target at this close range. He apparently understood the safety because she saw him look for it, then fumble to put it in the FIRE position.

Sonyea used the only thing she had at her disposal. She sucked in a deep breath and released a bloodcurdling scream, praying that Robert would hear it over the sound of his engine.

He did, but it was too late.

At the same moment Robert heard the scream, a round from the AR ripped through the Plexiglas windshield and sliced through the side of his bicep. He flinched and cried out at the searing pain. A second round punched through the windshield and impacted his chest plate. The round splattered and sent bullet fragments spraying into the underside of his face.

Robert craned his head, looking for his attacker between the spiderweb of shattered plastic. He couldn't see anything.

Then he caught movement in the weeds at the side of the road. In a flash, it registered that the barrel of a weapon was being pointed at him at nearly point-blank range. Not through the windshield this time but aimed through the door opening. He caught a glimpse of a familiar face above that rifle barrel. It was Jeff.

Out of a reflex motivated by pure self-preservation, Robert stomped the gas pedal at the same time a burst of flaming gases erupted from the short barrel. There was the whine of a bullet veering off the steel roll cage and Robert felt like a hot blade had been jammed into his shoulder. At the same time, the Razer accelerated beyond Robert's ability to steer it with his injured arm and beyond his ability to see through the damaged windshield. He lost control, hitting a high bank to the right of the road. A tire caught a rock and the vehicle flipped, tumbling several times before dropping off the opposite shoulder of the road.

Sonyea screamed again when she saw the vehicle tumbling in the distance. Unrestrained, Robert was flopping around like a ragdoll as the heavy vehicle tried to shake him free. She got to her feet, climbing toward Jeff, toward the road. She had to get to Robert.

Jeff seemed stunned as she climbed toward him, as if it was only now occurring to him that he may have killed another human being for the first time. Sonyea was almost to him when he spun on her. "Stay here!"

She hesitated, momentarily frozen by the rage in his expression, a vitriol she'd never seen in him even at his worst. He mistook her pause as compliance and scrambled up the bank away from her. Sonyea was far from compliant. All she saw was a man she hated crawling away to kill her friend. She dropped her cuffed hands to the pouch where she'd concealed her knife and dug it free. She lunged for Jeff, clutching the knife in both hands, determined to plunge it into the only thing she could reach.

He screamed when she sank the blade into the thickest part of his calf and tore downward. He jerked away, swatting at the knife reflexively, like someone stung by a bee and batting blindly at the injury. He twisted his body and stared at the offending blade, somehow mustering the strength to grip the handle of the knife. When his hand touched it he roared and yanked it free. He stared at Sonyea with a wounded rage that made her think he was going to come after her to kill her with her own knife. He didn't, instead flinging the knife far into the woods where she'd never find it.

Sonyea laid on her stomach in the rocks and weeds. She'd never felt so defeated. Her attack had not been enough. She hadn't killed the bad guy. She had not saved Robert, nor had she saved herself.

She also lost her only weapon in her rushed and poorly-executed attack.

Jeff crawled away, more concerned about Robert's fate than either his injury or whatever remaining threat Sonyea presented. At the top of the bank, Jeff staggered to his feet, wincing when he tried to flex his calf and bear weight on the leg. He glanced down at the spreading bloom of blood on the back of his pants leg and scowled at Sonyea. He shouldered the AR and pointed it at her. He wanted to shoot her so bad he trembled in his attempt to restrain himself. He finally cursed and turned away from her, limping off toward the Razer.

Sonya sucked in a gulp of air, not realizing she'd been holding her breath as she stared down the barrel. She scrabbled her way up the slope until she was on the forest road, then got to her feet and jogged after Jeff. Everything hurt and her gait was pained, awkward. She found a small satisfaction in the idea that however bad it hurt her to walk, it had to be hurting Jeff more.

Lurching ahead of her, Jeff reached the point where the Razer left the roadway. Ragged scrapes in the dirt marked the points of impact where the vehicle hit as it tumbled and bounced toward destruction. Jeff raised the AR as he closed in on the shoulder, peering over cautiously. With the earth-toned gear Robert was wearing, it took Jeff a moment to locate the body in the dense weeds. He had been tossed from the vehicle. Robert lay in an awkward position, his face and torso bloody, limbs splayed.

Jeff found the amount of blood to be satisfying. A sob behind him was the first indication that Sonyea was nearby. He lowered the AR and glared at her. "I told you to stay put."

Ignoring him, Sonyea continued toward the shoulder, wanting to make her way down to her friend. Jeff clamped a hand onto her shoulder, digging into her flesh and yanking her backward. She stumbled and went down hard on the same hip Jeff had taken a boot to earlier.

He stepped across her body and leaned over, jabbing a finger in her face. "Forget him. He deserved what he got."

"He might be alive!" Sonyea sobbed. "He might need our help!"

"If he's not dead now, he will be soon," Jeff said. He winced and stepped away from Sonyea. Crouching over her must have strained the damaged calf muscle.

Jeff limped around for a moment, tears pouring from his eyes as he fought to manage the pain. He stopped and raised his pants leg. Sonyea saw the jagged tear in his calf, blood streaming down his sweaty leg and saturating his sock. Jeff glared at Sonyea with murderous rage. "I should kill you."

"I wish I *had* killed you," Sonyea said.

Jeff dragged a grubby bandana from his back pocket, folded it into a bandage, and knotted it around his calf. He grimaced when he tightened it, giving Sonyea a small degree of satisfaction. "Get on your feet," he hissed through the pain.

Sonyea did as he asked. "What now?"

"Well, since we don't have a vehicle, we walk."

"We won't make it tonight. There's not enough time. We should stay here for the night. You need to rest your leg anyway so it can clot."

"Nice try," Jeff said. "You're just hoping your little boyfriend down there is still alive and coming to rescue you. Well, he's not. He's dead, and that's how you're probably going to end up too. Now let's go."

When she didn't start walking fast enough to suit him, Jeff grabbed her by the shoulder and slung her in the direction they needed to go. "If you know what's good for you, you'll stay ahead of me. If I get another hand on you, I'm not responsible for what might happen."

Sonyea started walking stiffly, heeding his advice to keep some distance between them. It would keep her out of his reach. Jeff fell in behind her. She could hear the difference in his gait, the injured leg dragging with each step. Her leash, the frayed rope, dragged behind her. He didn't even make an attempt to reach it.

"Why?" Sonyea asked, speaking over shoulder, her voice raspy from screaming and sobbing.

"Why *what*?" Jeff growled.

"This? Why all of this?"

Jeff didn't answer.

"I mean, those were your people back at that campground, right? You could have just delivered me down there and not had to deal with all this. Your dad's men would have me under guard at this very moment and you could be riding in an air-conditioned RV, eating cookies. It didn't have to go this way."

"Those guys get enough credit," Jeff said. "Dad sees a badge or a uniform and it's like magic. Those people are worth something and I'm not. Those people can do things and I can't. Those people are capable and I'm nothing but trash." The level of spite in his voice increased the longer he talked.

"So this isn't really about the compound? It's about a boy and his dad?" Sonyea was trying to be serious, to omit the sarcasm she was feeling at having to go through all of this just so he could mend his grievances with his father.

"You make it sound like nothing," Jeff said, "but it's something."

Sonyea sighed, noticing that it took effort, like she had to draw on every muscle in her body to wring the bad air from herself. "In the scheme of things, it's a small thing, Jeff. In the scheme of your life, it's a small thing. Going to all this effort just to prove something to your father is just wrong. You're still a young man. If you go down this road of letting other people define your worth, you're in for a long, hard journey. In the end, it will be a disappointing journey as well."

"What do you know about *anything*?" Jeff snorted. "What could you possibly know about me?"

Sonyea shook her head, unable to push away the sadness in what this young man was saying to her. She wanted to kill him. In fact, she'd already tried and failed. At the same time, the mother in her, the teacher in her, wanted to impart something. She wanted to make him understand that what he was, what he became, was up to him. People were fragile and could be damaged, broken even, but it was your own decisions that mattered in the end. It was all you could control.

Jeff couldn't make his father feel different about him or treat him any differently. The actions of others were always beyond one's control. The thing an individual could control, the piece that remains with them, was how they reacted. People could choose their response. In so doing, they kept the power.

"Don't let him define you," Sonyea said. "Don't give him that power over you."

"Haven't you noticed? My dad has all the power in *any* situation. He's a control freak who lives to wield power over other people."

"Don't think of who he is to other people. Think of who he is to you. This is about you and him. Nothing else. You said it yourself. That's why we're doing this."

"I'm tired of you talking."

Sonyea was tired of talking too. Her legs felt heavy and walking took more effort than it had ever taken before. "Think about one thing for me, Jeff. Don't tell your dad everything you told me. He'll only use it against you, use it to manipulate you. If you're going to turn me over to him, just do it and let him draw his own conclusions. Let him figure out how you did it and why you did it. Only then will you have any chance of changing him."

Jeff never did respond, though he was still dragging along behind her, occasionally stumbling or banging the AR against his leg. She thought she heard him crying quietly but she didn't dare turn and look. She didn't want to see.

34

T he security detail guarding the families at the campground was bored and frustrated. They had not received the go-ahead from the congressman to proceed to the compound, as they'd been expecting for several days now. They'd also been entirely out of radio communication with his group. That made them anxious and they weren't sure what to do. Some wanted to send a team ahead to the compound to find out what was going on there. The rest of the group, knowing how serious the congressman was about people obeying his orders, felt it was safer to wait until they heard something from him.

While the families fished, rode bikes, and pretended this was just another camping trip, the security detail patrolled and searched the grounds for things that might be of use to them. They took naps or worked out, played basketball at the playground. Still, they felt like they were wasting time. This was not what they had signed up for.

The men were understandably surprised when their midday routine was broken by a voice coming from one of the handheld radios.

"It sounds like Bradshaw," said one of the detail, a beltway-area security guard named Carrier. He raised the radio to his lips. "Go for campground. Is that you Bradshaw?"

"Roger that campground. Bradshaw here."

Carrier looked around at the rest of his group. For the last hour since they'd eaten lunch, they'd been lounging in camp chairs and trying not to nod off. They'd all jumped back to life, anxious to hear any news. "What happened to you guys? Is everything okay?"

"Things haven't gone as expected but that's not a discussion for an open channel. We can talk about it in person."

"Are you ready for us to head toward the compound? Do I need to get folks packing? We are so ready to get out of here."

"That's a negative," Bradshaw said. *"We're coming to you. In fact, we're turning into the campground now. I just wanted to give you guys a heads up so no one would get trigger-happy and open fire on us."*

Carrier looked stunned. "The campground? What happened? I thought we were supposed to join you at the compound?" He was dumbfounded. It was the call they'd been waiting for but totally without the news they'd been expecting to hear.

"I said we'll talk about it when we get there," Bradshaw barked. *"Bradshaw out."*

Carrier dropped the radio into his lap, shook his head, and looked at his cohorts with disgust on his face. "Well that's a kick in the teeth. What the hell happened?"

One of the men, York, got to his feet. "Like the man said, I guess we'll find out when they get here, but I think we should get on our feet and act like we're earning our keep. Why don't one of you go tell the families? The rest of you come with me. Let's make sure these guys don't have anyone trying to follow them in here."

Everyone grumbled but got up. This was the first real activity since the failed trap they'd tried to set up with Jeff. They got to work. A guy named Crabtree went from camper to camper and spread the word among the families, who peppered him with questions. He assured them that he had nothing to tell them. He supposed they would all learn the details of what happened at the same time.

York, Carrier, and Bryant slid their sweat stained web gear back over their heads, ready to act like they were hard at work maintaining security around the place. When they were geared up, they jogged to their truck. York and Bryant climbed in the cab while Carrier dropped the tailgate and planted himself there.

York cranked the loud engine, made a U-turn, and cruised down the campground road toward the entrance. The campground was spread out, the main entrance gate nearly three miles from the collections of cabins where the families were staying. The pickup only made it half that distance before they met the approaching caravan of RVs.

He started to swing the vehicle out of the way and let the caravan pass but that meant it would be that much longer before he got any answers. If they let the congressman proceed to the campground, they would hear the same version of his story that the families heard —a sanitized version suitable for family consumption. It would probably be a stripped-down version that didn't tell him anything. It would be better to stop now and try to squeeze the dirt out of them. He killed the engine and threw open his door. Bryant followed suit and slid out of the clammy vinyl seat. Carrier dropped off the tailgate and joined the others in front of the vehicle.

"What's so damn important it can't wait?" Bradshaw asked on the radio.

"I want to hear the truth," York said. "Wasn't sure if it could be told in front of the others."

It took a moment for Bradshaw to respond. He was likely consulting with the congressman. *"Might be a good idea,"* he finally agreed. *"We'll be right out."*

Even if the men in these RVs were anxious to reunite with their families they understood there might be an advantage to having a frank discussion beyond the ears of children and wives. The men in the forward-most vehicles exited their rides and joined the other men in the barren stretch of asphalt road.

York nodded at the approaching entourage. "Good to see some familiar faces. Now what the hell happened out there?"

As usual, everyone deferred to the congressman. They shuffled their feet and watched him out of the corners of their eyes. They were all hesitant to state their personal opinions just in case the congressman had a contrary spin he wanted to put on the narrative.

Honaker shrugged, tucked his shirt into his pants, and slicked back his hair with two hands. He looked a little road weary, a little frazzled. "We had faulty intelligence. Place was a tougher nut to crack than we'd been led to believe. Bridges and his people were dug in like Japs in the Pacific. Not sure we could have driven them out with ten times the men."

The men in the security detail, who'd been waiting for their chance to move into the compound, looked at each other dumbstruck.

"So where does that leave us?" Carrier asked, holding his hands out as if to beseech an answer from the politician. "This is all we had. This was our only plan. We all spun the wheel and put everything we had on this one number. Where else are we going to go?"

"Pipe down," Colonel Jacobs snapped. "You'll get answers when the rest of us get them."

Bradshaw stepped in at this point to deflect the heat from the congressman. It was what a good aide did. "It couldn't be helped, son. As the congressman said, the intelligence we got was faulty. The men in that compound had more significant weaponry than we'd been led to believe. It's clearly some homespun militia training ground harboring a bunch of suicidal mercenaries and their illegal weapons. The cost to take it was just too high."

Carrier let his hands drop, frustrated, but finally understanding that this was really as much of an answer as he was going to get.

"So we stay here in the campground?" Bryant asked. "Is that the plan?"

The congressman shook his head as if irritated at being badgered, like he was facing reporters at a press conference. "No, we're not staying here. We have a fallback plan."

"This is the first I've heard of any fallback plan," Bryant said.

"Because I don't have to run every damn thought by you!" the congressman barked. "I don't want to go into the details until we're all together. I don't see any need to chew my fat twice."

"I'm sorry, sir," Bryant said. "The guys and I have just been going a little stir crazy."

"Maybe we should just go on in," Carrier said. "I'm sure you guys want to reunite with your families."

Bradshaw raised a hand. "About that. Before we go in, you need to know that we suffered several casualties. Some of them had families who are in there right now waiting for them. This is not going to be easy."

"Who?" Carrier asked.

Bradshaw rattled off the names. Some of the lost had been their friends.

The congressman raised a finger and everyone stopped. "Have you seen my son Jeff? Is he here?"

York, Carrier, and Bryant exchanged glances, then York took over. "As a matter of fact, that's kind of a weird thing. We got this radio message out of nowhere. It's Jeff, and he says he's on the road with these two people and he's being held prisoner. He says there was somebody at the compound who gave him a radio so he could reach out to us. He wanted us to be on the lookout for these people because they were headed our way and we could spring a trap on them."

The congressman smiled at this, pleased to know that Carlos, despite his shortcomings, had managed to accomplish something while on the inside. "Did it work? Did you catch them?"

York shook his head. "That was the last radio transmission we got from him. I don't know if they found the radio or what, but we stayed on alert for them to show up. Sure enough, some tricked-out operator-type comes strolling into camp one night with night vision and we pounced on him. Jeff told us on the radio that he had a hidden knife. His plan was to take the woman prisoner once she and the man separated. Jeff thought we might be able to use her as a bargaining chip to get access to the compound."

"Exactly!" The congressman said, smiling broadly.

"Yeah, but Jeff never showed up with her. I had men all over the place. We looked nearly all night for him. We called out and no one ever answered. We never found any sign of him in the woods. We still don't know what happened."

"Did you ask the man you captured?"

York shook his head. "No, we didn't exactly capture him. We sprung the trap and tried to sweep him up but lost him in the dark. We caught up with him again later but he fled into the mountains on an ATV. He killed one of our men."

"Dammit!" The congressman erupted. His face turned red and he paced angrily.

York tried to console him. No one liked giving the congressman bad news. "It's okay, right? I mean, we don't want the compound anymore anyway."

The congressman looked at York like he was an idiot. "*Jeff*. His mother is waiting in camp wanting to know where her *son* is."

York winced at the sharp rebuke. "Right, I'm sorry."

"Look, these guys probably went back to the compound. They don't know we pulled out of there," Bradshaw said. "They're probably going to get back there and find out we've gone. They'll be stuck with Jeff. He'll be useless to them if we're not there trying to get in. Maybe we just need to send a team back to negotiate his release. They'll probably hand him right over."

"If he's still alive," the congressman mumbled.

Bradshaw gave the congressman a warning shake of his head. "You can't be talking like that, sir. He's gonna be just fine. That's exactly what you're going to tell his mother too, right? That's how we need to play this. Jeff isn't missing, he's just on the road somewhere else."

The congressman reluctantly nodded, like a child forced to acknowledge something he didn't want to. He understood that Bradshaw was right. "Pick three men. Send a team in a truck. Now. I want them to either come back with Jeff or with news of what happened to him. I've got to have something to tell his mother."

Bradshaw looked at Colonel Jacobs. "Who do you think?"

Jacobs considered the question for a moment before replying.

"Decker, Voorhees, and French. They're solid men who can think on their feet."

Bradshaw patted Honaker on the shoulder. "We'll make it happen. Don't worry about this part. Just enjoy your reunion with your family."

The congressman looked doubtful. "For the families, it's been fun and games up until this point, like an adventure. A long camping trip. It gets serious now. You've lost a man and we've lost several. I hoped to shield all of our families during this dark time. I guess it's just not possible."

"Then we use it as a rallying point," Jacobs said. "We assure the families that these sacrifices were not made for nothing and we're obligated to continue moving forward toward the goals these men died for."

"Spoken like a soldier. Thanks, old friend," the congressman said. He addressed the rest of the men. "No sense delaying this any further. Let's get on with it."

The three from the security detail hopped in their pickup truck and made a U-turn to lead the caravan back to the campground. While the rest of the command team returned to their vehicles, Bradshaw jogged toward the rear of the convoy. He flagged down the men that Jacobs had recommended, giving them their instructions. They asked a few questions then said they were good to go.

Bradshaw stepped out of the way and allowed them to turn their vehicle, returning back the way they'd come. He'd intentionally picked men without families, men who wouldn't have to make excuses about why they were immediately heading back out. Bradshaw jogged back to Honaker's RV and climbed inside so the caravan could continue its somber journey to the waiting families.

THE REUNION WAS everything that the congressman and his men expected, joy dampened by loss. Families comforted one another. Assurances were made that each family would help the others. The congressman cried harder, moaned louder, and hugged tighter than all of them, an accomplished showman and manipulator.

When the worst was over, he took to the stump. It was an actual, literal stump from a pine tree, the yellow faded to light gray and sap streaming down the leathery sides like amber. He wiped tears from his eyes with his grubby pink paws, casting sorrowful glances at those families hit the hardest. He shared their pain.

"I know some of you have heard that things did not go as expected. All I can say is that the people I had on the inside failed to provide us with accurate intelligence. We expected to encounter little more than a shooting club. A small group of men with a love of firearms who had planned on weathering this period of hardship on this shared property. What we encountered was a hardened militia group, practically a terrorist organization, and they were far better armed than we were. As painful as it was, we had to accept that we needed to develop another plan."

Hands shot up in the audience but the congressman gestured they should lower them.

"I will answer all your questions, I assure you, but let me say my piece. You see, we were forced to regroup and take stock after we lost men. In fact, my own son was taken prisoner by those scoundrels and has yet to be released. It was obvious that we needed a softer target. I now have reason to believe that an associate of this group has an offshoot compound that may be suitable for our needs. It's located a couple of hours north of here in Damascus, Virginia. It belongs to a man named Robert Hardwick."

There was an eruption of questions and comments.

"Virginia?" complained one woman. "Do we even have enough fuel to get there?"

"What if we get turned away there too?" asked another.

The congressman gazed on them stoically, the model of a sincere politician delivering a heartfelt oration. "I don't have all the answers. As much as I wish I did, I simply don't. All I can do is promise to each and every one of you that I will do my best to provide for you. I will do my best to find a place where we can weather this storm in safety."

Despite their concerns, his audience was moved. A single person in the crowd started to clap, a plaintive gesture of support, and it grew until even the sobbing mourners clapped. The congressman burst into tears and climbed down from the stump, embracing his family in a side hug that would not block him from the news cameras, had there been any.

35

When awareness seeped into Robert's body it brought with it a palette of pain so vivid it surpassed anything he'd ever experienced before. Every pain brought with it dozens of nagging sub-pains. It was bones, muscles, bruised and torn flesh. He also thought it included blindness until he realized that the pain-induced starbursts in his vision were intermingled with real stars within the night sky.

He must have been out a while. Instinct urged him into motion, but even the gentlest attempt to raise himself caused his many pains to impact together like the crashing of cymbals. His stomach heaved and he threw up, vomit running down his face, his neck, and around his ears. Only then, feeling like he was going to choke, was he able to force himself over to his side. He threw up again. Each involuntary arching of his body, each heave of his stomach, stimulated some pained and damaged part of him. It was hard to comprehend just how much pain there was in the world until you crossed paths with it.

He was laying on his left side in a tangle of branches and boulders that had been pushed over the bank when the forest service made the road. In the darkness it felt like he was caught in some mountain man's trap, woven of branches and anchored with stones.

He had to make himself more comfortable so that he could assess his injuries, or at least be able to think clearly. He put his right hand on the ground, trying both to turn and raise his body at the same time. Pain flickered and flared within him.

"Oh God," he groaned.

His efforts proved futile. He was tangled and couldn't see what he needed to do to free himself. He groped along the front of his plate carrier, tracing the loops of webbing. The movement of his arm stirred a mélange of pain—the dull burn of raw flesh, the sharp sting of damaged nerves. A finger brushed against the aluminum tube of the pen-sized Streamlight flashlight he carried and he shoved it upward, pulling it from the Molle webbing.

He clicked the rubber bulb, emitting a harsh LED light that seared his corneas. It also revealed that he was covered in blood, both dried and fresh. His clothing was torn and he was no longer in the vehicle he'd been riding in. It wasn't anywhere within the circle of light created by the little flashlight. He played the light over his arm since that appeared to be the source of a lot of the blood. It was messed up, or at least looked that way.

The sight of his gore-encrusted arm provided new motivation to get on his feet and take stock of his injuries. Using the light, he found that one boot was trapped in the crotch of a branch laced deep into the undergrowth. That was what had been holding him back. Raising his knee, he threaded his foot out of the underbrush and was free.

He rolled over onto his stomach, cursing when he realized that he was rolling through his own vomit. It was already covering him at this point, so he wasn't sure what the big deal was, other than that he found the very idea offensive. He finally managed to get one elbow underneath him and pushed, raising himself. His spine sang with pain. Every other part of his body harmonized along with it—shoulders, muscles, neck.

When he made it to his knees he began to examine his visible wounds. A slug from his own rifle, wielded by Jeff, had ripped through the edge of his right bicep. It was a grazing wound but deep enough that there was muscle damage. He flexed his arm and worked his fingers. It all functioned well enough but the pain was eye-watering.

The act of turning his head that small measure to look down at his bicep pulled at the dried blood on his chin. He brushed a hand along his neck, finding dozens of scabs throughout the stubble of his beard. The whole attack, wreck, incident, whatever you wanted to call it, was a blur. He remembered vignettes of it but not the entirety.

He looked down at his plate carrier and figured out what happened to his chin. He wore an American flag morale patch over his heart and there was a frayed bullet hole going right through it. Shredded nylon around the patch told him that the bullet had shattered on impact with his body armor, sending shards in all directions. It was one of the unpleasant side effects of steel plates but certainly less unpleasant than a penetrating bullet wound to the heart.

Another wound to the back of his shoulder hurt every time he moved. His back felt damp from the blood seeping from that wound. There would be no way he could see it without a mirror, nor could he easily bandage it by himself.

He turned his head to each side, confirming that his neck still worked and his head was attached properly. He twisted his body and the pain in his spine was electric. He felt like he'd leaned into an electric fence. He couldn't tell that anything was broken but it was the kind of pain that would have taken him down for days in his old life, at least until the chiropractor worked his magic.

Robert played the light around and found the Razer resting on its side against a tree. The distance between him and the vehicle he'd been ejected from gave him pause. He was lucky to be alive. He stumbled to the vehicle and clutched the flashlight in his mouth. He shoved against the vehicle with both hands but it was wedged in tight. Even if he could turn it over, he didn't think he could drive it back up the steep bank. Maybe in better times with a winch, fewer injuries, and a clearer head.

He located a bottle of water in a cracked plastic tote still strapped to the Razer, took a drink, and washed his mouth out. Running his tongue through his mouth, he found all his teeth present and accounted for. It was a small blessing.

Needing to tend to his wounds before he could do anything, he unfastened the Velcro that held his plate carrier in place. Even the flexibility required to do that was challenging and took him a ridiculous amount of time. When every fastener was undone he lifted the heavy piece of gear over his head and dropped it to the ground beside him. He unhooked the plastic buckle of his battle belt and lowered it to the ground a little more carefully since it held his Glock 19.

His pack had been sitting loose beside him in the Razer and it took him a moment to locate it. Just like Robert himself, the pack had been launched from the Razer as it rolled down the hill. Inside the pack was his individual first-aid kit. He struggled for a moment with whether to ignore his wounds and get on the road or take a little time for self-care.

Not knowing what was ahead of him, he decided he'd be in better condition if he cared for his wounds. It would reduce the chance of infection, and that was the last thing he needed right now. The bicep wound was the most concerning of what he'd seen. It had clearly bled a lot while he was unconscious and he'd reopened the wound while moving around. He used an alcohol pad to clean the grit and dirt from it, then bound it with gauze and tape so it would stay closed when he moved his arm. Although it was difficult to bandage himself one-handed, the job was passable.

Still a little scrambled from everything that had happened to him, Robert tried to get his head together. He dug out his headlamp, turned it on, and replaced the Streamlight in his plate carrier. He finished his water and ate a nasty protein bar from his pack before beginning to gear up again. He put on the plate carrier and the battle belt, making sure nothing had fallen out in the process. He searched the vehicle, taking a few more bottles of water and a pack of jerky.

He looked for the KSG shotgun. Jeff had his AR pistol, and the KSG was all Robert had besides the Glock and his backup pistol. He emitted a small cheer when he located the buttstock buried in the leaves at the base of the vehicle, but his satisfaction was short-lived.

The shotgun didn't immediately pull free and, when he finally worked it free, the barrel was bent.

"Dammit!" Robert growled, sailing the useless weapon off into the dark.

He was angry, but realized he'd wasted all the time he had to waste. Sonyea and Jeff could still be moving away from him or they could be holed up for the night. Either way, he wasn't catching them standing still. He leaned forward and began painstakingly working his way up the steep bank on all fours. It was grueling work that required he use injured and damaged parts of himself that no longer wanted to cooperate.

What would have taken him less than a minute yesterday took him several today. When he finally crested the shoulder of the road and stood upright he was coated in a clammy sweat and his pulse was racing. He remembered that he carried some Vitamin I—ibuprofen —in his plate carrier. He tore open two paper pouches and took four of them. He washed them down with a mouthful of coppery-tasting water and started walking.

The movement began to feel good after a while, loosening up tight muscles and introducing a stream of endorphins into his system. He walked with the headlamp for a while, then realized he should probably transition over to the night vision to avoid walking into an ambush like the one he'd driven into earlier. He'd removed it from his weapon once he'd gotten back in the Razer, afraid it would get damaged bouncing around in the vehicle. It was a good thing he had. If it had still been attached to the shotgun, it would have been as crushed and useless as the shotgun itself.

He couldn't remember putting the PVS14 in its padded pouch but there it was. He raised it to his eye and turned the switch, praying that it still worked despite what it had been through. When the green glow swelled to life it was another moment that made Robert want to cheer. The joy passed quickly, leaving a void that was immediately filled with negativity. He experienced doubt that he was up for what- ever lay ahead of him; guilt for not being with his family; fear for them and what they might be experiencing.

A gnawing depression, a gaping blackness, was opening up inside him. There were people in this world who loved him but they were so far away he might never see them again. Here he was, injured and alone, hundreds of miles from those people. His friend Sonyea, as far as he knew, had no one to depend on but him. He was glad he wasn't in her shoes because he felt like a pretty poor resource at the moment. To have her life hanging in his hands surely meant nothing but disappointment and certain death.

"Pull yourself out of this, asshole," Robert said aloud as he walked. "You going to whine all the way home? You going to give up? Is this the kind of father you're going to be? Is this how you want your kids, your friends, to remember you?"

He knew he had to pull it together. If he let the dark thoughts take control, it would be like spiraling down a funnel of blackness. Nothing good could come of that.

"If you have time to think, you're not pushing yourself hard enough," Robert told himself. He started walking faster, taking longer strides. It jarred his spine in a way that made his back muscles spasm. There was stabbing pain that took his breath. The good news was that the pain filled him in a way that left no room for other thoughts. No room for the blackness. As the saying went, the pain was indeed *weakness leaving the body*.

36

Sonyea and Jeff walked the forest service road until the light faded, moving stiffly and zombie-like. Sonyea was handcuffed and trailing a rope behind her, while Jeff brought up the rear, his damaged leg protesting every attempt to use the muscles Sonyea had severed. Around them, the forest road lost its color as the world slid into the gray of late evening. The ambient sounds changed from the chattering of squirrels and songbirds to the more aloof melodies of mysterious night birds. Cicadas chanted behind it, their sound like that of hooded monks chanting by torchlight in medieval chambers.

They were within a few miles of the compound now and Sonyea saw no escape. Despite the fact he did not hold her leash, she was too broken to run, and could not lope away without anticipating his bullet in her back.

She had resigned herself to ending up in the congressman's greedy little hands. She dreaded that above all else. He was a shrewd manipulator, so much more experienced than his sheltered son. She would not be able to toy with his thoughts and emotions the way she had with Jeff's. The odds would go from one-on-one, as it was now, to her being at the mercy of a whole team of armed guards. She was certain nothing good awaited her there, yet the result was as certain as the coming of night around her.

This close to the compound, she was sure they'd push through, but they didn't. It wasn't the night that stopped them. Jeff still had Sonyea's night vision and could've continued into the night, leading her behind him like a whipped dog. Instead it was Jeff himself who gave out, his body and will failing in tandem. In the waning light he stopped several times to lean against roadside trees, visibly struggling with whether he had what it took to push through. With each previous break, he'd found some inner reserve to tap and fuel his progress. This time he could not. There was nothing left. He was empty.

"I can't go...any further," Jeff said, his voice cracking with the desperation. "My leg is killing me. Every step feels like you plunging that knife into me over and over again. Why didn't you just go ahead and kill me? It would have been much more humane."

"I intended to," Sonyea said matter-of-factly. "But you got away."

Jeff's face was pressed against the coarse bark of a tree. It appeared to be all that held him vertical. He screwed a single eyeball around to glare at her. "Do you still want to kill me?" he asked. "Because the way I feel now, I would just about let you. Just to be done with this whole bad dream that my life has become."

"I never wanted to kill you at all, Jeff. I just want you to let me go. If you're willing to do that, I'll walk away now and you'll never see me again."

Jeff turned his face back to the tree. "Don't be ridiculous. You know I can't do that."

"It's no more ridiculous than you wanting to die just because you can't hack it anymore. Toughen up, buttercup."

Jeff raised a middle finger at Sonyea, a sign of both his frustration and his inability to respond to her coherently in his exhaustion. Perhaps that meant it was time for her to continue pushing, to try to wear him down. Sometimes tired people agreed to things just to shut you up and secure a little peace.

Sonyea sat down, awkward with her hands cuffed, and crossed her legs. "So, are you going to turn me over to your father?"

Jeff nodded, his head bobbing up and away from the tree each time he pushed it forward. It had to hurt, the bark grinding and scraping at his forehead like that.

"After all the trouble you went through, I'm not sure why you want to do it that way," Sonyea said. "Your dad, as usual, will get all the credit for the move. He'll get the appreciation and adoration of all the people he moves into the compound. Nobody will ever remember that you delivered me there. No one will ever remember your sacrifice, your suffering. You will simply be a small, insignificant footnote in this story. *Small. Insignificant.*"

Jeff didn't respond, not taking the bait. Too weary to do anything —to sit down, to lie down, even to push himself away from the very tree which supported him.

Sonyea was picking up steam, strategizing on the fly. Her weary and dehydrated mind freed up and began to spin with more fluidity. Ideas began to coalesce. This was her opening; she needed to pick at it with her fingernails, worry it until it broke loose. She had to do everything she could to keep from being turned over to Congressman Honaker.

"If you're the one who started this, you might as well be the one to take it to the end zone, Jeff. Deliver me to the compound gate yourself and state your demands. There will be no doubt then as to who secured the compound for your people. Everyone will see it. No matter how your dad tries to spin it, all of his men will witness it and they'll carry the story to the rest of your group. This will become *your* victory and not *his*. With your success, you get the additional satisfaction of that extra little twist of the knife. You'll be rubbing it in his face that you did this. You! Not him."

Jeff summoned the energy to resurrect himself away from the tree. He fished half-heartedly in his grubby jeans pocket and retrieved the handcuff key. He dragged Sonyea to a sapling as big around as his thigh, unlocked a cuff, and had her wrap her arms around the tree. He checked the cuff to confirm she'd actually locked it back. She started to protest but Jeff quashed it before she began, with a blood-encrusted finger raised to his parched lips.

"Shhhhh. I don't care if you're comfortable, I don't care if you're warm, I don't care if you sleep a wink. All I care is that you're here when I wake up."

Jeff limped away to a plush carpet of thick moss and half sat, half fell onto its green gloriousness. He hesitantly peeled up his pants leg and probed tenderly at his injured leg. Each touch brought searing, teeth-clenching agony. Each burst of pain reinvigorated his fury, his anger at Sonyea. She bore the full responsibility for his suffering.

When she'd cut him, she lost any chance of gaining his sympathy. He wasn't certain he could actually kill her unless it came down to him or her, but she would not have an easy ride. She deserved to suffer at least as much, if not more, as he did. When he woke up in a few hours they would get back on the road. He would get her to that gate if he had to drag her by the hair.

As much as he hated to admit it, she even had a point about him delivering her to the compound gate himself. Maybe he would do it just as she suggested, not allowing his father to steal the glory of his work and accomplishment, the fruit of his suffering. That would piss his dad off so much. That alone was incentive for doing it. The lowly cook, the son Congressman Honaker didn't even trust with a gun, would save them all. The embarrassing spawn took the compound when the United States congressman could not.

Despite his pain and weariness, the idea made him smile.

JEFF AWOKE to the pleasant song of morning birds, so subtle and understated that it seeped into his sleep like a lullaby. He cracked his eyes to find splashes of golden daylight laying across his body, warming him one area at a time. When he laid down, he'd fully intended on napping for only a couple of hours before getting back on the trail, wanting to be at the gate when the sun came up. The sun was already up now and he was still several miles from where he wanted to be. He'd slept too long and too hard. He didn't quite feel right either. It felt like he had the flu or a really bad hangover. Disoriented.

Feverish.

That reminded him of his leg. The leg didn't want to bend like it had yesterday, swollen like something set upon by angry bees. He tried to get a closer look at it and found it difficult to raise his pants leg. Had his jeans shrunk tight around the wound? No, it wasn't that. The leg had swollen to fill the jeans. That was bad. He gave up trying to raise the jeans when his attempts created a tearing sensation. What would seeing it accomplish at this point anyway? By the way the offending limb felt, he could imagine the sight of it, red and yellowed, streaked with infection, oozing a mixture of pus and blood. He could do nothing to address either of those circumstances. His only direction was forward, following this to the end.

With the remembrance that he was not alone, Jeff craned his neck and found Sonyea knelt against the base of a tree, slouched awkwardly against it, hugging. She watched him with interest.

"I hate to tell you this, but you're probably going to lose that leg. The compound has a doctor. He's got IV antibiotics that would save it but once you drive them out of the compound he'll leave with Arthur and his people. He's certainly not going to stick around at that point to render aid to the enemy. On the other hand, if you *surrender* me at the gate, I can probably get you in."

Jeff didn't respond to her resumption of tactics from the previous night. He understood she was just trying to trick him. She only wanted to be set free, she didn't care about him at all.

He tried to stand. Just getting to his feet was a complicated orchestration that produced several outbursts of pain and filled his eyes with tears. He walked tentatively in a circle, like he had a leg cramp, seeing if the wound would loosen up, but there was no indication of it. His leg felt like an odd and alien thing, the muscle grown rigid in the flesh, packed tight within its casing like a stuffed sausage.

"Let me go," Sonyea said. "I can get you some help. There's no use suffering like that. If you lose the leg, you won't even be able get a prosthetic under these circumstances. No one will be able to help you."

"Shut. Up."

Sonyea did as he demanded, sensing the potential for violence in the air like the whiff of ozone after an electrical short. He was likely weak from fever, although perhaps he wasn't thinking clearly either. He might just shoot her out of frustration, desperate for the quickest route to silence.

Jeff slung her pack across his shoulders and ambled, gasping and grimacing, toward her. He unlocked a single cuff, stepped back, and leveled a handgun at her while she stepped away from the tree and refastened the cuffs. He grabbed the chain and gave it a solid yank, testing that it was locked.

"Ouch!"

He scowled at her, his eyes red and glassy. "Don't even talk to me about pain."

She bit her tongue, trying not to provoke him lest he want to share some of his pain with her. She was already hurting but knew there was room for more. It was an opening she did not want to fill.

Struck with an idea, Jeff pawed at the pouches on the body armor he was wearing. It had been Sonyea's and the pockets were packed with her gear. He flipped up Velcro flaps and probed canvas for whatever he was searching for. When he found it, he smiled, pulling several long zip ties from the pouch and dropping half of them. He fastened two together to make a longer one, then looped it around Sonyea's neck.

"What are you doing?" she asked.

Jeff threaded one of the free ends of the zip tie through the flash hider on the AR pistol. He missed the opening several times, squinting his bleary and watering eyes to focus. Once he had it through the holes in the flash hider, he had to thread the loose ends of the zip tie together, which took additional effort. When he was done, he tightened the zip tie until it held the rifle barrel directly against her spine.

"Not too tight!" she said, panicking. "I can't breathe."

"You'll be fine," he said, a sadistic tone overtaking him. "But this way you can't duck and dodge. You can't get away. If they shoot me, I can still pull the trigger before I die. If I do, you're a dead duck."

Sonyea couldn't help but wonder at that comment, so childlike and inappropriate, like something stolen from a cartoon. "Just don't pull too tight. I have this thing about stuff around my neck."

"I have this thing about being stabbed in the leg," he retorted. "I guess life isn't always about our own personal comfort, is it?"

Sonyea raised a hand and slipped her fingers beneath the zip tie.

"What are you doing?"

"I need room to breathe. The weight of the barrel is pulling it tight. I'm not getting enough air."

"You're wasting time. Let's get on with it."

She lingered for a moment, considering her situation. The handgun he'd stolen from her was in his belt. Earlier, considering his dazed condition, there was a chance she could have fought him and taken it. Battered as she was, she was uncertain. If she lost again, what would he do? Probably just kill her. There was no way she could fight back now. He just had to pull the trigger, no aiming required.

"I'm ready," she said.

"Then let's get on with it."

She did as he asked, walking slowly, biding her time. Her sympathy for this boy ebbed and flowed. Sometimes she understood his simple psychological state and thought he'd be a decent guy under different circumstances. Other times, she felt he was already too damaged to be salvaged. Right now she cared nothing for him or his fate. She could slit his throat herself and watch the light fade from his eyes as he bled into dirt.

If she had the chance, she wouldn't hesitate.

37

"There's your camp," Sonyea said, approaching the final stretch of road leading to Arthur's compound.

"My tent," Jeff said, pointing to the backpacking tent he'd stayed in. The slash in the side reminded him of his abduction, of Brandon hitting him with the Taser and carrying him off through the woods.

She'd had her back to him a long time, but something in Jeff's voice made Sonyea turn to look at him. He was sickly looking, his face shiny with an oily fever sweat. Broad blooms of dampness encircled his neck and beneath his arms. He winced with each loping step. His eyes were the worst—crazed with fever, delirious.

"We keep going, right?" Sonyea asked. "You're running with this. You're taking it to the end."

"Shut talking," Jeff mumbled, unaware of the way he jumbled the words. It didn't matter. Everyone should know what he meant.

They passed the dense wall of foliage that separated Jeff's camp from the congressman's main camp and Sonyea was surprised at first. This had to be the spot because she could see the compound gate in the distance. No one was there. They'd left.

"Where are they?" Jeff moaned.

"Up ahead," Sonyea said. "We're not there yet."

Jeff bought it for a moment, continuing to move forward, then he froze in his tracks. "No, this is it." He looked around wildly.

"I don't think so," Sonyea assured him. "The woods can be confusing."

"Dammit, don't lie to me!" he bellowed.

Sonyea went silent while Jeff scanned his surroundings, taking in what he saw. What he didn't see.

"They left," he finally said.

Despite what they'd been through, despite her anger toward this young man, Sonyea could not help but hurt for him. It seemed almost a ridiculous emotion, considering that this very moment he had the barrel of a gun strapped to her neck. She couldn't help but wonder what it would feel like to be in his shoes at this moment. He had to be processing this on so many levels. For one, they'd apparently left without attempting to rescue him. They'd just gone on, leaving him behind like an unwanted puppy.

Secondly, he'd been deprived of his whole reason for taking on this endeavor. The entire point of bringing her back here instead of turning her over to the security detail at the campground was so he could have the pleasure of seeing his father's face when he successfully accomplished what he'd set out to do. Whether he turned her directly over to his father or presented her at Arthur's gate to negotiate their surrender didn't matter. Either way he'd have the satisfaction of having done what his father had not been able to do.

Except now that satisfaction had been stolen from him and he sagged with defeat. His miserable condition took on an even more pitiful form in that light.

Sonyea turned slowly, her neck turning within the confines of the zip tie until she was facing him, the gun barrel against her throat. "Jeff—"

"Shut up! I don't want to hear anything you have to say!"

"I'm sorry."

"You think I want your sympathy?" he spat. His eyes bore into her with a rage so deep she wondered if he might kill her just to vent the surge of emotions within him. Coming to some conclusion, he jerked the rifle, the movement whipping her head forward. "Let's go."

She was terrified the rifle would go off from his erratic movements. She couldn't see if he had the safety on or not. She started to turn and walk, accepting that this next part was inevitable. Without his father to turn her over to, they would go directly to the gate and something would take place there. She didn't want to admit that she suspected what Jeff's fate would be there. They would kill him. He didn't have any chance of prevailing in this. Why did she feel so bad about that?

She turned away from the empty campsite, ready to lead them to the gate, then stopped. Jeff stared at her in frustration. He didn't have much left in his tank, either in terms of willpower or patience. He couldn't afford for this to drag out too long.

"What is it?"

She raised her cuffed hands, extended a single finger, and pointed back the way they'd come. Jeff turned and squinted, experiencing a little difficulty focusing with his bleary, fever-ravaged eyes. Then he saw it. A bedraggled and slouched form, moving with the same pained and broken gait as his own.

Jeff sighed, a protracted grunt of disappointment. Even at this distance he knew it was the man he'd left for dead, broken and bleeding at the bottom of the embankment. He didn't know how he could still be alive, nor did he understand how the injured man had managed to catch them. It must have been the time lost sleeping so long. Perhaps this other man, nearer to death, already withdrawing from the physical needs of the body, had continued moving through the night, powered by some supernatural force.

Robert was not going to stop him. His dad had already stolen part of his victory and he would not allow this dead man to steal what remained. Jeff pushed the gun barrel against Sonyea's throat, prodding her into stumbling backward.

"Let's go. Now!"

〜

JEFF WAS WHOLLY unaware of the stir his appearance created within the compound. His arrival with Sonyea had been so slow as to be undetected by the sentries until he began shouting angry commands at her. The confused sentry went on alert, whipping his binoculars around and finding Jeff and Sonyea at the abandoned camp.

"Gate for command," the sentry whispered into his radio. "I need command at my position immediately."

The sentry waited, and was preparing to repeat his urgent plea when Arthur replied.

"Go for Arthur. What's going on?"

"Sir, that cook that we captured is approaching the gate on foot. He's armed and has Sonyea Brady as a prisoner."

"Everyone hold your fire," Arthur said. *"I'm on my way."*

The whine of an approaching side-by-side confirmed to the guard that they were indeed on their way. Less than two minutes after getting the call, Arthur and Kevin were piling into the observation post. Arthur didn't say a word, going straight for the binoculars that the sentry extended to him. Kevin took a position behind a tripod-mounted spotting scope and began making his own assessment.

"I'll be damned," Arthur said. "Those two look rough. Makes me wonder if Robert is dead."

"That would be a negative," Kevin said. "Look behind them. Maybe two hundred yards back. Just coming into view at the crest of the road."

Arthur adjusted his viewing angle and let out a low whistle. "Talk about the walking dead. These guys look like they were dragged here behind a vehicle."

Kevin hit the mic on his own radio. "Gate for Brandon."

The reply was nearly immediate. *"Go for Brandon."*

"I need you on the gate with your long-range kit. Need it now."

"Camo?"

"That's a negative," Kevin said. "Just need you on the gate with good glass and a tuned rifle. Confirm when you're in position."

"Roger that. On my way."

"I don't suppose this kid has a radio," Kevin said. "I'd like to ask him what the heck he thinks he's doing."

"We'll find out in good time," Arthur said, assessing the three bedraggled figures in his sight. He lowered the binoculars, then handed them back to the sentry. "Let me know if there is any change in circumstances."

"Where you going?" Kevin asked. "Think you got time for a nap or something?"

Arthur shook his head. "Figured I'd meet them at the gate and talk this out."

"What?" Kevin asked, stepping away from the spotting scope and staring at Arthur in surprise.

"Yeah, the kid doesn't have a radio and I'm too old to hear what he's shouting from here. I need to get closer."

"The kid has a weapon," Kevin pointed out. "An SBR or AR pistol trained on the woman and a handgun tucked in his belt."

Arthur shrugged. "I've got the backing of a small army. I've got a sniper on the way. Plus I've got my personal weapons. I think I've got this covered ten different ways."

"I'll go with you," Kevin suggested.

"The hell you will. That will just make the situation more stressful. I'd rather have you back here providing cover fire if things go south."

"At least take the side-by-side. You can take cover behind it if bullets start flying."

"I can do that," Arthur said.

"Brandon, give me an ETA," Kevin said into his radio.

"*Settling into position,*" Brandon replied. "*On target in less than thirty.*"

"Roger that," Kevin said. "Do not fire unless directed to do so. We clear on that?"

"*Affirmative. Do not fire unless directed to do so.*"

Arthur smiled at his friend. "Okay, let's get this dog and pony show on the road."

Arthur hopped into the side-by-side and started the engine. He made the short drive down to the gate and killed the engine. He remained in the seat, watching through the windshield. Sonyea was leading the way, probably seventy yards from him. She had a hand to her neck, like she was tugging against something. It made Arthur suspicious but he couldn't see anything.

The congressman's son, Jeff, remained hidden behind Sonyea. To the rear, remaining at least two football fields behind them, Robert Hardwick was limping along like some wavering mirage, only the vestigial remnant of a man, what remained when the body was too damaged.

Arthur couldn't see if Robert was carrying a weapon or not. He raised his rifle and peered through the optic but the adjustable one to four power optic didn't tell him a lot. When he turned it on Jeff and Sonyea again, something just didn't seem right. Maybe it was his angle. He hit the mic on his shoulder and spoke into his radio.

"Arthur for Kevin."

"Go for Kevin."

"Get on whatever the strongest optic is you have up there and dial in on Sonyea Brady's neck. There's something weird going on. She keeps tugging at her neck but I can't tell anything from here."

"Roger that."

Sonyea and Jeff had moved another twenty feet closer. It was about time to intercede.

"Kevin for Arthur."

Arthur keyed his mic. "Go for Arthur."

"This is some of that third-world terrorist bullshit. The kid has his barrel strapped to her neck with something. Could be a zip tie, could be wire, I don't know. It's like a dead man switch. We drop him and he'll probably still have time to top her."

Arthur sighed. This complicated things. "Roger that, Kevin. I'm stepping to the gate to address them. You guys don't make a move unless things go south. I don't want this woman hurt. She's one of ours."

"Roger that."

"Brandon?" Arthur asked.

"Affirmative."

Arthur slid out the door and stretched. He adjusted his plate carrier, then leaned back in and got his rifle. He snapped it to the buckle on the sling and double-checked the chamber, then walked toward the gate. He assessed what cover he had available to him, both to each side of the gate and behind the ATV.

Sonyea was ahead of him, close enough that he could see the fear in her eyes. Her hands rode looped into whatever devious device the kid wrapped around her neck. Jeff stared at him over Sonyea's shoulder, looking more like a kid sick with the flu than some combatant there to make demands. They were about forty yards away now. It was time to get this figured out.

"That's far enough!" he called out.

Jeff lurched to a stop. His sudden movement pulled the zip tie around Sonyea's neck tight and she jerked to a stop.

Rather than address Arthur, Jeff turned and nervously scanned for Robert coming at him from behind. Robert had gained some ground and was probably a little more than a hundred yards behind his quarry. He staggered forward with the unwavering rhythm of a damaged machine that knew no direction but forward and no speed but for that which it was originally set.

"Stop FOLLOWING me!" Jeff bellowed.

Robert did not reply or slow, only limped onward. Jeff drew the handgun from his belt, Sonyea's own Glock. With his right hand still holding the grip of the AR bound to Sonyea's neck, Jeff was forced to shoot the Glock with his offhand, the left. He fired twice, hitting nothing. He fired twice more.

Robert didn't parry or dodge, didn't break pace. Dust kicked up around him, the two shots going low.

Unsatisfied with the results, Jeff dumped the mag to no more affect. Robert didn't slow or flee into the woods, nor was he hit. The bullets hit the ground or went wild. There was the ping of a ricochet skittering off a rock somewhere.

When the gunfire began, Arthur raised his rifle but did not have a shot. Sonyea's eyes widened and she shook her head. Arthur kept the rifle raised but didn't shoot, prepared only to fire if fired upon. If he did so, he understood that it would probably be the death of Sonyea. At the same time he was worried that the kid, so distracted by engaging Robert, might accidentally pull the trigger on Sonyea.

"Stop following me!" Jeff screamed again, his voice cracking.

Robert kept coming.

38

"You have a shot, Brandon?" Kevin said into his radio.

"*Sir, I can easily drop him but I can visually confirm that the safety on that weapon is in the OFF position. A spasm or the movement of his body falling can discharge that weapon. It is securely fastened to the female prisoner's neck with perhaps a two inch gap between the barrel and her spine. If he fires, he will not miss.*"

"What's your range?"

"*Three hundred and sixty-seven yards.*"

"Relocate," Kevin ordered. "I want you at two hundred yards or less. This could come down to a matter of millimeters."

"*Affirmative.*"

"Confirm when you're in position."

"*Roger that.*"

Kevin knew Brandon was just as good at this distance as he would be at a closer range, but getting closer would reduce environmental factors such as the updrafts common in these high mountains. He continued to study the scene through the spotting scope. He could see Robert better now and the man appeared to be injured. He was covered in dried blood and was moving at an awkward gait, due to either exhaustion or injury. He held a handgun in his hand, pointed at the ground, and he walked with a steadfast determination.

Kevin could also see that Arthur had his own rifle at the ready but couldn't take a shot for the same reason that Brandon couldn't. There was no shot that didn't mean certain death for Sonyea.

"In position, sir," Brandon announced. *"I'm ranging one hundred and eighty-three yards."*

"What's your caliber?" Kevin asked.

"6.5 Creedmoor."

"What can you do with it at that range?"

"Sir, I can choose which pupil to place the round in," Brandon replied with confidence. *"If it wasn't for the woman strapped to the barrel of the gun."*

"Stay in position. Don't fire unless cleared to do so."

"Affirmative."

Kevin was too far off to hear what words were exchanged but saw Arthur speak to the cook. Despite verbally engaging with Arthur, the beaten-down cook couldn't keep the approaching Robert off his mind. He kept turning and watching the man come toward him. Then the handgun came out and he fired. None of the shots hit and Robert didn't slow his approach.

"All teams! Hold your fire!" Kevin ordered into the radio. He didn't want anyone to hear the shots and get carried away. There was nothing they could do at this point to resolve or deescalate the situation. "The gunfire is outside the fence and does not pose a risk at this point. I do want Fire Team Alpha to take a concealed position to the northwest of the gate with a view of the approach road. Over."

"Roger that," came the reply from the team leader.

This was all Kevin could do at this point. Get people in an optimal position to respond to whatever might happen. He hoped it would resolve peacefully but he had little faith in that outcome. These men outside the gate were exhausted, injured, and apparently simmering with rage at each other. Such men were poor decision makers. They were men who killed or got themselves killed.

39

"Son!" Arthur barked at Jeff. "If you don't pay attention to what you're doing you're going to accidentally kill this poor woman. Is that what you want?"

Jeff was staring down at the Glock in his hand, the slide locked back, and the chamber empty. He seemed to be trying to figure out why it had quit firing and what he needed to do to make it go boom again. He looked down at his body armor, hoping he might see a pocket obviously containing a fresh magazine, but he had no hands available to open the flaps on any of them.

Jeff's distraction worried Arthur, who watched from behind a raised rifle. "You need to drop that handgun and focus on what you're doing. If you keep moving, you're going to put too much pressure on that trigger and that rifle will go off. How about we put the safety on?"

At that, Jeff raised his pale, sweaty face and glared at Arthur. "How about you kiss my ass?"

Arthur could see how sick the boy was now. That wasn't good. His decision-making would only be worse. He was sweating profusely, had red-rimmed eyes, and his skin had an odd pallor.

"If you wanted to kill Sonyea, you would have done it already. You wouldn't have brought her to my doorstep. If you're here with her, it's for a reason. Drop that handgun, focus on what you're doing, and let's talk about why you're here. Tell me what I can do for you."

At the mention of the handgun, Jeff recalled why he had it out. *Robert!*

He whipped his head around so violently he nearly lost his balance. He staggered, tugging against the rifle, and Arthur flinched, knowing it would certainly fire. Somehow, it didn't. Jeff found that Robert had closed the distance between them and was getting even closer.

"Stop or I'll kill her!" he screamed.

Arthur was uncertain if Jeff would intentionally kill her or not but he was going to accidentally kill her if he didn't quit moving so erratically. "Stop, Robert! Let me handle this!"

Robert paused his forward movement but did not break his intense concentration. Arthur could just make out the laser-focus, the glare of pure hatred and murderous rage. Robert was determined to finish this. He wanted to kill Jeff.

"Robert, let me speak to Jeff for a moment," Arthur said. "Let us try to resolve this. You're making him nervous and I'm afraid there's going to be an accident." Hopefully the logic of that would seep into Robert's head. His message was *don't think about killing Jeff, think about accidentally killing Sonyea.*

Satisfied he'd at least been granted a temporary reprieve from Robert's pursuit, Jeff dropped the Glock. Arthur couldn't be sure if it was an intentional move or simply from a lapse in attention. Jeff stared down at it as if he couldn't figure out what happened or how to fix it, then he looked at Arthur.

"Where's my dad? What happened to my people? Did...you...*kill* them?"

Arthur lowered the barrel of his rifle. He was still ready to whip it up in an instant but he didn't think talking to Jeff over the barrel of a gun was going to instill any confidence. "I didn't do anything to them, son. They packed up of their own accord and left. Made it sound like they had a fallback plan or something."

Jeff rolled his head back on his shoulders and stared at the sky for a second. It was a gesture of utter frustration and hopelessness. Arthur could see it on his face. Jeff had come all this way with a plan, with a particular expectation of how this was going to play out. All that had gone out the window. The game had changed entirely in his absence and now he didn't know what to do.

"You doing okay, Sonyea?" Arthur asked.

She threw him a weak smile. "Okay considering the circumstances."

"She's not responsible for any of this, Jeff," Arthur said. "There's nothing to be gained from putting Sonyea in further danger. She has family."

That revelation only inflamed matters. "I had family, too," Jeff growled. "Part of it was here when I left. Now I don't know where to find any of them. I don't know if I'll ever see any of them again."

"That's no reason to punish an innocent woman," Arthur said. "Could you live with something like that? Is that the kind of man you are?"

Jeff retreated into his head but Arthur couldn't tell if he was considering what kind of man he was or if his fevered state simply overwhelmed him for a moment.

"You did it, Jeff," Sonyea said, a fake smile plastered on her face, a cheery lilt in her voice.

This seemed to reanimate him and his head turned toward her. "What?"

"Arthur asked what kind of man you are and I think you know now, don't you? You're the kind of man who did what your dad couldn't do. You were determined to get me here and you did. You were determined to show your dad you were a better man than he gave you credit for. You've done it." The entire time she spoke, Sonyea made eye contact with Arthur, trying to say just enough with her expressions that he would understand the dynamic, that he could perhaps follow her lead.

It took him a moment but he eventually caught on. "That's right," Arthur said. "Your dad would be pissed that you were able to do something he couldn't. He'd be spitting nails right now if he were here. He'd be pacing back and forth in that camper of his cussing and complaining."

The image of that brought a smile to Jeff's tortured face.

"But it's over now, son," Arthur said. "Let's put down the gun and you can go find your family." Arthur said it in a gentle, soothing voice that he rarely had to call upon. He wasn't even certain from where he resurrected it.

Jeff shook his head. "It's not over until you go."

"Go?" Arthur asked.

"Jeff, they're not going anywhere," Sonyea said, starting to fall apart now, crying. She thought she'd had this but he was still hung up on pushing them out, something she understood would never happen.

"You have to leave the compound," Jeff said.

"That's not happening," Arthur said. "I didn't do it for your dad and I won't do it for you."

"I'll kill her."

"Then I'll kill you," Arthur said. "If I don't, then Robert will. If he doesn't, the gunmen I have watching this position right now will. You see, you don't have a play here. We don't negotiate with kidnappers."

Jeff looked around nervously, his movements erratic and bird-like, apparently not having thought there might be other people watching him. *Aiming* at him. He *should* have known. He should have expected it. Sensed it.

"Lay down the gun," Arthur repeated.

Jeff appeared to be considering it, seemed to be wavering.

"Take this victory," Arthur said. "Leave knowing that you did something your dad couldn't. If you die here, you lose."

Jeff looked down at the front of his body armor, then fumbled around with his free hand. Arthur sensed he was looking for a knife. This was over. The kid was done. He was going to take his personal victory and move on.

With Jeff unable to lay a hand on a knife, Arthur reached for his own blade. His hand was closing around the grip when he heard the roar of an approaching diesel engine. A crew cab pickup crested the hill, a plume of gray dust rising behind it.

The appearance of the truck broke whatever conciliatory mood Jeff was in. He snapped to attention and panicked, back-pedaling. Sonyea's hands shot back to her throat, slipping fingers beneath the zip tie to prevent it from choking her.

"Stop!" Jeff shouted.

Arthur was wincing. This was it, the gun had to go off now. Arthur leapt up onto the side of the gate. "NO!"

Then there was a shot.

40

Brandon didn't get clearance for the shot. There wasn't time. He didn't want a headshot. People didn't always fall limp when they died. People with a bullet in their head could stiffen like they were having a seizure. Brandon felt the only safe way to prevent the falling body from pulling a stiff finger into the trigger was to sever that physical connection between the brain and trigger.

When he heard the truck, he knew negotiations had failed. Things were about to go upside down. Then it got worse. The cook staggered backward, pulling Sonyea with his rifle. She was going to die.

Brandon had already adjusted his zero for the distance. He dropped his crosshairs to Jeff's wrist, where it protruded behind the grip of the AR. Before Jeff could pick up momentum, before his gait became erratic, Brandon squeezed the trigger and Jeff's wrist exploded into bloody strings. Whatever flaps of flesh and muscle remained were outside of his ability to control.

Jeff yelped, at first thinking he'd accidentally pulled the trigger and fired his own weapon. Then he stared in bewilderment at the gushing crimson and the exposed stark white bones of his wrist. The

AR disentangled from his limp fingers and fell hanging against Sonyea's back.

She had no idea what was happening and screamed. She felt the weight of the weapon against her and interpreted that as Jeff preparing to fire. She had no idea he was injured and assumed she was going to die at any moment.

Arthur had no idea what was happening at first either. He couldn't believe that one of his men had taken a shot under such circumstances. He couldn't believe Kevin would have given them clearance to do so. Then Jeff raised the mutilated remainder of his hand in front of his own face and he knew what had happened.

"Sonyea!" Arthur shouted.

In her panic she fell backward, landing on the rifle. She was still terrified of choking, her eyes wild as she tried to process what was going on around her—the approaching truck, the gunshot, the bleeding Jeff, and the shouting Arthur.

Arthur was scaling the gate, trying to get to Sonyea. The truck barreled toward Robert. He was distracted by the shot, trying to figure out if Sonyea was injured, and didn't see its approach. When he finally processed the urgency of the growing roar of its engine, it was nearly too late. It was bearing down on him, murderous glee in the driver's eyes.

Robert leapt for the ditch, the impact stunning his already battered body. His eyes watered and his breath left him. The passenger leaned out his window and opened fire on the gate. A round struck Arthur center-mass as he tried to top the gate. It hit armor but the impact knocked Arthur off the gate and onto his back.

There was another shot and the driver's head peeled open. He sagged onto the wheel and the truck veered off to the side, quickly losing momentum. The passenger door sprang open and two men rolled out. Robert, still flat in the ditch, opened up on them with his Glock. His shots were followed by a barrage from the compound as Fire Team Alpha tried to take down the two attackers.

"Watch for friendlies!" Kevin bellowed into the radio. "We have three friendlies downrange!"

The fire team was aware of this and the men were placing their shots as judiciously as possible. Still, there were pounds of lead flying. Robert was certain he hit one of the men but their body armor was absorbing it. They didn't slow. Instinctively, they seemed to sense that the high-value target there was Sonyea and that was where they were headed.

Arthur, flat on his back, struggled to breathe. He heard the men running toward Sonyea but he couldn't do a thing about it. Bullets whistling around him, he rolled onto his stomach. He crawled for what little cover he had, moving agonizingly slow. When he finally got behind his side-by-side, he rolled onto his back again, uncertain if he was going to live long enough to see how this ended.

The two surviving men from the truck closed on Sonyea and the fire tapered off, no one feeling they had a shot with her so close. Robert got to his feet and loped toward them. They were sixty yards away now. A close distance for anyone but an injured, dehydrated, and nearly broken man.

Each man looped an arm under Sonyea and dragged her toward the woods. This pulled her hands away from the zip tie around her neck. Her face reddened as she choked. The men either didn't understand what was happening to her or didn't care.

There was a lone shot from a high-powered rifle and one man dropped like his plug had been pulled, a spray of red mist surrounding his head like an angry aura. Before Brandon could take out the remaining attacker, they hit the trees and disappeared into the concealment of deep forest.

Robert lurched into the woods, burning pain as fuel, and setting an intercept course. The other man had to be fast but he was dragging Sonyea like an anchor behind him. That would slow him down.

The woods were alive with the sound of running feet, like herds of fleeing animals. There was Robert, Sonyea and her attacker, plus whatever men from the compound had been dispatched to join the fight. There were gunshots now, spaced evenly. It sounded like only one weapon, like the man with Sonyea returning fire in an attempt to discourage pursuit. Arthur's men would be afraid to shoot unless they had a certain shot.

Then Robert saw the man pass through a clearing in the woods. He dropped Sonyea at his feet and Robert couldn't see her for the dense underbrush. The man pulled out a knife and Robert raised his handgun but the man dropped out of sight.

Robert panicked, thinking the man might have stabbed Sonyea. He staggered in that direction with all the stealth of a moose in a Maine forest. Robert broke into the clearing, uncertain of what he'd find. The man was over the nearly unconscious Sonyea, slicing the zip tie from her neck. At Robert's appearance, the man sprang up with the knife.

Robert didn't think. He jumped onto the man, grabbing the knife hand with both of his and using his momentum to propel them backwards, away from Sonyea. Robert was not a fighter in the best of times but he knew he needed to stop this man and he needed to control that blade. He thought he had that dealt with until they hit ground and he lost his grip.

He felt pressure on his back as the man tried to stab him with several quick thrusts. There was no pause, nothing but reaction on the man's part. He knew what he was doing. Robert was just reacting, trying to stay alive. Fortunately, the steel plates in his armor deflected the knife blade but it gave the man the feedback he needed. He knew his next strike needed to be outside of a protected area. He raised the knife to plunge it in Robert's neck.

Sonyea tried to scream, thinking Robert was dead, but only a croak escaped, her throat raw from the zip tie that had just been cut loose. Robert raised his body and hooked both arms around his attacker's, trying to lock him up. The strength he normally had for such a maneuver was not there. His bicep, injured by a bullet, burned from both the raw flesh and the damaged nerves. His shoulder, injured and perhaps still carrying a bullet, felt like it had already been stabbed several times. Couple that with too little food and water and you had a man who was about to die.

Before Robert even sensed what was happening, the man rolled them. Robert was on the ground then, trying with his failing strength to ward off the knife blade coming closer and closer to his face. He wondered what had happened to his pistol, perhaps lost somewhere when he leapt onto this man. It didn't matter. He certainly couldn't free up a hand to reach for it. He tried to look for Sonyea but could not see her. He was going to die.

When he finally looked up into the face of the man who would kill him, he saw a grimace turning into the smile. The man could feel that Robert's muscles were failing. This was going to be over soon. Then Robert saw a shadow rise behind the man. A red face, ligature marks on the neck, dirty, stained with tears, and holding an AR pistol like an avenging angel.

When Robert smiled, his attacker looked at him in confusion. It would be his last expression before his head puffed up, absorbing the energy of two nearly simultaneous rifle rounds at point-blank range. Then Robert closed his eyes and the warm blood hit his face like stepping into a hot shower.

The body thudded forward onto Robert, the soggy mass of his head settling onto him like a warm sponge. He rolled to his side, shoving the body off, and dragging a sleeve across his face. Sonyea dropped to his side and started wiping at his face with a bandana. Unable to see if it was someone come to his aid or a renewal of the attack, Robert started to move away.

"It's me, Robert," Sonyea said. "Let me help you."

There were people crashing through the underbrush around them and Robert began to panic again. Sonyea put a gentle hand on his shoulder.

"It's okay. It's our people," Sonyea said. "We're safe now. We got them all."

"What the...?" It was Kevin. He'd thundered into the clearing with two other men. Brandon was just behind them, carrying the sniper rifle. He dropped at Robert's side, wasting no time tearing open a trauma kit.

"Most of this blood isn't his," Sonyea said. "He was fighting the guy that had me. When I shot him, he bled all over Robert."

Kevin pulled another bandana from his own pocket and helped clean Robert. "Brandon, get Arthur on the radio. Tell him we're all clear."

"Roger that," Brandon said, standing and tugging his radio out of a pouch.

"Let's get him to his feet," Kevin said.

Sonyea stood, then staggered. Brandon rushed to her side and steadied her.

"You two!" Kevin called to two other men in the group who were still scanning the woods at high ready. "Get over here and help me. These two have nothing left."

The men swooped in and helped Robert to his feet. Robert groaned as he stood.

"Any injuries that need immediate attention?" Kevin asked.

"I don't think so," Robert replied.

"Then we'll let Doc tend to you when we get you back over the fence."

41

The facilities in the infirmary were field-hospital crude. The building was of recent construction, with solar power and running water, but it lacked the equipment of most basic doctor's offices. This was a station where people got patched up and sent back to work. There was a homemade exam table and a couple of cots against the wall. Sonyea was in one cot, behind a curtain, cleaning up. Robert was on the exam table and Doc was going over him inch-by-inch.

"Not sure how you made it back here, Robert," Doc said. "The bicep wound is ugly. It has to hurt pretty badly. You're also going to need a couple of dozen stitches."

"You're right. It does hurt."

"I might have laid down and gone fetal," the doc mumbled.

"Sometimes the only direction is forward," Robert said. "That's kind of how it felt out there. Like there was only one choice, once I ruled out packing up my toys and going home."

The doc was focused intently on cleaning Robert's bullet wound. "It's a grazing wound but there's muscle damage. You'll have to baby it a while to let it heal, then do some physical therapy to regain the flexibility. I really need to put your arm in a sling or the wound won't heal properly. It's going to hamper your mobility."

"Physical therapy?" Robert asked. "A sling?"

"Maybe two slings. One for the bicep wound, one because I'm going to need to dig around in your shoulder and make sure there aren't any bullet fragments floating around."

"I don't think that's going to work," Robert said. "You do the best you can and I'll wear a sling if conditions allow it."

The doc didn't look satisfied with that answer but continued to clean dirt out of Robert's wound with an irrigation syringe. "How you doing back there, Sonyea?" the doctor called.

"Wishing I had a hot bath waiting on me," she said. "It would take about three of them to get all the road grime off of me."

"We can probably arrange that," Doc said. "Arthur has a tub and shower at his place, unless you've got a hankering for a galvanized washtub and heating water on a fire."

"Did I hear my name mentioned?" Arthur said, cracking the infirmary door and sticking his head in.

"Speak of the devil," Doc replied.

"Can we come in?" Arthur asked.

Doc nodded. "Sure."

Arthur pushed the door open and entered, Kevin behind him.

"Stay over there," Sonyea said. "I'm getting dressed."

"I respect a lady's privacy," Arthur said. "Especially one who can shoot."

In other times the comment may have brought a laugh but it didn't even raise a smile among this worn down group.

"You okay, Arthur?" Robert asked. He'd been told that a gunshot to the chest had taken Arthur out of the fight when the truckload of men showed up.

"Nasty bruise and a broken rib. Hurts to breathe and hurts to move," he replied. "Things happened fast and I didn't think ahead. I was wearing light armor instead of heavy. Almost cost me big time."

Robert nodded. "Armor saved my life. The guy running away with

Sonyea tried to stick a fighting knife in my back. The plate blocked it."

"Deflected it," the doc corrected. "It still sliced your back beyond your plate, just didn't penetrate."

"He glued me back shut," Robert clarified.

Sonyea popped out from behind the curtain. She was wearing clean clothes and had scrubbed off the worst of the dirt, which only served to make the numerous cuts, bruises, and scrapes more evident.

"I'm sorry for what you all went through," Arthur said. "I appreciate the effort you made, though I know things didn't turn out like you planned."

"Story of my life," Robert said.

"I'm assuming Jeff didn't make it?" Sonyea asked. There was a weight in her voice that implied a desired outcome. She wanted him to be alive. She wanted him to have a chance to mature and find his place in the world.

No one leapt forward to respond to that. Kevin and Arthur looked down, probably trying to find a neutral explanation.

"I'm guessing that's a *no*," Robert offered.

"If someone had gotten to him immediately a tourniquet may have saved him," Arthur said. "In all the chaos, no one pursued that. He crawled off into the weeds and died. Never made an attempt to staunch the bleeding or apply a tourniquet on himself."

Sonyea sighed, processing that. "He was crushed when he got back and his dad was gone. He didn't expect that."

"We didn't expect that either," Kevin said. "Them leaving took us all by surprise."

Kevin and Arthur knew the basics of what had taken place. Robert and Sonyea, despite their injuries, had explained bits and pieces as they transported to the infirmary. Robert had discreetly informed Arthur that he suspected Carlos was a spy only to find that he was correct and that Carlos was now dead.

"So where did they go?" Robert asked. "You think he has a list of survival retreats operated by preppers and he's going to work his way down that list until he finds one he can take over?"

Kevin and Arthur exchanged a glance.

"No," Arthur said, looking Robert in the eye. "We think he put all his eggs in this basket. We have reason to believe that he pulled out only when he learned of a softer target."

"Any idea who the target is? We should probably warn them if we can," Sonyea said.

Arthur and Kevin exchanged another uncomfortable look.

"What is it?" Robert asked. "You're making me nervous."

"We think he's headed to Damascus, Virginia," Arthur finally said. "Carlos said he was asking lots of questions about you before they left."

Robert sat bolt upright in the bed.

"Hey!" Doc protested. He'd been intently cleaning impacted dirt out of Robert's infected bicep wound.

"I have to go," Robert said.

"We know you do," Kevin said. "You've got to let the doc finish his work first. You can't travel or fight until you're patched up."

"You don't understand," Robert said, getting to his feet. "Every second I sit here, the congressman could be closing in on my family. My kids can shoot but they can't turn back an army. They'll be slaughtered."

"We won't let that happen," Arthur said.

The doc put a hand on Robert, trying to steer him back onto the table, but Robert pulled loose.

"And just what are you going to do to prevent it?" Robert snarled. "How could you possibly stop it from down here? The only way it gets stopped is if I get on the road right now and try to take them down before they reach Damascus."

"We don't even know where they are," Sonyea said. "They could be closing in right now."

Robert's mind raced at the possibility. Panic rose in his eyes.

Kevin stepped forward. "Sit down, Robert. Let the doc do his thing. We're pulling in a favor."

"What kind of favor?" Robert asked, distrustful of such things.

"Kevin's pilot friend, Chuck," Arthur said. "We've already been on the horn with him and he's headed this way."

"I thought he was working," Sonyea said. "How's he managing to get away with that chopper for a personal mission?"

Arthur reached into his pocket and pulled out a handful of clear plastic discs. The warm yellow glow radiated from them even in the dim room.

Krugerrands.

"I can't take that," Robert said.

"Yes you can. It's already done," Kevin said. "It's the necessary bribes for all parties involved—to get the chopper, the fuel, and for Chuck's trouble."

"I don't know what to say," Robert said, sitting back down on the exam table.

"He'll be here in two hours," Arthur said. "That gives you time to get patched up, clean up, pack your shit, and be waiting on him."

"After the way I acted, I..." Robert trailed off, words failing him. "Thank you."

"You risked your life to try to help us," Arthur said. "You put yourself in danger. That's all I remember."

Sonyea moved forward and hugged Arthur, then Kevin. Robert started to rise and shake their hands but the doc tugged him back down.

"We're going to need every second we have," Doc warned. "Sit still and let me work."

"I would hug you too," Robert said. "I don't have words."

"You don't need them," Arthur said. "Friends do what they can. This is something we can do."

42

I n two hours, Robert and Sonyea were at the chopper pad with their gear.

"This is a hot landing," Kevin said. "He's not hanging around for lunch this time. When he lands, you guys will board and be off."

Robert nodded. "Got it."

When the chopper arrived, the folks on the ground covered their eyes while the rotor wash raised a dust cloud. Quickly, it set down and lowered the engine speed. Kevin opened the door and helped toss in their gear while Robert shook Arthur's hand one more time. Sonyea had to get another hug.

Robert and Sonyea boarded and strapped in. They were ready to go but Kevin still hadn't closed the door. Robert tried to yell at him, to get his attention, but no one could hear over the noise. Robert caught his eye and shrugged as if to ask what the hold up was. Kevin held up a finger, indicating that he should wait just one more moment. Robert struggled to be patient. It was not a skill he'd mastered.

Two more men arrived at the door. One tossed in a green duffel bag, the other slid in two padded green rifle cases. When they moved aside, Brandon stepped up and boarded the chopper. Robert caught

Kevin's eye again and got a thumbs up gesture. Yet again, he was overwhelmed by the generosity of his friends, their willingness to help him.

Brandon settled into a seat, strapped in, and put on a headset. Robert and Sonyea slid theirs on as well.

"Brandon, this is unexpected," Robert said. "Are you sure?"

"I volunteered for this mission. I'm there to help, Mr. Hardwick, for as long as you need me. When this mess is done, I'll ruck back here to the compound."

Robert patted the younger man on the back. "Damn glad to have you, Brandon. Damn glad."

"Everyone ready?" Chuck asked.

When there were no dissenting voices, he lifted off and set a course for Damascus, Virginia. It was only then Robert began to think again about what lay ahead of them. There were a lot of things he was uncertain about and he tried to push them to the side. The important thing was that he would be seeing his family soon and there was nothing more important than that.

BONUS CONTENT

Please enjoy this sample chapter from *The Mad Mick*, the first book in
The Mad Mick Series

MEET THE MAD MICK

Conor Maguire felt the approach of colder weather in the morning air. He wore short sleeves but caught a slight chill on his front porch until the sunlight hit him and warmed his skin. He sipped coffee from a large mug, his favorite, embossed with *Coffee Makes Me Poop*. It had been a Father's Day present from his daughter Barb, who really knew how to pick a gift.

There had been no frost yet, but that would come soon. The previous night had probably gone as low as the upper forties, but if the recent weather pattern held they should see upper sixties to lower seventies by the end of the day. It kind of sucked to not have a goofy weatherman updating them each evening on what to expect. It sucked not having an app on his phone that would allow him to see a current weather radar. All that technology had disappeared with the nationwide collapse.

Goats and hair sheep wandered the fenced compound nibbling at clusters of grass poking through crumbling fissures in the asphalt, dry leaves crackling beneath their hooves. Chickens trailed the goats, searching for bugs, worms, or anything unfamiliar to eat. Crows cawed in the distance, making their plans for the day. Conor dreaded the winter. He dreaded the cold and the inevitable discomfort winter brought. He dreaded the misery and suffering. Not so much for himself, as he was well-provisioned and had wood heat, but studies both public and private had shown that the first winter with no power would result in a massive loss of life.

As a statistic, those lives meant little to him. He was a solitary person. But when you zoomed in on them, those lives were neighbors, they were kids he saw playing in the yards of homes he used to drive by; and elderly folks who waved to him from the porches of humble houses with white aluminum siding and cast iron eagles over the garage door. When spring came, when the crocuses pushed through the cool, damp earth, the world would be a changed place. Conor could not help but be very concerned about what stood between the world he looked at now and that future world he could not even imagine. Between those two bookends lay volumes of death, sickness, suffering, and unthinkable pain.

Conor's friends called him "the Mad Mick," and if you knew him long enough you would understand why. He walked to the beat of his own deranged and drunken drummer. He had his own code of morality with zero fucks given as to what others thought of it. He lived with his daughter Barb in what he referred to as a *homey cottage* on top of a mountain in Jewell Ridge, Virginia. His cottage had once been the headquarters of a now-defunct coal company. It was a massive, sprawling facility where there had once been both underground and longwall mines. Numerous buildings scattered around the property held repair shops and offices.

When Conor first looked at the property he thought it was absolutely ridiculous that a man might be so fortunate as to live there. It reminded him of the lair of some evil genius in an old James Bond movie. It was surrounded by an eight-foot high chain-link fence and topped with barbed wire. There was a helipad and more space than he could ever use. There was even an elevator that would take him to an underground shop the coal company had used to repair their mining equipment.

The ridiculous part was that the facility, which had cost the coal company millions of dollars to build out, was selling for just a fraction of that because it was in such a remote location no one wanted it. In the end Conor came to own the facility and it did not even cost him a penny. His grateful employer had purchased the property for him. It was not an entirely charitable gesture, though. Conor was a very specialized type of contractor and his employer would do nearly anything to keep him at their beck and call.

In an effort to make the place more like a home, Conor had taken one of the steel-skinned office buildings and built a long wooden porch on it, then added a wooden screen door in front of the heavy steel door. Going in and out now produced a satisfying *thwack* as the wooden door smacked shut.

Conor placed his coffee cup on a table made from an old cable spool and sat in a creaking wicker chair. Barb backed out the door with two plates.

"I hope you've been to the fecking Bojangles," Conor said. "I could use a biscuit and a big honking cup of sweet tea."

Barb frowned at him. "You're an Irishman, born in the old country no less, and you call that syrupy crap *tea*?"

"Bo knows biscuits. Bo knows sweet tea."

"Bo is why you had to take to wearing sweatpants all the time too," Barb said. "You couldn't squeeze that big old biscuit of yours into a pair of jeans anymore." She handed her dad a plate of onions and canned ham scrambled into a couple of fresh eggs.

Conor frowned at the insinuation but the frown turned to a smile as his eyes took in the sprinkling of goat cheese that topped off the breakfast. "Damn, that smells delicious."

"Barb knows eggs," his daughter quipped.

"Barb *does* know eggs," Conor agreed, shoveling a forkful into his mouth.

Conor was born in Ireland and came to the U.S. with his mom as a young man. Back in Ireland, the family business was bomb-making and the family business led to a lot of family enemies, especially among the police and the military. After his father and grandfather were arrested in *the troubles*, Conor's mom decided that changing countries might be the only way to keep what was left of her family alive. She didn't realize Conor had already learned the rudiments of the trade while watching the men of his family build bombs. Assuming Conor would one day be engaged to carry on the fight, the men of the family maintained a running narrative, explaining each detail of what they were doing. Conor learned later, in a dramatic and deadly fashion, that he was able to retain a surprising amount of those early childhood lessons.

He and his mother settled first in Boston, then in North Carolina where Conor attended school. In high school, Conor chose vocational school and went on to a technical school after graduation. He loved working with his hands to create precise mechanisms from raw materials, which led him to becoming a skilled machinist and fabricator.

Conor was well-behaved for most of his life, flying under the radar and avoiding any legal entanglements. Then he was married, and the highest and lowest points of his life quickly showed up at his doorstep. He and his wife had a baby girl. A year later a drunk driver killed his wife and nearly killed Barb too. Something snapped in Conor and the affable Irishman became weaponized. He combined his childhood bomb-making lessons with the machinist skills he'd obtained in technical school and sought vengeance.

How could he not? Justice had not been served. There was also something deep within Conor that told him you didn't just accept such things. You continued the fight. There was the law of books and there was the law of man. The law of man required Conor seek true justice for his dead wife.

When the drunk driver was released from jail in what the Mad Mick felt was a laughably short amount of time, the reformed drunk was given special court permission to drive to work. Conor took matters into his own hands. He obtained a duplicate of the headrest in the man's truck from a junkyard and built a bomb inside it. While the man was at his job, Conor switched out the headrest. A proximity switch in the bomb was triggered by a transmitter hidden along his route home. One moment he was singing along to Journey on the radio and enjoying his new freedom. The next, his head was vaporized to an aerosol mist by the exploding headrest.

No one was able to pin the death on Conor despite a lack of other suspects. He had a rock-solid alibi. The proximity trigger detonated the bomb because the man drove within its range. No manual detonation was required on Conor's part at all. After putting everything in place, Conor took his young daughter to the mall to get a few items. Dozens of security cameras picked up the widower and his daughter.

Oddly enough, his handiwork resulted in a job offer from an alphabet agency within the United States government. A team of men who made their living doing such things were impressed with Conor's technique. They recognized him as one of their own and wanted to give him a position among their very unique department. He would work as a contractor, he would be well paid, and he would be provided with a shop in which do to his work. There were no papers to sign but it was made quite clear that any discussion of his work with civilians would result in his death.

Conor knew a good opportunity when he saw it. He accepted the offer and, as he proved his worth, his employer decided it was worthwhile to set Conor up in his deep-cover facility in Jewell Ridge, Virginia. On the surface, Conor presented himself to the local community as a semi-retired machinist who'd moved to the mountains to get away from the city. Mostly as a hobby and to help establish his cover, he took in some machining and fabrication work from the local coal and natural gas industry. Behind that façade, Conor was *the guy* that certain agencies and contractors came to for explosives and unique custom weapons for specialized operations.

Over his career, Conor created pool cue rifles that were accurate to 250 yards with a 6.5 Creedmoor cartridge. A rifle scope was integrated into a second pool cue and the matched set was used for a wet work operation in Houston that never made any newspapers. He once made a music stand for a clarinetist turned assassin that transformed into a combat tomahawk. It was used for an especially brutal assassination in Eastern Europe.

He turned automotive airbags into shrapnel-filled claymore

mines that replaced standard air bags in most vehicles and could be triggered remotely or by a blow to the front bumper. For another job, he'd created a pickup truck that appeared to have standard dual exhausts from the rear. In reality, one exhaust pipe was normal while the other was a rear-facing 40mm grenade launcher.

He routinely created untraceable firearms, suppressors, and unique explosive devices. His explosives contained components sourced from around the world which made it difficult to ascertain the bomber's country of origin. It gave his employer plausible deniability. He had resources in every shadowy crevice of the world and they were always good to send Conor the odd bit of wire, circuitry, and foreign fasteners to include in his handiwork.

Like many bomb makers, Conor was fastidious in his level of organization and preparation. That carried over to his home life. His compound on the mountain had backup solar, available spring water, and food enough to last him for years. Even with those food stores, he maintained a little livestock just to freshen up the stew pot.

"What's on the agenda today, Barb?" he asked. "What do you have planned for yourself?"

"There's a girl at the bottom of the mountain, JoAnn, who I've become halfway acquainted with. It's just her and her dad. Kind of like us. I ran into her yesterday and she said she was going to be doing some late-season canning so I offered to help. She's canning things I've never done before, like French fries."

"Canned French fries. That sounds bloody magical," Conor said. "Plus I'm sure it would be nice to get some girl time, huh?"

Barb smiled back at her dad, a wee drop of mischievous venom in the expression, and yet another demonstration she'd been aptly named. "Actually, it would just be nice to be around somebody who's not telling the same old tired jokes and boring stories all day long. Somebody who doesn't think they're God's gift to humor and storytelling."

Conor faked offense. "I always thought you liked my stories. I thought they were part of our familial bonding. Those stories are your heritage."

"You need new stories, Dad. I don't know if you've noticed or not but, when you tell a story, I'm usually sitting there beside you mouthing the words along with you. I know exactly how they all go. But I guess sitting there making fun of you also counts as bonding."

Conor looked smugly at his daughter. "I had a new story for you when I went over to Damascus and helped that girl Grace and her family. You were on the edge of your seat."

"Yes, but as much as I'm tired of the old stories I don't want you putting yourself at risk just to bring home new material. Besides, you're getting too long in the tooth for those kinds of adventures. You're not an operator anymore. Your days would be better spent puttering around the garden in a cardigan, half-drunk on Guinness, cursing at the beetles and weeds."

"Don't be so quick to put your old dad out to pasture, Barb. I've got plenty of good years left in me. And plenty of good fights."

Barb raised her cup of tea toward him in a conciliatory toast. "Well, here's to hoping those fights die on the vine. I hope you never have to use them."

"I'll toast to that," Conor said, raising his coffee mug.

"So what's on *your* agenda today, dear father?"

"I spoke to a man the other day who lives down in the valley near the Buchanan County line. Since the shit hit the fan he's been taking in horses people could no longer feed. Now he's got more than he wants to take care of over the winter. I told him I might be willing to trade for a few so I'm going to go look at them."

"Ah, a horse would be nice. It could take me an hour to walk to JoAnn's house this morning. It would be half of that on a horse and a lot less effort."

"It will damn sure be easier to carry a load on a horse than on a bicycle," Conor added.

"So you've given up on your bicycles, have you? I'm shocked. I thought you were training for the Tour de Bojangles, twenty-one days of bicycles and biscuits?"

Conor shook his head. "I've not given up on bicycles but my tender arse has. It's become *delicate* in my golden years."

Barb smiled at that. Despite her banter with her father, she loved him dearly. It was just the two of them in the world and that was fine with her. One day she may have room for a husband and children but she was in no hurry. She would try to wait the world out and see if things got back to normal one day.

"An hour is still a long walk," Conor said. "Take your full load-out."

Barb rolled her eyes. "You know I don't go out without my gear."

"It doesn't hurt to remind you. We check and we double check. That's what we do and that's how we stay alive. Not just your rifle and your pistol, but your go bag and your radio."

She gave her dad a thumbs up. "Got it, Dad."

"You better," he warned. "Some things are joking and bullshit. This is not. This is life and death. Every single day."

"Roger that."

"Plates too," he insisted. "Plate carrier and armor plates."

Barb groaned. "It's too hot, and it's heavy."

Conor gave a conciliatory smile. "Well, if you're too weak to carry the weight..."

"I'll take them," Barb said, getting up from her seat. "You're driving me nuts with this." She went into the house to get her gear together. She had no intention of carrying those heavy plates. She would have to find a way to slip out without him seeing her.

This story continues in
The Mad Mick by Franklin Horton
Available on Amazon

Made in the
USA
Columbia, SC

77868095R00163